The Syndicate 2:

Carl Weber Presents

The Syndicate 2:

Carl Weber Presents

Brick & Storm

www.urbanbooks.net

Urban Books, LLC
300 Farmingdale Road, NY-Route 109
Farmingdale, NY 11735

The Syndicate 2: Carl Weber Presents
Copyright © 2017 Brick & Storm

ISBN 13: 978-1-62286-495-9
ISBN 10: 1-62286-495-6

First Mass Market Printing October 2017
First Trade Paperback Printing February 2017
Printed in the United States of America

10 9 8 7 6 5 4 3 2 1

Distributed by Kensington Publishing Corp.
Submit Orders to:
Customer Service
400 Hahn Road
Westminster, MD 21157-4627
Phone: 1-800-733-3000
Fax: 1-800-659-2436

Chapter 1

Javon

"We have a problem . . ."

"Talk to me," I stated; then I listened.

I stood there, stunned then furious, with a tiny thread of fear coursing through me due to what was being relayed to me. My home was, yet again, breached and this time it was by the law. The FBI had implemented a raid all while I had been away from home. Never in my life had anything like this happened in our neighborhood, with good reason. My mother's choice in neighborhood was picked not so much as just comfort for her, but also as a cover, and now that shit was being picked apart, piece by piece. On top of that, motherfucking pigs had attacked my family?

Oh, hell no. That just wouldn't go.

When it came to family in the street game, there was no point in thinking shit out. It was time to react and that was what I did. I briskly walked away, stepping over the red wetness of the floor. Dead bodies had been there just moments before the cleaners had come to get rid of them. Fury had me aggressively pushing through the doors of our secret location while reaching for my Glock. Behind me were a few of my Forty Thieves—basically my personal group of highly skilled bodyguards—also checking their ammo. A brotha had to think smart about this shit. Logically I understood that. However, I also knew that there was no way in hell that I was about to lose my family in the system again for some bullshit power play by the law.

I'd go down before I allowed that to happen. See, even the law needed to be taught a lesson, just to get everything in line. Which was what I planned to do. I was going to reverse all this shit and get the motherfuckers who had my family to understand exactly who the hell I was. There was no backing down from that shit.

I was a "made" man now. All due to design.

After all the hoopla with the Syndicate, I was sure the game had more than changed. It was still odd to me that I was now the head of a criminal enterprise, but judging by all that had happened in just a few short days, it was my reality.

First, Mama Claudette, the woman who had adopted me, my fiancée, Shanelle, and the rest of my siblings, had been gunned down senselessly. At first we thought it was because she was just in the wrong place at the wrong time. Come to find out she was the head of the Syndicate and none of us kids had had any idea. It was a rude awakening. One that I, initially, had no intention of being any part of . . . until one of the Syndicate foolishly kidnapped two of my siblings. Once that happened, all bets were off.

I ended up taking the seat Mama had left vacant and, in doing so, I made enemies. Enemies I took care of swiftly. Mama had people in high places who owed her plenty of favors. I'd called on my ace in the hole and it had paid off. Everything had been going according to my plan . . . until now.

I could remember the heated summers when I was kid, wilding out while Mama Claudette was sipping either sweet tea or some other sloshing liquid on the front porch, thinking in her chair with Uncle Snap smoking his cigarillos. Or, Mama with a big bucket at her feet, shucking peas while he barbecued in the back. I could remember the scent of fresh bleach and lavender drifting through the house while she and some of us kids were cleaning the house as he fixed whatever was broken in the house.

Chuckling to myself, I sighed. They had a unique system. No one would have guessed who Mama really was.

I could vividly see Mama Claudette in my mind's memories, bent over, ass swallowing her shape, while digging in the dirt at the front of the house, setting flowers and fussing at Uncle Snap. I smiled in thought, remembering her pulling weeds and gardening while talking to me or us kids, spitting wisdom. I also could remember the way her face would contort in anger while going in on my bad ass after gathering me from the principal's office.

In all those memories, I could clearly recall the sweetness of Mama Claudette's voice saying, "Now, Javon, the Lord said ya enemies will become ya footstool. You hear me, boy? Those who attack you will always be made to stumble and fall at ya feet. Remember that always or be made a fool."

I used to laugh that shit off as a kid, not really understanding the power of those words until now. My enemies had stumbled and fallen. At my feet was a river of their blood mixing with flowing water, detergent, and other chemicals. I had just erased certain members of the Syndicate with one calculating move: a power play and alliance with an old-school crime base, the Commission.

This move garnered exactly what my adoptive mother, Claudette McPhearson, had spent years cultivating with the fostering and adoption of me and my eight siblings. She had single-handedly had planned the restructuring and longevity of her crime family, the Syndicate, through us. Yeah, that's right; sweet, old, Southern Claudette McPhearson was a true-to-the-blood mobster, along with her right hand, our uncle, Raphael Wilson, aka Snap. It all started long ago, which is a story for some other time, and it all led to me stepping in as the lead of the family due to her murder.

Before finding out her true story—that she wasn't some sweet, old lady wishing to help some bad-ass foster kids like myself and my foster siblings—I was just your average, mundane white-collar analyst, working at a Fortune 500 financial advising firm. My world was good and I had my woman by my side, Shanelle. She was the savvy of the family. Yes, I say of the family. She's my foster sister. We were not related by blood and we never thought of ourselves as actual brother and sister. Frankly, she wouldn't allow me to see her that way but I digress.

Shanelle was my fiancée. She was the additional glue of the family. In her job at the same firm as me, she was lethal in how she handled her business; and her aim with a gun could rival any sniper or hunter. Which was why, as I reformed the Syndicate, I'd gradually move her in place to be my second set of eyes on the business front. She and I were the heads of the kids. Our mother, Mama Claudette, chose all eight of my siblings for our varied personalities. When the truth about her criminal dealings came out, we all slowly started to learn exactly why that was.

Now, dealing with that truth, the fractures in our family became wide and the eight of us dropped down to six. Like Mama Claudette, we lost two other siblings, this time due to bullshit that could have been corrected had I known about it. My blood, my personal counsel, and my right hand, Cory, my baby brother, and our foster sister Inez were both gone in the blink of an eye after we all found out that they were in a secret and abusive—on both ends—relationship.

Shit broke my heart when I found out.

Cory was my best friend, not just my brother. But, he had a problem with fucking around with pussy and drugs. Shit all stemmed back to before Mama Claudette adopted us. He always had issues and I'd always helped him manage it. But with Mama's murder and finding out about her secret life of crime, and even before that, with being swamped with work and trying to make life good between Shanelle and me, I ended up dropping the ball.

I allowed my baby brother to fall between the cracks and leech off Inez, something that should have never happened. Shit turned my stomach when I found out the truth of it all. But, as they say, the bond of family can be one's support or downfall.

I learned that my brother was an addict and now liked to put his hands on women . . . I should say one woman. Nigga was an abuser. Shit was foreign to me because he never learned that crap from our time growing up. Hell, whenever us kids would fight, Mama Claudette would always say, "Any man who puts his hands on a woman for fun ain't worth shit stuck on a donkey's ass, and any woman who thinks she's a man and puts hands on her man for fun is no better than cat piss in a bucket. Don't let me catch any of y'all fighting each other again or I'll shoot ya then put ya back in the streets, hear me?"

The memory was fond, but it scared us as kids. So, where Cory picked up fighting a woman from I didn't even know. I just knew that that shit was dishonorable and wack as hell.

When I learned Cory hooked Inez on drugs, that she was crazy in love with this nigga now, and that she also was fighting him, I was livid.

The people before me weren't my siblings. Hell, the people I knew had sense. They were individuals who had made it out of the system and were now achieving their goals, not the people who died in a car accident caused by the Irish. My sister Inez was hella young, twenty, so she was a pre-med student in college on track to be a surgeon. Whereas Cory, shit, he was supposed to be a grown-ass man, and in his second year of criminal law. They had so much ahead of them.

Both of those fools hooked up and, apparently, the shit hit the fan. When I found out, I went off. I fought my brother then tossed him out, along with Inez when she tried to attack me on his behalf. They sped off during a war at our house and went out in a flame like some crazy ride-or-die tragic love tale. Cory and Inez: toxic to each other, even in the end.

Even in my anger at them, I was ashamed that I pushed them to their deaths. That shit burned in my spirit because I let them both down by not knowing the truth. I didn't uphold my responsibility in keeping them both on the right path. We lost them and now the family was broken even more. I wished I could have saved them.

Sadness made my temples throb at the memories.

In the mix of the family drama, there were my three younger foster brothers and foster sister: Lamont, Naveen, Jojo and Melissa. Lamont, or Monty as we called him, was training to box. He never felt a connection with extending his education. He was about the streets and fighting, so we never pressed him about it.

Twenty-year-old Melissa was an accountant. I'd put her over the club, one of the only legal businesses Mama had left behind. Melissa was good like that. Really, she was only managing the club. Shanelle was running everything else, being that she was the business maven. Naveen and Jojo were our youngest. Jojo was the baby at seventeen and a genius in high school, while Naveen was a fresh graduate and in tech school for civil engineering. We all came from different backgrounds and walks of life. Oh, and cultures: Native American, Black, Filipino, Bangladesh, Latina, and White. A few of us were mixed all the way up, as none of us knew what Jojo was mixed with. In the end, we all were bonded like blood family.

Keeping us in line after the death of our mother and siblings was our Uncle Snap. Old head was like a father to us all, but he, too, was living a secret. He wasn't our dapper-dressing, eccentric, old-ass uncle who loved to sing us the blues while sipping moonshine and quoting Ralph Ellison's *Invisible Man,* and Shakespeare. Nah, he was a crazy-ass country gangsta, who was our mother's right-hand man and body-guard. He was once full of vibrancy but now, because of Mama Claudette's murder, he was quiet and withdrawn, until it was time to handle business.

That was when he'd return to being my mentor, keeping me straight and making sure that I didn't break while being the leader of the family and the Syndicate. See, it was my responsibility to keep the McPhearsons together. If we broke, we'd lose everything we built in our real lives and everything Mama built as a legacy for us. No matter what, I couldn't let us fall.

We were all we had.

So for them, I chose this life of darkness and intrigue. Besides, Mama felt that I could carry on the legacy, and I intended to honor her wishes no matter how bloody it might be while looking for her killer. I didn't want this life, but I could see why Mama chose me. This shit was coming too easy and natural for me.

"Nephew, are you good?" came from my right side.

My fingers were digging in my palms. The adrenaline from the meeting and watching a few members of the Syndicate die was still flowing sharp through me. I had a partial hard-on from the intensity. So, fuck no, I wasn't good. But, I wasn't about to verbalize any of that. Besides, the buzzing from my cell phone was drawing my attention again.

Calming down from my thoughts, the hazy red that filmed over my eyes was now gone. I gave a nod, noticing everyone was gone and that it was just me, Uncle Snap, the Forty Thieves, and the cleaners. Exhaling with my arm stretched out by my side and my Glock in my hand, I looked toward my uncle.

"Make sure they go through this place more than once. Any drops of blood, any splashes of it from the cleaning, any trace needs to be erased," I said, reaching for my cell only to feel it stop buzzing.

"This is what they do, nephew; don't worry about it," Uncle Snap said, almost too calmly.

A frown spread across my face and I turned to fully face the old man. "What's going down?" I asked.

My uncle was staring at me with his flip phone in his hand and speaking to me without even talking. A sudden anxiety attack had my spine tightened like steel and I knew that there was a problem with the family.

"Monty, Navy, and Jojo were taken by the cops," he finally said, getting closer.

What?

All thoughts paused in my mind in that moment. Any types of *what the fuck* didn't have a chance to flourish because I was already acting. I let out a sharp whistle. Stepping from where they stood at the side, my Forty Thieves appeared behind my uncle and me. I turned and motioned for everyone to follow me. In one fluid motion, I pushed through the doors of the building, then pulled out my Glock, making sure the clip still was good.

From my side, my uncle kept up with my strides as a blacked-out Escalade pulled in front of us.

"Nephew—" he started, but I stopped him.

Pulling off my jacket, I changed quickly behind the open door of the truck, tossing clothes in the back seat. "Run me down how deep our connections are with the police, in our area and ATL as a whole."

"I sent ya mother's lawyer to handle the situation and report back to me. Melissa dropped the message but Shanelle gave the rest of the intel," Uncle Snap briskly mentioned.

"I didn't ask you all of that. Answer my question . . . though I appreciate it," I said between constrained emotions.

The old man cleared his throat then swiftly broke it down. "Overall we own a small five percent of the law. It's one of the things your ma made sure to have secured in her reign."

Climbing in the back, I slid over for my uncle then looked at him. "Make that ten and find out who in the districts are watching us to the point that they feel justified in going after our family."

"Nephew, first of all, this is the Feds and you need to think calmly before you step to them," he said, tapping the roof of the ride to signal for our driver to pull off.

"Don't I always?" Smoothing a hand down my button-down that I changed into, I reached up and rubbed my chin, repeating myself. "Don't I always?"

When my uncle chuckled low, I glanced at him and he adjusted his brimmed hat over his eyes. "The names are Special Agent in Charge Andy Monroe and his partner Special Agent Stillwaters. The same ones who tried to question Shanelle."

"Humph," was all I said in thought with my fingers pressed to my lips. Eventually, I spoke up after thinking. "Have Shanelle meet us near the station. I take it she's there?"

"Of course. That girl is your shadow when she has to be in situations like this, nephew," the old man stated in a tone that had pride in it.

"Good. Find out their life stories. We need ammo."

"No doubt, nephew, I'm on that." Uncle Snap whipped out his flip phone and he got to business. "Seems like it's always something. Welcome to the game."

The ride felt like forever, but once we pulled up and I pushed open the car door, reality hit hard. Shanelle quickly climbed in, and the car whipped around. The urgency in the air was thick. It had me reaching out to take Shanelle's fisted hands in my own, and staring into her big brown eyes. My woman was pissed off. I saw that fury clear as day and it didn't have to take reading the tension in her body, the locked jaw, the slightly flushed red of her skin, or the way her leg shook to tell that. I knew my girl. She was ready to kill.

"Debrief us, Shanelle," I softly asked of her, holding her hand.

"They . . . they . . ." she stammered. "Baby? They kicked in Mama's door and came at us hard. Roughed us up. A motherfucker put their knee in my back. I was pressed to the floor. They had Navy by the hair. Knocked Jojo's glasses off his face and broke them. I know he can't see shit."

Shanelle bristled in her constrained anger then immediately went to detailing everything else that had happened. "We have to get them out."

"You went in and tried?" I asked calmly when really I was ready to jump out of the car. *They put hands on my family? They put hands on Shanelle?*

"Yes, but they are playing stupid and won't tell me if they will be released on bail," she explained.

"Let's go," was all I said. I climbed out, helped Shanelle out, and walked near my uncle.

With a slap to my chest with his hand, Uncle Snap gave me a look that had me chilling for a second. "I'll speak for them since I'm Jojo's guardian now, and I'll see if our lawyer is here," he said.

"Yes, sir," was all I had to say at that moment just to keep calm.

Once we stepped into the precinct I made sure to observe everyone. Cops and nobodies moved around us as if we were invisible. White noise indicated the busy atmosphere as people moved through the place. Stale cigarette smoke mixed with old coffee annoyed my senses. Then Shanelle bristled at my side as she squeezed my hand near her side.

Copping her from the side of my eye, I noticed her nod ahead of us. I wondered who she had noticed and a part of me hoped it was one of our family; but it wasn't. When my gaze focused on an older white dude who reminded me of Andy Griffith, I grimaced. Next to him was his plump, Homer Simpson–looking friend.

"Stillwaters and Monroe," she whispered to me, never breaking her poker face.

"Of course."

I chuckled and it was as if they heard me, because both men looked our direction, locked eyes on Shanelle, then chuckled themselves. We watched them come our way. Uncle Snap was busy talking to a receptionist who played like she hadn't seen Shanelle before or heard of our brothers.

"Ms. McPhearson, what a joy to see you again. Come to drop off more trash?" Stillwaters taunted.

"You know what? I will . . ." Shanelle made her way to him, but I stopped her by stepping in front of her, blocking her with my body.

Adjusting my blazer, I looked down at the floor and shook my head while inwardly chuckling at the disrespect. I knew that I was going to let Uncle handle this, but shit didn't always go the way it was supposed to, now did it?

"Very unprofessional of you to taunt my fiancée like that. Aren't we supposed to be on the level of showing why *some* cops' lives matter? Huh?" I asked snidely, stepping close to Stillwaters while staring down at him.

That tension was back. Stillwaters took to his full height as if to intimidate me, but wasn't shit I was scared about in the building, not even the fucking roaches hunting for doughnuts. So, we both stood glaring at each other. My jaw tensed and my lips curved in a slanted smile, taunting him.

"What did you say to him, McPherson? That sounded like a threat," I heard the Andy Griffith lookalike say. Stillwaters smelled like beef jerky and ass.

Silence overcame me and I never took my eyes off Stillwaters while I ignored Monroe. All it would take was one snatch of his fucking windpipe and me falling on him to slice his throat, then lights out for his ass. That's all it would take and I could kill him in a blink before anyone would even know it. Or, I could light him and his partner up with my Glock. No remorse for either kill. I'd say I was provoked and that it was self-defense. You know? Standing my ground. All he had to do was get froggy.

I knew I was thinking foolishly. No matter how angry I was, I knew I couldn't harm a fed in a police station and get away with it.

"McPhearson, I know you're angry about your brothers, but it would be ill advised to go head up with us in the middle of a police station, son," he repeated, adding emphasis on the "son" as if to stir my already rising anger.

Because I had leather gloves on, all you could hear was the slight straining of that fabric as my fists clenched, and our breathing.

"Gentlemen, please. We don't have time for pissing contests and marking territories. Please break this up. There are civilians here." The scent of light perfume brushed against my nose, with that of a woman's hand urging me and the assholes apart.

The face of a sista appearing in front of me had me stepping backward just to get her out of my space. I was too pissed to register her beauty, but I could hear others around me murmuring about it.

"Who are you?" I asked as I slid my hand back to take Shanelle's.

No more than five seven with a bushel of breast-length curly, natural hair, the woman who spoke was dressed in dangerously form-fitting slacks, and an African screen-printed blazer that accented breasts any man or woman would want to touch. She stood looking back and forth at us with black half glasses and a slick smile across her brown face. For a swift moment, I swore she had a Glock hidden on her; but there was no way that she'd be allowed to bring that in, so I was tripping.

"Unless you want me to file a formal complaint for harassing my clients, especially Ms. McPhearson, I'd advise you to please give us some space, Agents, and go back to your work."

We watched the woman before us turn on her heels and stare undauntedly at both cops. Stillwaters snarled at me and Monroe only gazed at me with a smirk before both men walked away.

As the hallway grew quiet, the woman turned back to us with an infectious smile then held her hand out. "Mr. McPhearson, I will be the woman getting your brothers out. Hello, I'm Jai St. Clair, your family lawyer, but today I'm you brothers' representative. Nice to meet you all."

At her lapel was a broach that, if you looked closely and knew where to look on it, had a symbol that matched my own on my ring. It was then that the name St. Clair rang in recognition.

The woman before us was one I had interest in bringing into the new Syndicate. One with a history rich in dealing with both crooked cops and mobsters, because her own ancestor was one of the baddest mobsters in Harlem back in the day. This woman's bloodline was rich with such connections and it had me glancing at my uncle in appreciation.

Before me was the great-niece of Stephanie St. Clair and I knew she'd hold us down without a blink of an eye. God bless my uncle Snap and Mama for having such provisions set in place.

Chapter 2

Shanelle

"Okay, now that we've spoken to Monty and Naveen, the more serious charges are on Jojo," Jai said.

The woman was beautiful. That wasn't lost on any of us, but she was also about her business. There was no way we should have been allowed to see any of our brothers because of the serious charges thrown at them, but Jai made it possible. She took no shit and gave a look of death that made the nuts of each man who tried to test her shrivel up into their stomachs.

Monty and Naveen had been charged with possession with intent to sell. Monty had an unregistered gun on him so they threw in a weapons charge.

"Talk to me," Javon said as we walked down the narrow hall to where they were holding Jojo.

Correctional officers passed us. They paid us no mind. The place was cold and dank. The correctional officers were like zombies who bullied the humans inside the jail no matter what the charges were. I'd seen them treat every last person like an animal. It sickened me. As tough as nails as I claimed to be, I knew I never wanted to see the inside of this place unless I was sure I could walk right back out on my free will.

"Felony drug possession. Felony drug trafficking. I know he's only seventeen, but in the state of Georgia that makes him an adult." She stopped walking and looked at us. "He was manufacturing drugs?" she asked with a frown on her face that said she didn't understand. "In the house? I know Mama taught y'all better than this," Jai said. She gave me and Javon a look, one an older sibling or adult would give to show their disappointment.

"I knew about the Mist, okay?" Javon admitted. "But all this other shit, I had no idea."

"He has a lab, in a basement. Nobody thought to check on what a seventeen-year-old was doing while locked away in a lab in a basement?"

"No, we didn't. We never suspected Jojo had it in him to manufacture and sell drugs down a freaking pipeline," I said.

"The boy was always down there working on some science project, Jai," Uncle Snap said. "Even when Mama was alive."

"We don't know how he was able to pull this shit off," Javon said.

"And right under your nose," Jai added sarcastically. "Not a good look for a leader of a syndicate, now is it?" she asked before pushing open the door of the room where Jojo was.

Javon bristled. I could tell he was about ready to snap, but he kept his cool. We had to remember Jai was on our side and just doing her job. At least, that was what I kept telling myself so I wouldn't punch the woman in her face. None of that mattered, though. As soon as we all walked into the dank room, Jojo stood from the black folding chair he had been sitting in. The room was no bigger than a bathroom in a one-bedroom apartment. The dark gray walls were in stark contrast to the white marble flooring.

I knew Jojo couldn't see worth shit. So the look of fear on his face while his hands were cuffed in front of him broke my heart. Without his glasses, his baby face was more noticeable. He was indeed just a kid. He backed into the wall behind him, looking as if he wanted to run away.

"Relax, Jojo. It's just us," Javon said.

Jojo visibly relaxed and sighed, but he still didn't sit. "I can't see," was all he said.

I went into my pocket and pulled out the spare glasses I was able to find in the mess the Feds had left in his room. "Here," I said.

I placed the glasses in his hand and watched his eyes come to life behind them. Jojo looked from me to Jai to Uncle Snap. He glanced at Javon then dropped his head. I hugged him. I just needed to feel my baby brother in my arms again. It was good to see he had no bruises, but the orange jumpsuit was way too big for him. The white socks and prison-like flip-flops he had on made him look awkward.

"Have a seat, Jojo," Jai said to him as she took a seat at the small, round table in the room.

He did as she asked him once I let him go. The rest of us stood as Jai spoke to Jojo.

"You have some pretty serious charges against you right now. So what I need you to do is tell me the truth from beginning to end. First, start by telling me how long you've been doing this. The only way I can help you is if you tell me the one-hundred-percent truth," she said.

Jojo brought his cuffed hands up to scratch his head. "Started junior year," he said.

"What the fuck, Jojo?" Javon asked. "Before Mama even died?" The disappointment in his voice was so real that it almost made me want to cry.

Jojo's shoulders slumped. "Yeah. I was . . . was trying to make . . . I had this idea that I could make enough money for her to go on a trip for a while when I left for college. Before I knew all this about who she really was, I thought she was some broke old lady, bro," he said with a frown as he shrugged. "So I was going to hand her this money and tell her to just relax for a minute."

"Jesus H. Christ, Jojo," Uncle Snap muttered.

Javon ran a hand down his face and took a deep a breath. By the time Jojo finished running down the list of all the drugs he had made and all the places he had been selling them, I was left speechless.

Jai pulled out all the evidence they had against Jojo, from pictures to video recordings. The more she showed us, the less and less I started to feel like my baby brothers would be coming home, especially Jojo.

"This is serious," Jai said once we had left the jail and were standing outside. "We're going to have to call in some favors. I'm going to have to maneuver things so we can get him in front of a friendly judge, if you get my meaning. They haven't set bail for any of them, but I can change that with one phone call."

"How soon before we know something?" I asked.

"You guys don't worry about that. Let me handle this. Understand, Raphael? Javon? Let me handle this. No underhanded tactics unless I'm pulling the strings. If done right, Jojo, Monty, and Naveen will be walking out of here with minor offenses, if any at all. What you need to find out is who snitched. They have an informant somewhere. Get rid of the informant and I can sink the whole case from there," she said. "For now, let me work on getting bail set."

"How much?" Javon asked.

"How much what?"

"If you get bail set, how much will you need?"

"Don't worry about it. Mama has provisions set in place. I have access to certain things," Jai assured us before walking off.

"The girl's good," Uncle Snap said.

"I for damn sure hope so," I said.

The ride home was a quiet one. We were down five siblings. Two dead. Three locked away. My body, soul, and heart couldn't take anymore. Since Mama had died, all hell had broken loose and it didn't appear it would go away any time soon.

I couldn't wrap my mind around the fact that Jojo had been slanging drugs since the eleventh grade. It didn't make sense to me. How did we not see that shit happening? Granted, Javon and I had moved out, had our own places, so we hadn't been around every day. But how did Mama not know with all those damn cameras she had around the house? Jojo had always been quiet, so we thought nothing of the time he spent in his lab. He always completed his homework and always had some new science project he was working on. Where in the hell had he found time to make and market new drugs?

"How did Mama not know or see that Jojo had been making drugs in her house?" I asked once Javon and Uncle Snap followed me into the house. The place was a mess. Furniture had been turned over. Pictures had been knocked from the wall. Papers and glass were strewn all over the place.

"I've been asking myself that same question," Javon said.

Uncle Snap shrugged. "Maybe she did know. Maybe that's how he flew under the radar for so long," he answered, causing Javon and me to stare him down.

"What?" I asked.

Uncle held his hands up like he was being robbed. "I'm not saying that was the case. I said maybe. Wasn't too much you could get past that woman, especially not in her own house."

"I ain't got time for this bullshit," Javon said, tossing his blazer to the side. "We have to get our brothers out of there. I just made a power play that isn't going to go over too well with a lot of families. The Commission has already prepared for war just in case, all because of a call I made. I can't be worried about if my little brothers are safe while locked away in a jail cell. And where the fuck is Melissa?" he thundered.

Javon had said so much that I didn't even know where to begin with the questions. "We need to talk about Melissa," I said.

He and Uncle turned to look at me. "What now?" Javon asked.

"Something odd was going on with her just before the Feds came through."

"Something odd like what?" Uncle asked.

"She kept looking at her watch, glancing out the window. Shit like that. And then when the Feds busted in, she was gone. Had disappeared before I could even blink."

"Like she knew they were coming," Javon said, lips pressed together in a tight grimace. It's like he was conflicted about what to think.

Uncle looked like he had aged another ten years. "This is too much. Too much coming at us all at once," Uncle said.

"I need time to digest this, to process all of this," Javon added. "Don't say anything to Melissa about her behavior. Let me scope her out on my own. See what my instincts tell me."

"Right, nephew. For now we got product to move and people to see." Uncle looked around. "And we gotta clean my woman's house."

Before we could say anything else, there was a knock on the door. The fact that all three of us grabbed guns and crouched low told of the paranoia we all felt.

"It's chill," Javon said once he had looked outside. "It's the old lady from across the street."

He unlocked the door and smiled at the lady while hiding his gun behind his back. Ms. Lily had been on this block for a long time, even before we had. She was an old German white lady who liked to smile and plant flowers in her front yard. She never did more than wave or speak in passing, unless she wanted one of the boys to move something in her basement or take some trash out.

"How you doing, Ms. Lily?" Javon greeted her.

"I'm well. First, I wanted to know if you children were okay. Lots been going on 'round here since Claudette passed on," she said. Her eyes roamed Javon's face like she was searching for some kind of answer to the madness.

"We're fine, Ms. Lily," he said.

"Neighborhood talking. People wanting to know what y'all got going on over here to have all this shooting and police presence. We never had no madness like this before."

Javon gave a wry smile. "We're just as stumped as you are, Ms. Lily."

"Naw, you ain't, boy. Saw your brothers being carted out of here in handcuffs. Claudette must be turning over in her grave."

Javon's jaw clenched and he moved his weight from one foot to the other. "Is there something you need, Ms. Lily?"

"Yes. Need you to come help me with this stuff I got in my basement and take out my trash."

"Is it possible I can help you tomorrow? We have a mess here we need to clean up right now," he said.

She tried to look past his shoulder but Javon was much too tall for her to do so. "Fine then. Don't take too long. I need it to be moved immediately."

Before Javon could respond, the old woman walked off. Ms. Lily may have looked like she was hours away from death, but she moved with the agility of a woman much younger.

"Nobody got time for that crazy old woman," Uncle Snap said. "Shit, she walked all the way across the street, past the trashcan to ask you to come take out her trash?" Uncle shook his head. "Don't know why Mama was nice to the gotdamn Nazi," he fussed while on his way up the stairs.

Javon slowly closed the front door. I sighed. I was drained, tired, mentally and physically. I looked around at the mess that had been made and I shook my head. The Feds had torn Mama's place to shreds. It would take me days to clean it. *May as well start now,* I thought while Javon paced the floor.

Chapter 3

Uncle Snap

No one man should have all that power . . .

I kept thinking that as I undressed. The day had been long. Javon was a made man. He had given the Commission a seat at the table of the Syndicate. Who in their right fucking minds would go up against Javon now? He had come in knowing nothing and, in a matter of days, turned the game on its head.

Of course, the streets would be talking. Of course, men would want to know how a boy not even twenty-five yet had managed to do what no man had before. Mama would be proud. That I was sure of. But I had to wonder how much more the kids had to lose on the journey to greatness. Losing Cory and Inez was like a blow to the heart after losing Mama. I couldn't afford to lose anyone else or my heart would give out on me. We had to get Jojo, Monty, and Navy up out of that jail.

I plopped down on the bed in the room I had been sleeping in and picked up Mama's picture. "Did you know what Jojo was doing, Claudette? I know shit like that wasn't going down right under your nose and you didn't know about it. You had been protecting that boy, hadn't you?"

I didn't know why I was talking to her. She wouldn't answer me, that I knew. But I still missed her like hell. I also knew my woman. I'd bet money she knew what her baby boy had been up to.

Wasn't no need in crying over spilled milk. We had work to do. I showered and dressed comfortably. By the time I made it back downstairs, Shanelle had made a dent in most of the mess left behind by the Feds.

"Where is he?" I asked her.

She nodded toward the fireplace, which meant he was in the secret bunker that they'd found out about the day of Mama's funeral. It was where they had learned that Claudette was more than just their foster mother.

I thanked her then made my way down. Javon was standing in front of the monitors, watching parts of the city like the leader he was. Nephew was deep in thought. Wide-legged stance with his hand up to his chin.

"I know you ain't in the mind frame to talk business right now, but we have to," I said.

He didn't say anything. He simply nodded.

"I think you've pretty much put the Irish in their place, but that doesn't mean they won't keep coming. Also, the Russians, the Romanians—"

"Anybody who step to us wrong at this point will be met with violence like they've never seen. I no longer plan to coddle or negotiate with anyone. If you come for me, you will be dealt with," he said.

I couldn't even argue with nephew there. Clearly, he wasn't the boy he had been just weeks before. Life had come in that quickly and hardened him even more than he already was.

I nodded. "All right, nephew."

Javon kept watching the cameras then turned to me. "I'm angry, Unc. No matter what I do, I can't quell this anger, this rage, inside of me."

"You need to grieve, Javon. Ain't seen you shed a tear since Mama died. Ain't even seen your eyes water for Cory and Inez," I said.

"Ain't gon' be able to do that until I find out who killed Mama. Up to this point, I've done everything she wanted me to do. I've rearranged the Syndicate, solidified my place at the head of the table, and kept all pipelines clear with suppliers still in place. Now I'm doing me. I'm going to find out who pulled that trigger. After finding out who she was and the fact that she knew somebody was aiming at her, I need to know who did it and I need them to suffer."

Chapter 4

Melissa

"Oh, my God!" ripped from my lips as I clutched my cell, texting Uncle Snap an SOS while panicking.

I was shaking. My heart was slamming in my chest, rising in my throat, making it hard to swallow or breathe. That was how out of sorts I was. Tears rimmed my eyes, and it felt entirely too hot for me; but that was the point. I had to keep the heat off me. That's the least that I could do in a fucked-up situation that had to happen.

There was no regret; though, there was shame for what I had just done. I slowly stood up then caught my reflection in the full-length mirror in front of me. Smoothing the flyaway hair sticking to my plump lower lip, I licked my lips and took in my looks as I heard Mama's comforting voice in my mind.

"Don't you ever let others take what is yours to give freely."

Five ten with a body slim yet thick and curvy thanks to growing up in a home that fed me right, I had a figure that made many of the bad bitches in Atlanta and in my neighborhood envy me. Running my hand over the black sweater jacket I wore, I unzipped it and glanced at my perfect, perky breasts. I was cream and honey, so I was told many times by the niggas I fucked and let pay me how I was taught to do. Turning, I glanced at my plump ass, never knowing where I really got that shit from, but thankful for the squat practices Shanelle taught me.

No matter where I went, I profited off the privilege of my beauty. Naturally, I had black hair, and dark features for a white girl. But once I dyed it blond, it was like if I wanted the world, it would fall in my hands. Niggas called me Amber Rose because of my physique, and at one time I almost took this gift of mine to the club to dance for Magic City. But, I opted not to once I met a rich African motherfucker who liked to lick me from my lips to my pussy and ass. He loved the sex I could give him, which kept me decked out in money, and which allowed me to take my gifts for manipulating money and numbers to school for accounting.

Money was my addiction and living the good life my cocaine. That's why I ran. I couldn't risk being caught up in the bullshit of my family. Well, not the getting locked up part. I was too pretty for all of that and I had sugar daddies to think of, because had I gotten snatched up, it could have messed up my whole game.

Walking around the club I was now an owner of, thanks to my big brother Javon's quick thinking since Mama initiated us all in the crime world, I undressed quickly, feeling disgusted in the quiet corners of my mind. Silencing my conscience, I showered in my office, oiled up, pulled on a flesh-tone bandage dress and gold stilettos, and fixed my silky hair.

Once I flipped on the power to the club for my staff coming in soon, automatic music began thumping, as I heard, "'Smoke a li'l bit/Pop a li'l bit/Aye get fucked up.'"

My cell vibrated in my hand, while I made sure my Glock and blade were hidden in my purse; and I grabbed the keys to my cherry red Lexus. I couldn't let none of the family find me off bat. I didn't have time for the drama. First there was Mama, then stupid-ass Inez and Cory still playing the "needing attention" card to the point that they both were killed. Pausing in my thoughts, I fixed my face with my makeup, then posed for my camera, posting it on IG. I loved them both, don't get me wrong, but it hurt too much to think that they were dead now because they had to be so chaotic.

Then there was Jojo. I had no words on that except that, like Mama said, "Sometimes, it takes being bitten for you not to mess with a garden snake."

Either way, I could only do what I could in that moment: leave Uncle Snap a message, and run. Besides, I had an appointment to keep. This pussy was hot. I had a meeting with a Brazilian and I had money to cop. Family could wait until later.

Swiping right on my cell, I gave a light, flirty answer in Brazilian Portuguese, *"Foi mal xodó!* I'm sorry, boo. I'm a little late, but I'm on my way . . . and, yes, it was handled as promised."

Chapter 5

Javon

A cool breeze kissed my face while I watched Melissa's club from across the street through my cracked tinted window. Knuckles to my chin and lips, I kept watch while my Forty Thieves also did what they did: stay hidden and observe from their own posts. Shanelle had explained that Melissa was acting shady and had run off as soon as the heat came. How that went down, it didn't sit well in my stomach. I knew Melissa was a different breed even as kids, due to her addiction to sex and using her body to get whatever she wanted when she needed it.

Even as a kid, I understood that either Melissa had had something bad happen to her or she had seen some shit that triggered her behavior and desire. But, I never judged her for that or saw her differently, because if you were a kid in the street and from the hood like me, nine times out of ten every young girl in the area had something sexual attempted, done to them, or they'd seen it too many times to count. Fucked up as it was, that's just how it was and no one was protecting us from that reality so we just lived through it. Melissa was that type of case, until Mama fostered her at ten.

When she hit puberty hard, Cory and I had to deal with her walking naked from time to time around the house when she was sixteen, until Mama and Shanelle got in her ass about it, thankfully. After that, there were the little niggas of all races trying to run up and through her; then Mama had to set her right on that shit, too, and help her gauge her sexuality in a healthy way. I tried not to get too involved in hearing what was taught, but Mama always made sure that what she taught the girls she also taught us boys.

Mama and the girls had a close relationship. When she died, I tried my best to keep an eye on all of them but, of course, I failed at that.

Sharply exhaling, I rapped my knuckle on the window of my ride. "She's not here. Head to Southlake."

Cars zipped past on the highway. I quietly sat with my legs wide while smoke curled from my lips as I took hits from my cigar in thought.

Uncle Snap was to the right of me with Shanelle next to him. She originally had to work, but she called off due to our brothers being jailed. I studied her: legs crossed, showing her bare thigh from the white dress shorts she wore. In her hand was her cell, which she was clicking on with her dark purple abstract-tipped nails. Her hair was smoothed back into a big pillow bun at her nape, and her hooped diamond earrings danced against the curve of her baby face.

"What is she saying?" I asked Shanelle in reference to Jai, our family lawyer.

"She said it was difficult, but she managed to get what we needed," Shanelle explained.

"Did she make a copy?" Uncle Snap questioned from the rim of his mason glass, finishing off the liquid in it, then setting it to the side. He smoothed his hand down his vest then glanced our way with questions in his eyes.

"Yes, sir, like you suggested. Do you think we'll find anything extra?" she asked.

Exhaling, Uncle Snap slumped his shoulders. "I do hope so. Worked hard to get it—"

"Most importantly, how is expanding our hold on the cops going?" I asked, interrupting.

"Inside is my connect. He is carefully rising through the ranks as best he can, considering how busy it is in there and the fact that all eyes are on us," Uncle Snap explained, watching me. "I'm also extending our pull to the upper rungs, and working carefully in recruiting the big hitters, like at least a couple in the Feds to cover our asses, nephew."

This was good. Uncle Snap upheld his part and we were making moves in trying to make sure that we were never surprised again by another raid.

"Whatever you can do is what's important. If it's going to take time just to smoothly get our footing, then do that, but don't sleep on it."

I looked up to hear Shanelle say, "I suggest you pull money from any cop departments that we're paying and let them feel that sting. Once they understand the power we are pulling, they'll get in line and pull in ranks, while effectively recruiting people who will do whatever we ask of them. It's simple supply and demand, and HR tactile results." Baby girl shrugged her shoulders as if what she said was simple logic; then she put her cell up to her ear.

"What she said makes sense, nephew. Don't want the pigs to continue to get too fat, then they'll stop being compliant and become sloppy."

Glancing at Uncle Snap, who sat chuckling, I gave a head nod while our driver parked our ride.

Chilling in our ride, we all sat in a partially full parking lot of a mall. Behind us were empty restaurant buildings, some being renovated for new businesses, and others empty thanks to the lack of patrons. Minimal cars drove past, which was nothing to worry about in our case of why we were here, because it kept what we doing low-key and without awareness.

"All right, do that, and monitor it, Uncle. Let them understand that this is also punishment for not giving suitable warning about the raid." I leaned then pushed open the door of our ride. "Mama never had work cross with the home life and we need to keep that going; otherwise, our image will only become worse."

Shanelle popped up then slid over and moved to my side.

"Don't know why you telling me that, nephew. I already know. It's now up to you and the kids to remember that." Snap chuckled. He leaned out and held his hand to the outside. Several plastic bags rustled around and I noticed that there were piles of books within.

Attached to those bags was Jai. She glanced around the car, and pointed ahead of her. "Open the door on the other side too, please," she said.

I watched her climb in, while I reached behind me to open the door. My brow rose as I assessed

Jai. She was dressed casually in dark jeans, and a white blazer. Jai, I could tell, was close to our age but older. Part of me was interested in learning how Mama knew her, but I put that on hold to look at the brotha with the streamlined goatee and bald head climbing in after her.

Immediately, my Glock rested against his temple as he got his bearings. Reassessing my surroundings, I realized that he had been on the bike parked near a car covered in advertising by one of the shops on the strip. He was dressed in a leather jacket.

Uncle Snap immediately checked his body, and ran a bug machine over the brother. He reached down to pull the dude's boots off, then continued his check before sitting back.

"He's with me, Javon. You can put the gun away," Jai quickly spat out, holding her hands up.

I gave her a cold glance then slowly put my Glock away while my uncle continued his search.

"Clear, like he had better be," Uncle Snap said, giving the brother a look before flashing a smile. "How you doing, nephew? Glad you made it."

Jai gave a gentle chuckle then set her bags down. "Trey, I can't believe you let him take your boots off."

I watched in clear confusion; then it hit me who Trey was. "Oh, shit! Cousin Tremaine?" I queried.

"Wondered if you'd recall my face, fam. It has been a long time." Trey extended a hand and we shook like back in the day with a flick of our hands, thumbs locking and fingers extending like wings as we slid them up and down, then pulled each other in for a shoulder bump.

"Damn, it has been. Never thought you'd turn into a cop," I said.

At that moment, Shanelle set her cell down and flew across the car to hug Trey with a huge smile. "Where have you been?" she asked.

Settling back, Trey gave Shanelle a fist dap, like they used to do when we were younger, before speaking up. "Undercover working and making sure nothing I did ever linked back to my involvement with the family," he explained, showing us his badge. "As you see, I'm one of your inside men at the district."

See, Tremaine was Uncle Snap's only surviving relative. For a brief time, he stayed with us at Mama's until he was sixteen. That was, until he mysteriously moved to Memphis then Chicago. None of us kids had heard from him after, but I was sure Mama and Uncle Snap did. Damn, I never knew that he turned into the law.

"Did you bring it?" Uncle Snap asked, his tone turning solemn.

"That I did." Reaching in his jacket, he pulled out a flash drive and held it out. "Jai used her pull to get a hold of the surveillance video of Mama's murder to view it, then passed it to me."

Jai gave a slick smile then rested her hands over her crossed legs. "If there's information, I'll find it and lay out the facts as best I can, by any means necessary. Bastards were trying all types of means to block me from viewing it, but thanks to young Jojo's case, I was able to argue that it was important to his case."

"Is he okay, by the way?" Shanelle asked. "He's too young being in there."

"Naveen and Monty are both protecting him for the time being," Jai said, looking toward Shanelle. "I was able to use our resources to move them together. So, for now he's safe and untouched by the cops and others."

"Oh, thank God," Shanelle whispered then sat back.

Jai gave a light nod. "Agreed. I want them all out of there, but for now they are safe. Now, to some unrelated news. We have an issue that needs to be addressed with the Syndicate."

"Which is?"

Glancing at me, Jai reached in her bags and pulled out a black zipper folder, then pulled out pictures and paperwork. "Apparently, we had rights to a new drug coming out of Brazil."

"Ah, yeah, Ink. The black cocaine pipeline is compromised?"

Jai frowned and nodded. "I received your requests for them to change out the shipment and place it in dry erase markers with usable marker tips, but as we made moves to do so, the product was seized by a rival, which has caused us to stop production."

Shit!

A frown creased my face and I sat back in thought. Part of this new product had been in Mama's notes. She had explained that the demand for black cocaine had been something she was carefully working on. However, it had been difficult to manage since her informants in Brazil all said that it was being carefully controlled by another who really wanted nothing to do with the Syndicate.

This crap was just another stressor on my already full plate. If we couldn't get Ink out and distributed, then it could mean a problem for me with the other Syndicate members.

"Since you have a history with what we are doing, Jai, tell me, do you think we can get our product back?"

"Yes," she said with a quick nod. "If we can find out who took it."

"Then, I need you to rectify our loss and get our hands back on Ink. Can you do that and get our brothers out?" Locking eyes on her, I waited for her response. Jai licked her lips and my body almost responded to the simple move.

She tilted her head to the side, looking at the roof in thought; then she glanced at Trey, who gave her nod. "I have you covered as security," he said to her.

Jai gave a sexy laugh then scribbled in her planner. "Manipulating gangstas to do my bidding for the family is what I'm good at. Yes, I can. I'll contact—"

"Shanelle. I want you both working on this," I interrupted.

I watched my baby's eyes widen. "Really?"

"Yes. I'm the head of the table and Mama put us all in a place to run the Syndicate from that spot." Resting my ankle on my knee, I tapped my fingers on my knee. "I got my hands full with other things as you see, so I need you to work your business mind and get Ink sorted out on my behalf."

"Then I'll do it," she said with a wicked smile.

Jai gave a nod and a smile. "I'll do my part as well."

"Good. Craft a team and report through the appropriate circuits."

Locked in my thoughts for a moment, I rolled my shoulders then ran my gaze over everybody. Uncle sat studying me, with weariness in his gaze. I then reached over to Trey and took the flash drive from him. Reaching up, I pulled down the viewing monitor from the roof then set it up.

"Let's watch the video. Before I do, you good, Unc?" I asked.

"I'll be good, nephew. Let's just see what happened to my woman," he said while noticeably clutching his glass.

Rolling my shoulders, I turned the video on and quietly watched the soundless video.

"There're two different camera angles from where everything went down: one outside of the juvie detention center and one near the bus stop. Had she not been thinking quickly, we wouldn't have anything," Trey explained. "If you look closely, you can see the area where she was attacked," he pointed out.

Studying it, my eyes narrowed. Whoever came after Mama knew the area well enough to know how to get to her. They understood that if they sent a nigga after her to take her purse as she walked to the bus stop, then all that they had to do was direct her away from the cameras. Which was what they did. However, Mama Claudette was smarter. She turned it around and I was now watching her run into an area where people were allowed to park cars on the side of street that had cameras.

Eyes widening, I realized from how she'd occasionally glance around then up that she was assessing the area and checking for the cameras. At my side, I felt Shanelle lay her hand on my thigh then squeeze. Through it, I wanted to comfort her, but I couldn't turn my eyes away. Our mother was fighting for her life. Mama was pulling out all the stops to make the fight last long enough to leave clues, I assumed, while unsuccessfully trying to escape. She must have known someone would get us the footage or one of us would ask for it.

"My woman could hold it down," Uncle Snap said, affection and pain in his voice. "Stick that bastard."

We watched as Mama slid her blade in the side of her attacker after she had sliced his neck. A black car came through spraying bullets. Each bullet that slid in her felt as if it had hit me too. My fists gripped my seat and I felt myself ready to rock back and forth until Shanelle's hand landed on my back, grounding me. I had an image to uphold in front of company who didn't know me that well, who was Jai. So, I reined in my emotions and continued watching, studying the tape.

I stopped it once it got where she looked in confusion at the person who stepped before her near a huge trashcan. All that we could see were the feet and a side glance at their torsos. The video distorted some, but my mouth dropped at Mama's confused face softening.

"Wait, wait! She knows them," I said, shifting forward, coming to that realization.

I reached out to hit the rewind button, then watched it close. I stared at the one in front of her then the one who showed up behind her to shoot her in the head. *That bastard.* I craved to find out who it was. "I need the one who put a cap in her skull."

A light thudding at my temple had me narrowing my eyes in tandem with my frown. I was trying my best to catch any clues about who it was Mama recognized and who had finished her off. Head tilting to the side while my mind worked like a processor, I shook my head, then rewound the video to watch it again, only to hit pause again. I had found something. "Did the station look into who owns that black ride?"

Jai shook her head with red eyes. She worked her mouth to speak but ended up staying quiet as Trey spoke for her. "No. For now they are sitting on it," Trey explained.

"Why?" Shanelle asked.

"Probably paid to ignore it by the same people who came for her," I quietly stated. "Let's run down what we caught."

"Two bullets to her back. From the make of the ride it was a 1973 Cutlass Supreme," Uncle Snap started.

"Three shooters. One in the car, one in combat boots, the other, smaller build in black Nikes," I said, glancing at my uncle.

Uncle Snap nodded, then continued, "The one behind my . . . my . . ."—he paused then cleared his throat—"behind Claudette, had a mark on his wrist. Couldn't see that clearly, though."

"I caught that the one who shot her from behind was left-handed," Shanelle added.

"If you go back to the first angle, the Cutlass was parked around the corner. Still couldn't see the face but we might be able to catch the license," Jai pointed out. "Also, I noticed in that Honda, right there, if you look closely you'll see another person."

Surprised, I paused and looked closer. "Shit, it sure is. Who is that?"

"Oh, my God. Good eye, Jai," Shanelle said, staring at the monitor.

"Damn, where?" Trey slid from his spot to study the video. "I see them. Hmm." Rubbing his chin in thought, he shook his head. "From the video, you can also see that she had a blade; but it wasn't found at the crime scene or just wasn't recorded. Yet, you see it there in the video." He pointed.

"Someone took it. Maybe like a trophy?" I asked in thought.

"It's a possibility. Either way, we'll figure this out, Von." Trey gave me a look of seriousness. "On my word. I already have it running through our system to break it apart and study every part of it to get more clues."

A low, guttural wail sounded and we all looked up to see Uncle Snap clutching his head, shaking in pain and tears. "They killed my woman in cold blood! Struck her down like she was nothing."

Pain shot through me and I reached out to Uncle Snap and pulled him into my hold. We all sat in silence as he let his pain out. I vowed that we'd get our revenge. "Do whatever you can to give us more details and find us that possible witness."

Meeting over, we all went home in silence. The image of Mama being taken down like an

animal was burned in my mind. It was clear that
a hit was put out on her and that it had gone foul
thanks to Mama's quick wit. Whoever was trying
to kill her had to take the matter into their own
hands because Mama had picked off the man
who went after her. Since that was the case, they
chose to blow their cover, which was a major
flaw.

Never reveal your hand, even in the last hours
of death.

Either way, I needed to think of a plan. "We
need to put ears to the street; and I want hands
on the goons who survived Mama's attack."

Chapter 6

Jojo

"Watch out, li'l bitch."

The tall dude damn near knocked my shoulder off as I passed him on the way to the round silver table with my food tray. Three days later and we were still locked away.

"Sure as fuck hope you get shipped to the same prison as me, pretty boy. That asshole gon' be a pussy when I'm done," another inmate said. This one was an old head. His wild hair looked like a used Brillo pad and he gave a literal meaning to the phrase "long in the tooth."

I'd been dealing with comments like that since I set foot in the jail. I was sick of it. I wanted out of this place. I knew damn well Mama would have been disappointed in me. Shit, I was disappointed in myself. I never thought about what would happen if I had gotten caught. Guess I wasn't thinking long term. It fucked me up mentally to know that as soon as I said I was out, shit had hit the fan.

I got to the table, hoping Monty and Navy were let out soon. They let us out to eat by levels. I was on the bottom while Navy and Monty were up top. Everything about the place annoyed me, from the light blue thick steel doors that separated us from the rest of the prisoners at night to the buttercream-colored stone walls.

I was hoping Javon would have us out by now. I didn't want to spend another night in here. I didn't try to cause any trouble. I didn't want it to find me, either. Just the thought of being locked away for a long period of time scared the shit out of me. If and when I got up outta here, I was never coming back. No matter what!

I looked at the bland food on my plate. The oatmeal looked like vomit. I bet the apple had worms and I refused to drink milk from a carton. However, I was hungry as fuck and the apple looked like the safest thing on the plate.

Just as the thought crossed my mind, someone snatched the apple from my tray. I took a deep breath and looked up to see, biting into my apple, the man who had all but threatened to butt fuck me if we ended up in the same prison.

"Problem?" he asked me while spittle flew from his mouth into my face and on the lenses of my glasses. He wanted a fight, I could tell. He was the type who got off on hurting people.

I didn't say anything. Just stared up at the man. The nigga looked like he was in and out of prison for fun. Damn it, I missed Cory more than ever. He could easily turn his crazy on and off when the time called for it. I didn't have that kind of buck in my system.

"Nah, fam, you got the problem," Navy said as he dropped his plate on the table next to mine, then stood toe-to-toe with the man. "You need to back the fuck up out my little brother's face or I'm about to walk the dog with your Billy Goat Gruff–looking ass."

Somebody yelled, "Oh shit. Think we got us one, fam!"

Another inmate yelled, "I put my lunch on pretty boy. Homie look like he 'bout that life."

We had an audience. Wasn't no need for me to tell Navy to chill because I knew he wouldn't. When people first looked at Navy, they probably didn't see the monster I knew lived just beneath the surface. Life had groomed him to be a chameleon. By the time people figured out my brother had the devil in him, it was too late.

The man sized Navy up. "You sho is pretty like a li'l bitch. All that pretty hair you got. Hope we make it to the same cell too. Make you lick my asshole while I'm fucking that li'l—"

I watched Navy's face contort. I knew the look. Knew what it was to relive the terror from our pasts. I thought Navy got it worse than I did when he was a kid. Just by listening to his story, by the time Mama had gotten to him he had already learned to defend his manhood by any means necessary.

Before Brillo pad could finish the sentence, Navy had punched the man in the throat. I jumped up from my seat, grabbing my plate as a weapon just in case I had to help Navy. I had to wonder where Monty was. The inmates were loud as Navy yelled out when the man punched him in the chest. I took my tray and cracked it over the man's face. Blood shot out from the man's nose as he hollered. He went down to one knee. Navy grabbed him by the collar of his jumpsuit. He brought the man's face to his kneecap over and over and over and over again.

Someone grabbed me from behind. By now, I thought I'd hear alarms going off and correctional officers yelling for us to get on the ground, but I heard nothing. It felt like a setup. I wrestled with whoever had grabbed me from behind, but a punch to the gut took me down.

I kept having flashbacks of the woman my real mother had sold me to coming into my room with men holding me down so they could do shit to me that shouldn't have been allowed. I heard something metal hit the floor beside me. It had thick tape wrapped around the handle and a long, sharp object protruding from the end. I knew a shank when I saw one. Navy had knocked the Brillo pad man out. But now two more guys were on him. I looked up to see Monty rushing in. He was naked and wet, but he jumped in the middle of the fight like he was fully clothed. Bodies went flying as soon as he started swinging. Blood soaked his face, which told me something had happened to him. Had he been in the shower and gotten jumped too?

Didn't matter. I couldn't think about that. It felt as if the men attacking me were trying to rip my clothes off. They may not have been, but in my mind I was that seven-year-old little boy again. A kick to my side sent me sliding but not before I grabbed the shank. It would have hurt but my mind was on survival. My glasses fell off and I couldn't see anymore. Any other time, this would have frightened me, but I couldn't afford to be scared. I wasn't about to let that woman or none of her friends do that to me again. Never again. I placed my back against the wall. All I saw were shadows and blurs, but as soon as they came for me, I tried to send every last one of my demons back to hell.

Chapter 7

Shanelle

For the last three days, I'd been scouring the places where Jojo mostly sold his product. From the high school he went to, to the colleges he supplied, back to the rich folk side of town where all the preppy kids hung out. After cleaning and trying to salvage any- and everything I could find in Jojo's room after the Feds left, I'd found notes and an old map in one of his science projects. In their overzealousness to scour his room for drugs, they completely overlooked those things. The warrant had said they could only search Jojo's room and the basement, which meant not only was there a possible snitch in the streets, but there was a snitch in the house. How else would they know to search the basement specifically?

Shit wasn't adding up. My phone beeped. A message from Lucky came through. I ignored it. He'd been trying to get me to talk to him for days.

It's not that he wasn't fine, because he was. It was just that Javon and I had already been down that road before. There was little to nothing that would make me step out on him again. Lucky caught me at a time when I had matured, and using other niggas to get back at Javon to make him mad was a thing of the past.

Walking around the Georgia State campus didn't yield me much, but it gave me enough to know that Jojo's name rang bells around the college. Students thought I was coming to deliver drugs and they were sorely disappointed that I wasn't. The weather wasn't too hot and wasn't too cool. It was hot enough to not need a coat, but not warm enough to not wear a light sweater or jacket. I was dressed in black: black leggings, a black turtleneck, and black combat boots. My hair was pulled back into a ponytail and my makeup was minimal. The college was alive with life. Students milled about, some wearing blue and white hoodies to show their school pride. Different kinds of music clashed when cars rolled down the street. All kinds of food rented the air as well.

"So you guys know nothing about someone going to the cops on my little brother?" I asked the small group of students who had been sitting around the big tree in the middle of campus.

"No, just know he's been MIA since Crum and Calista were found dead. He used to sell to them all the time," someone said.

There was no need for me to ask who they were. X-clusive had been one of the gangs that Jojo had been selling his product to. When he wanted out, they decided that they'd rather kill him before allowing him to walk away from their business deal. While running for his life, Jojo had called Cory. Cory had killed Calista and Crum just before he was killed himself. They were two of the leaders of the X-clusive clique.

I paid close attention to the dark-skinned black girl who had been watching me since I'd asked the group of people she was hanging with if they knew anything about Jojo. She kept trying to hide her face, and any time I looked in her direction she looked away. At first I thought she was trying to avoid me, but when she picked up her book bag and walked away, she glanced over her shoulder at me.

I followed her until we made it a few blocks away from where all the students were. As soon as I rounded the corner, she was in my face.

"Who are you and what do you want with Jo-nathan?" she barked at me.

The fact she called him Jo-nathan, pronounced Joe Nathan instead of Jonathan, told me she knew him well. Jojo hated his real name.

He would curse anybody to hell who called him by his real name as opposed to Jojo.

"First off, back up out my face. Second of all, who are you?" I asked.

The girl studied me for a moment. Distrust was all in her eyes. Her dark skin had a glow to it. Her natural hair blew wild in the wind. She was dressed like most of the kids on campus: skinny jeans, brown combat boots, and a coat that was way too big for the weather we were having.

"She told me about you," the girl said.

I quirked a brow. "She who?"

"The white girl. She said you would be coming down here, asking questions and shit. Told me not to tell you anything."

My mind immediately went to Melissa. "What did she look like?"

"Why should I tell you anything? She said not to trust you. Said you always fussed at Jojo. You and your little boyfriend."

I took my cell from my pocket and pulled up a picture of me and Melissa at the gym. "Is this the girl?" I asked.

The girl nodded. "Yeah, that's her. What's going on? Where is Jo-nathan?"

"He's locked up," I told her.

Tears sprang to her eyes. "I told him. I told him to stop and he wouldn't listen."

I really wished I had the patience to comfort the girl, but unfortunately I did not. I needed information and I didn't care who I got it from. "Look, I need you to tell me what else the white girl said to you," I said.

"She didn't say a lot. Just told me not to talk to you. Tell him I'm sorry. Tell Jojo I didn't know the black lady was a cop."

"Whoa wait, what black lady?"

"A few days ago, she came down here. Rounded a few of us up asking about Jojo and his dealings with X-clusive. She knew he was my boyfriend. Said she'd seen us around town. Told me if I didn't want Jojo to die, I had to tell her what he was up to so she could help him."

I frowned for many reasons. One, Jojo was seventeen with a college-aged girlfriend. Two, who the fuck was this black lady? Three, why the hell would Melissa tell this girl not to talk me or Javon?

"What's your name?" I asked.

"Danielle. Jojo calls me Dani."

"How old are you?"

She hesitated a moment then glanced at the ground. "Just turned twenty-one yesterday."

"Do you know Jojo is only seventeen?" I all but yelled.

"I . . . I do, but—"

"There are no buts! You're a grown woman. He's a kid!"

"I told him that. He wouldn't take no for an answer. He kept asking me out, buying me things, showing up places."

"How old was he when you met him?"

"Sixteen."

"Which means you were twenty."

"Was nineteen going on twenty."

"He's a boy."

"He's nice to me. He doesn't make me do things I don't want to do. He doesn't hit me. That makes him more man than any man my age."

"He's a boy!"

"He's seventeen. He'll be eighteen soon."

I had a good mind to take my gun from my purse and shoot that bitch. I knew I was probably overreacting. Knowing what happened to Jojo as a child made me want to protect him, even from himself. We all knew Jojo had a thing for older women, so to speak. When he was fourteen, I beat down some eighteen-year-old he had set his sights on. Then when he was fifteen, Inez choked some twenty-year-old chick out. Mama had laid into a few other older women Jojo had gotten himself involved with. It was never ending. It was like the boy couldn't help himself, but he was still just a child and I would always beat down any adults who couldn't control themselves when it came to children.

"Let me tell you something: you stay away from Jojo. Do you understand me? He's a child—"

"She said you would try to keep us apart."

"Danielle, Dani, whatever your name is, stay away from Jojo. I won't say it again."

"No."

I tilted my head to the side. "Excuse me?"

"I said no. I . . . I can't."

I slid my phone in my back pocket. I was about to put that bitch flat on her big ass until she stepped back and opened her coat. I took a breath so deep it got lodged in my throat. Her stomach protruded just enough for me to see she was pregnant. It was small and barely there, but she was clearly pregnant.

"Oh, my God. How far along are you?" I asked.

"Four months."

"Does he know?"

She nodded.

"Oh, shit, Jojo," I whispered.

I was so undone, I had no idea what to say next. I gave Dani my cell number and told her to call me if she heard anything else. That was all I could do for now. The urge to strangle her was so strong, I had to leave before I did just that.

I didn't know what to say or what to do as I rushed to my car. Nausea overtook me. I rummaged in my purse and popped a Phenergan. Seeing Dani pregnant made me remember I was too. I had yet to tell Javon. Dr. Ahn told me there was a very big chance I wouldn't carry this child or any other child to term because of the damage done when I lost the last baby. It was as if the chick I'd been fighting with had literally kicked my womb loose. My cervix was so damn thin the doctor was giving me P17 shots to try to prevent premature labor.

Javon wanted a baby, but there was no way I would get his hopes up only to lose the child, then have to see the pain in his eyes afterward. No, I couldn't tell him yet, not until the doctor said I was in the clear.

I couldn't worry about that, not when Jojo had a grown woman pregnant. And not while he, Navy, and Monty were locked away. Not to mention that the way Mama was cut down like a dog in the middle of the street kept replaying over and over in my mind. I was so caught up in my own thoughts that I never saw the black car trailing me as I pulled into traffic.

Chapter 8

Uncle Snap

"There was a problem at the jail," Jai said as soon as she walked into the house. The panic in her eyes alarmed me. Dressed in a cream two-piece business suit that fit every curve she owned, she looked every bit of the lawyer she was.

"What do you mean?" I asked.

"Where's Javon?" she asked.

"Upstairs in the shower."

I watched Jai's expression. Clearly there was something going on or something had gone on between her and Javon. I couldn't be sure. But I saw the way nephew looked at her and I saw the way she regarded him. I didn't want no bullshit, but I knew what would happen if Javon had done something stupid like cheated on Shanelle again.

I wouldn't even confront nephew about it. Sooner or later, the shit would hit the fan. For that very reason, I kept Jai at arm's length. Wasn't for nobody coming in trying to cause havoc. It was the same reason I fed Lucky with a long-handle spoon. He may have thought he was nickel slick but I had his penny change.

"Will you get him? Or I'll do it," she said and made her way to the stairs.

I stopped her. "I got it," I said. I took the stairs two at a time. I rapped on Mama's door three times.

"Yeah?" Javon yelled.

"We got some trouble," I said. "Jai's here."

"I'm coming," he said.

I headed back downstairs. I tried to call Shanelle, but I got no answer. Javon came downstairs five minutes later. Dressed in jeans and a hoodie, he looked like he was ready to go hang out at the park or something. Jai's eyes danced over him like he was a suitcase with millions of dollars in it. He noticed it because the fool-ass boy smirked.

"Get to the business, Jai," I said.

She came to her senses. "Your brothers were attacked in jail this morning."

That wiped that silly-ass smirk right off his face. "What?" he asked.

"Yes, apparently it was a setup."

I asked, "Anyone hurt?"

"Yes. Jojo killed two inmates."

"What the fuck? Say what?" I blurted out.

"They're going to charge him with those murders."

"You were supposed to have them out of there by now," Javon snapped.

"I was working on that. Had gotten bail set for Navy and Monty—"

"And what about Jojo?" I asked, cutting her off.

"I have to play this smoothly, Raphael. I can't just walk in there and walk out with him without even attempting to go through the proper channels. If we don't want him to be seen as this drug lord, we have to not treat him as if he is one."

"Fuck all that, Jai. If you had done what you were supposed—"

"Wait one damn minute," Jai snapped. "I'm doing my fucking job. Don't come at me like I'm not. I got to the jail to bail out Monty and Navy and they told me what had happened once I got there."

"Did they let you see the boys?" I asked, just to stop her and Javon from having a pissing match.

"They did. Monty and Navy are pretty banged up, but they're well. It's Jojo who, I fear, has had a psychotic break."

Javon frowned then folded his arms across his chest. "Meaning?"

Jai sighed then set her briefcase down. "I have footage from the jail of the fight. See for yourself."

Jai pulled her MacBook from her briefcase then opened it. She took a flash drive from the bag as well then inserted it. It took a few seconds for the video to pop up. I watched as Jojo took a seat. Watched as some old-ass prison-built nigga took his apple from his plate. Saw when Navy stepped in. All hell broke loose then. Navy punched the man. Jojo took his tray and broke it across the man's face. Two niggas grabbed Jojo from behind while Navy was still putting in work on the other dude.

Jojo was on the floor fighting for his life. I'd never seen nephew fight with such aggression. Hell, I didn't even know he could fight. My heart dropped when a shank hit the floor. Heart sank further when two men grabbed Navy and tried to take him down. I had no worries that Navy could and would defend himself. There was a naked blur that rushed into the camera. Bodies went flying everywhere.

"What the fuck was that?" Javon asked.

"That was Lamont," Jai answered. "He was attacked in the shower first. Needless to say, he won. But pay attention to Jojo."

Javon's cell went off upstairs.

"It's probably Shanelle," I said. "She called earlier."

Javon made a move to go upstairs, but Jai stopped him. She grabbed his arm. "She can wait. This is important," she said to him.

I almost told Javon to go answer the phone anyway, but my eyes were locked on the screen. By now, Jojo's glasses had fallen off. I watched as nephew picked up the shank then put his back against the wall. Monty or Navy must have put the bug in his ear to always fight with your back against the wall when outnumbered. As soon as niggas rushed him, Jojo wasted no time lashing out. He used that shank like he had been trained to do so by a master swordsman.

By the time nephew was done, bodies lay at his feet. Two nonmoving. Jojo looked like something out of a horror movie. Both hands fisted, shank in one. Blood raining down his face and, although I couldn't hear him, the wide mouth and wild look in his eyes told me he was screaming. More like roaring. They'd placed him in a jungle and he came out king.

The video stopped. Javon and I were both left speechless. His phone started ringing again.

"Get to the jail to get my brothers out of there. I don't give a fuck who you have to call and what favors you have to call in. I want them out of there. *Tonight*," Javon ordered.

"I'll see what I can do," Jai said.

Javon got in Jai's face. "No. Don't see what you can do. Do it or I'll find someone else who can."

With that, Javon stormed back upstairs. Jai looked after him like she wanted to chase him down and make him forget his brothers.

"Jai, leave him alone," I said.

"I'm not bothering him. I'm just trying to do my job."

"That's not what I'm talking about and you know it. Shanelle is his woman. Leave him be."

Jai gave a snide chuckle as she closed her MacBook then put it back in her briefcase.

Before walking out the door, she said, "If I want him, I can have him, and Shanelle being his woman won't stop that. Again, I'm here to do my job, but if something else comes up, I won't stop it."

I watched the young woman walk out the front door. My nephew was a good man, honorable even, but I knew the wiles of a woman could tempt even the best men. I prayed Javon was over that phase in his life. Prayed even harder that Shanelle knew better than to let Lucky get too close.

My phone started ringing. It was Shanelle.

"Hey, niece. Where are you?" I asked.

It took me a minute to realize I heard gunshots in the background.

"I need help, Uncle. I got ambushed. I called Javon but he didn't answer. I crashed my car trying to get away."

I didn't even have time to explain to her why he didn't answer. "Where you at, niece?"

"Cleveland Avenue just off exit 241. I'm stuck. I'm in the parking lot behind the legal aid office. I took out a few but my ammo is low."

"We coming, baby girl. Javon," I yelled.

He came barreling down the stairs. "What?"

"It's Shanelle. We have to go."

Chapter 9

Javon

There was no pause in my actions. As soon as Uncle Snap said Shanelle's name and that we had to go, I felt it in my gut that we had another situation going on.

"Hit me with the level of the situation, Uncle," I quickly said.

"We have a Queen's Gambit going on, nephew," he responded in worry, tossing me a bulletproof vest while he slid his on.

Fear flashed across my mind. A Queen's Gambit, or QG, was a term I saw written in Mama's diary. It was code that either one of the Syndicate's female heads was being attacked or any wife of one of the Syndicate's heads was being attacked. Had Mama Claudette been able to get to a phone and put out a message to the Syndicate, that was exactly what she would have either said or texted: QG.

In a QG, it could go in favor of the queen taking out her enemies or those who attacked her, or it could all go foul and turn on her. Right now, Shanelle was without protection and backup. Immediately, all I saw in my mind was Mama being surrounded and taken down. I couldn't have that happen to Shanelle. I was already dealing with Jojo being attacked.

The image of him screaming on the video was burning fresh in my skull. I knew exactly why he was screaming and why he was able to take those motherfuckers down as cleanly as he did, with no glasses on top of that. He was locked in a PTSD and manic attack and the added fact that it was a setup for all my brothers to go down like that, whoever was gunning for us was going to show their hand eventually. When they did, I'd be right there ready.

Moving to my silver Charger, I kneeled near my license plate, changed it out, then hurried toward the driver side. "I need all street cameras and security cameras to be put on blackout around and near Cleveland Avenue, immediately," I shouted in my Bluetooth to the Forty Thieves. Worry and rage had me clutching the wheel of my ride. My knuckles were white from the pressure I had in my grip as we sped through our area to get to Shanelle. "We have a QG going on," I explained. "Get on it."

Silence was my friend until my uncle decided to speak. "I've been going over and over in my head on who is gunning for us, nephew."

"Yeah? Did you figure that shit out? Because the family is being attacked. We need Jojo out right now, and Shanelle . . . Fuck." There was no way this was reality. "Never should have taken on Mama's plan for us. We keep losing."

As I sped on, I wished that Monty and Navy were with us. Considering how they protected Jojo, I knew they would be the best eyes outside of Uncle to keep Shanelle safe while we took out whoever was after her. But, since they were in transition to being released, wasn't much else for me to do.

"Don't say you never should have taken this on!"

I glanced at my uncle then made a sharp turn, slowing down as he spoke with passion.

"Boy, you've single-handedly moved a mountain that even my woman had trouble pushing. You got the family sitting all in their perspective roles. This ain't your fault that we all are having difficulties right now, okay?" As he spoke, he reached under the seat and removed a part of his compact long-range Remington. He set one part on his lap, then ran his palm against the side of the door to remove another component.

"There's a helluva lot that you and your siblings need to learn. I'm tryin'a give you that, nephew. You just gotta let these seeds sprout then trim them when you see they are growing in the wrong directions. Get me?"

I glanced at him as he put the rifle together then locked it with force. He was right, but it wasn't something that I could fully accept right then and there. There was just too much that had happened that wouldn't allow me to have that same type of wisdom as my uncle. I just needed everyone to back the hell up off us and give us some breathing room, but I guessed I had to show it from a different angle then.

"Yeah." I exhaled, flipped my hoodie up, and slid low in my ride, rolling down the windows as we approached a four-way. "Yes, sir. I get you."

"Good. Here." Slapping a semiautomatic on my lap, Uncle Snap cocked his cap over his eyes, then shifted his seat back and lay with the Remington pressed against his chest.

One look at my uncle and it was time. Gripping the wheel, once the light changed, we rolled past the legal aid office. It was a tall white cube building with various windows with parking at the back. Immediately we heard gunshots ringing out. Cars were chaotically zooming by, while my uncle and I hit a quick U-turn then drove near the building, taking it to the back of it.

I could see, in the parking lot connected to the legal aid office, Shanelle's car parked haphazardly half on a curb, half off near an exit fence of the lot. Across from her was a black car with people climbing out of it. In front of it was a second car, a navy blue Cutlass, which also had people spilling from it. She was surrounded and the shit smelled like a setup.

Jaw clenching, I zoomed the car up, nodded at my uncle, then aimed my ride at the people who shot at her. Immediately I saw a parked black car. Guns were pointing from it at my baby. Several of my backup were blazing bullets at that black car. Whereas, me? I swiftly backed my ride up, hit the gas, then ran my ride into that bitch. The sharp crash of my car into the side of it had my uncle and me jerking around.

"Gotdamn, nephew!" Uncle Snap shouted out.

I didn't have time for a snappy comeback but I gave him a quirked eyebrow as I climbed out of the car. He moved with me, kicking open the glove compartment, pulling out any identification, then climbing out to aim his Remington at the shooters.

"Shanelle!" I shouted, using my automatic.

Tension had my vision narrowing as I looked around. People in hoodies came from my left and right. Others broke apart and scattered like rats away from the gunplay. I watched the Forty Thieves chase after them, as others took it upon themselves to run up on me trying to take me down. I had to inwardly laugh. They just didn't understand who the hell I was. Rolling my shoulders back, I ducked down, flipped my gun in my hand, fisting it, then countered with several punches to the face of a goon.

Gravel crunched under our feet as the bastard stumbled backward. Quickly, I ran forward, chucked my foot up, then sent a solid slam of my kicks into his chest, followed up with a bullet to the face once I got my footing. I dropped to one knee, lifted the body up, and used it as a shield against the blaze of rounds aimed my way. As I held that body, I pushed off the mask and saw it was a brotha. There were no gang-affiliated markings on this nigga at all and it had me wondering what the hell was going on.

"Who the fuck are you all working for, huh?" I shouted.

I threw the body back down, pushed back up, then turned toward the black car, which, funny enough, had no driver because that door was open and that side of the car was empty. Had Shanelle gotten to them?

"Uncle Snap! Von!" cut through the noise.

"Shanelle, gal! We're here fo' ya!" Uncle Snap shouted between squeezing out rounds. "Where ya at?"

Bullets sizzled past me, a few grazing my clothes. The attack had me dropping low to run as I saw Uncle Snap covering my back. From my angle, I saw the bopping of hair, a familiar hairstyle, along with a scarf-covered face and familiar brown eyes. Several bodies were littered around, forming a pattern near what I knew was Shanelle's ride. From how the car was haphazardly parked on a curve in the exit of the parking lot, I could tell that she had chosen this small location as a means to isolate the fight.

Bullet holes peppered the car. There was a large scratch on the side of her ride and her right blinker was going off and on. Looking her way, I saw her partially covered face pop back up where she was behind her car and some hedges. Baby girl was resourceful in using her surroundings as protection, and I mentally smiled at knowing it was Shanelle.

"Got her, Unc!"

As I ran forward, everything seemed to switch to slow motion once Shanelle's and my eyes locked. I glanced left and right. I saw her rise up, two automatics in her hands, from behind where she hid on the opposite side of her car and the bushes. As she spread them wide, I spun on my feet as if reading to catch a football while I ran.

Swiftly, we shot off rounds. I acted because she acted and she was seeing behind me what I wasn't. The result of that was several masked bastards were simultaneously hit with our rounds. Due to the propulsion of my movements, I slid hard against the side of Shanelle's ride. I gasped from the wind being knocked out of me and I fell to my knees, hands flat on the gravel dirt.

"Can you reach me, baby?" I shouted.

White dirt and gravel from the uncared-for parking lot asphalt coasted in the air creating a cloud. I thanked the Based God above for not being hit by anything as I leaned to my side, tucked, and rolled out of the way.

When Shanelle shouted, "Yes," I slid her several extra clips and a fresh Glock. Sweat leaked in my eyes. I used the back of my sleeve to wipe it clear as I caught my breath. All around me was bedlam. Goons ran. Cars did their best to avoid the area and flashing lights indicated that it was time to haul ass. However, Shanelle had another idea in mind.

I watched her stand up, reach down, and grit her teeth as her body tensed while walking slowly forward. Rolling to my side, I pushed up and noticed her pulling a body behind her. A smirking grin flashed across my face when she dropped the hulking body at my feet. Glancing at me, she literally did a standing skip and kicked her boot into the side of the face of the masked man.

Staring down at him, she dropped down, ripped his mask off then looked past me, letting off a round. Her actions had my dick rising with the intensity of the situation. I took the time in that moment to memorize the face of her captive. My stomach clenched in awareness as I saw a mark, a branding, on the wrist of the guy. He was the one who landed the killing blow to our Mama.

Jaw clenching, I dropped down and gripped that nigga by his neck, burning my gaze into his face. "Clear the area and move our ride, baby. We need to go," I said without looking her way. I reached up and slapped her ass, then finally looked up. "You did good, baby."

Eyes twinkling with a smile, she nodded. "I know."

With that, Shanelle strode forward and cleared the area as Uncle Snap came to her side. He was breathing hard like me, sweating and covered in blood. A blade was in his hand and he held his Remington in a tired, slacking way.

As they cleared the area, doubled back, and opened the passenger side to Shanelle's ride, I worked on binding our prize captive. His head lolling, I waited for him to open his eyes, which he did. I listened to him murmuring something in another language that I couldn't readily identify yet, because he spoke so low; then I chucked him over my shoulder.

"Save that shit for later, my friend. We have a lot to talk about," I said.

"Ain't that right," I heard at my side with a loud cracking of a fist against a face.

Turning, I smiled at Uncle Snap then stuffed this fool into the trunk of Shanelle's ride.

A sharp whistle let me know that several of the Thieves were around. I made a signal for them to back off but also to clear our area, which I knew they would as protocol. They would remove any traces of my ride belonging to me then leave the rest for the cops to play with.

Satisfied that Shanelle was safe, we all climbed into her ride and unhinged it from the curb then sped off. We all ended up near our undisclosed shipping facility. It was set up with everything we that we needed if we ever found ourselves in a bind. There were clothes, food, cash, and extra vehicles just in case shit like this happened. We dropped Shanelle's car off, changed out of everything, and then tied up our guest.

"Uncle, meet the nigga who put the killing blow in Mama's skull," I said while putting a pair of gloves on and standing in my black combat boots, white beater, and jeans.

Behind me, Shanelle was in a matching outfit, and a cropped hoodie sweatshirt. Uncle stood in overalls with his Remington in his hand. We all studied the face of one of Mama's killers. Anger was definitely in us, but there was something else. I wasn't sure if it was grief or something darker than anger in our spirits while we watched this hanging dude. But, whatever it was, it had me bristling and ready to cut the guy open like a fillet.

"How do you know?" Uncle calmly asked.

Reaching up, I grabbed the guy's arm, unhooked it from its cuff, then flipped his wrist up and snapped it just for the pain. Our guest gave a sharp grunt then began tugging on the chain he hung from by his other arm. See, from the looks of this guy, he was mixed up with something while appearing more Caucasian than other.

Shaved buzz cut, peppered hair around his chin, dirty nails, blue eyes, and a crooked nose. Dude wasn't anything special. There were several sleeve tattoos on the upper parts of his arms. His now bare chest was covered in several markings as well, in Spanish and some other language. Splashes of vibrant colors were inked in his flesh as well.

"Mark on the wrist," I stated then walked around the guy. "I know you're awake."

Uncle walked up to the guy. He poked a burn mark against the ribcage of the guy then used his Remington to push the guy's chin up. "He's formerly São Africana. Don't kill him."

Whipping around, I opened my mouth to go off but Shanelle beat me to the punch.

"He helped kill Mama!" she shouted incredulously while pointing her finger at him with tears rimming her eyes.

Spitting on the ground, I watched Uncle back up and walk to her car, pulling out a bag. "I know, baby girl, which is why I'm saying don't touch him. Sãos are our allies with the pipeline in Brazil. They are who we manage through, so think on it, baby girl. They have a turncoat, and we have him."

"I don't give a damn!" Shanelle ranted.

My arms crossed over my chest as I realized what my uncle was doing. He was right. For him to have that burn mark let us know one of two things: either he was kicked out of the Sãos or he ran. Either way, they'd still want him in order to permanently erase him. We needed to secure our partnership with them and move them on our permanent pay grade. But, the main thing was this: we needed information and if we had to bleed this nigga dry we would, in order to get that information.

"Shanelle, watch your step," I calmly said, rubbing my chin. "Check out Uncle."

We both turned to see Uncle Snap removing a steel container from his bag. He unscrewed it, then walked up to our hanging guest. "Like I said, don't kill him. But we for damn sure will harm him," he growled low then tossed the container at the guy.

Clear liquid splashed and our hostage let out an animalistic scream that put a grin on my face. Hell yes, we were going to get some answers; but, for now, it was time to play. Shanelle's hand slid to my arm. She gazed up at me, then kissed my lips. I watched her walk up to the guy then reach down where she had laid a bat with needles it in. One swing and a hit, and more screams rent the air.

I stood there watching as liquid sloshed down our captive's body. The smell of burning flesh mixed with the scent of a strong sulfuric stench thanks to the liquid lye Uncle carried around stung my nose. While I reserved my own play with our guest, I enjoyed watching the two people I loved the most in the world work out their rage and dish out a little eye for an eye. As they did, my cell began to vibrate and I reached to answer it while walking out of the storage area.

"Talk to me," I said, finger to my Bluetooth bud.

"Von? Where you at? Why aren't you here?" I realized it was Navy on the other end.

"Where's Monty? Is he with you?"

A rustling on the other end of the phone kick-started my worry and I started pacing where I was. I hadn't expected Navy to call me, let alone have access to call yet. I knew they were in transition to be released but it wasn't supposed to happen until Jai hit me up with that information on when to pick them up. Now, I was busy with the man who helped kill Mama and listening to a brother who I was too relieved to hear from.

"Yeah, yeah, he's by my side. Jojo isn't here."

"Do you want me to go back in to protect him?" I heard Monty shout in the background.

"No! Both of you chill. I'm on my way right now. If it's not me or the FT then don't trust a damn thing. I'm on my way. And we working on Jojo," I quickly added, jaw clenched in anxiousness. "Tell me where y'all at."

"The Waffle House. We walked from the station there," Navy let me know.

"A'ight, I'm on my way." I quickly hung up and sprinted to the storage area. As I did so my cell went off again. I didn't have time for my cell to be fucking blowing up like this. Annoyed, I quickly answered, "Yeah?"

"Jojo is being released. I pulled some strings, made this look as legit as I could, and I have him out due to his mental state and age. He'll have to wear an ankle monitor, but he'll be out and we'll be waiting for you or the others to pick him up."

Relief hit me heavy in my gut at the sound of those words coming from Jai.

"I tried Raphael first but he's not answering. Is the old man okay?"

"He will be. Listen, thank you, and keep doing what you doing for my brothers, especially Jojo." I stared at our swinging guest then added, "Tell the Syndicate that we will need to meet up for a meeting on a secure feed for those who can't fly back in quickly, a'ight?"

"I'll do that. Bye, Mr. McPhearson."

Once the line went dead, I shook my head then sprinted inside. "Jojo is being released on house arrest for his safety. We need to get to the courthouse and pick him up, but also get Navy and Monty. They are at the Waffle House."

There was a blank look in both my uncle's and Shanelle's eyes. As soon as I mentioned our brothers, though, that humanity flickered back in their eyes.

"Uncle, find out whatever you can from this dude," I stated. "Shanelle, you coming with me or staying here?"

"I'll be good here," Uncle Snap said with a wave of the hand.

"You sure?" Shanelle asked, walking to him and placing a hand against his shoulder.

"Yes, baby girl."

The weight of the world was on our uncle's shoulders and I could see that Shanelle saw it. She mouthed for me to go ahead, and I gave a nod, doing just that. We needed our brothers out, but we also needed to know who was gunning for us. I wished Cory was alive.

With Shanelle by our uncle's side, I knew that he'd be okay and able to focus on finding out what we needed. Besides, I knew he would be able to teach Shanelle some things in interrogation. So without a thought, I hopped in our extra ride then headed to the Waffle House then the courthouse, picking everyone up without a hitch.

Chapter 10

Melissa

"What do you mean, you can't pay me? If you want a happy pussy, then you need to pay this pussy. I have to keep my rent up or we are done, Diambu . . . Hold on. My cell is ringing, baby."

The lap of luxury was so exhausting when breaking off pussy for rich men. I mean, I never thought I'd be in an era where more men were acting like women instead of dominant men. Hell, Diambu was from Nigeria and acting like a punk. He was sexy, thick like the country boys of Georgia. Unfortunately, he wasn't Hershey's Syrup cocoa like I usually enjoyed my black men to be, but he was good enough. He was light caramel with hazel eyes, the son of a Dutch oil tycoon and a Nigerian educator. I really didn't care as long as he paid me and kept me looking pretty. I had bills to pay, and a savings account to stack up.

I also had appearances to keep up. Climbing out of a white linen bed, naked and covered in the afterglow of good sex, I flipped my hair over my shoulder. I glanced out the window to see the midtown skyline, then headed to where my cell sat on a dresser. I had several texts from other lovers of mine, but one stood out and had me worried.

"Who are you on the phone with?" Diambu called out to me. "This is our time and I need more of you."

"Baby, I'll give you all you need, but you just told me you can't pay me . . . help me with my rent, and now I'm sad about it," I said while texting urgently and biting my lower lip.

There was a problem, a major one. Shanelle had talked to Jojo's girlfriend, and now my lovely sister knew about his nine-month situation. *Damn it.*

"I'll help you but I want stock in your club, Lissa," I heard Diambu state.

A deep sigh came from me as I texted and ignored him. There was no way that I was allowing his hands on the club. It was mine! I finally had something that I could make into my own thing and I planned to keep it. Besides, it was a good cash cow thanks to its prime location and clientele. I had met Diambu there, anyway, so there was no way that I was giving him that gem.

Going through my texts, I saw another one that made me clutch my cell hard. This one was from Javon, asking me where I was at and telling me that Shanelle needed me. I inwardly laughed at that crap. Shanelle needed me? As if. If anything, she needed a doctor. I typed a lie that I was stuck in traffic and couldn't make it, then tossed my cell on the table. Whatever, with Von. I mean, I was thankful for thinking of me with the club, but I had too many eggs that needed tending to.

"I'm not doing that, Diambu. I already linked you up with help to bring you more money to your father's business; yet, you're trying to take from me at the same time? This isn't how partnership works, baby. Now, pay me my two hundred K, please."

Men loved a weak-willed woman, so when I spoke to Diambu I always had to soften my language and approach him in a way that tailored to his childish ego. I also had to seduce him. While I stood near the bed, I ran my nails over my stomach then my hairless mound. My teeth grazed my lips while I stared at his dick growing in his hand. That large palm of his rose up and dropped down, working his head, and I laughed then sighed when my cell rang again.

"Hold on. I promise I'll give you everything you need, Diambu," I said.

"And I'll pay you what you asked, princess," he responded. "Just turn that shit off."

Giggling, I went to my phone. The only reason I answered was because it rang with a special ringtone. "Hello?"

"We have a problem."

"And?" I asked.

"No 'and.' Tell us what you need to have done or we are exiting the equation, boss."

Who the fuck did they think they were? That almost spilled from my lips, but I remembered that I wasn't in polite company. I always had to be careful with what I said around him. Every word I said to him or detail I gave had to be constructed in a manner that worked for my needs and kept everything easy. Sashaying to the bathroom, I closed the door then addressed the thorn in my side.

"Don't give me ultimatums. I control you and I can end you, do you understand that?" My hand laid flat on the counter while I gazed at my reflection in the mirror. Tears suddenly rimmed my eyes. My aroused, plump lips were now going back to normal. The love marks on my body were fading from their rose tone against my flesh. My hair slid over my right eye, veiling it in its golden curtain. I was not who I grew up to be.

This part of me was something different, a beast bred out of desperation and a need to survive. I hadn't meant to kill Mama. All I wanted was to scare her and put her in the hospital. That way I could convince the family to give me control over her insurance. After that, I mean, then she could have done like old, sick people do: die and make me rich.

But, it didn't go that way. When I chickened out of that plan, another one was forced in my lap. I really, really, really didn't want Mama dead. Especially after everything she had done for me. But as I tried to flip my situation in her favor, it flew out of my hands. Now, I was a boss, with a partner who had an iron-clad hand on my every movements and who was turning my life upside down. I didn't mean to kill Mama . . . and I didn't want to send those men after Shanelle or my brothers.

What the hell was wrong with my life? I had no control here, but I would act like I did. "Find Almir right now! Before Elias ends you for me!"

Abruptly hanging up, I soon got another text, this one saying my brothers had survived and were out, currently being picked up by Javon. My mouth dropped and I screamed silently in my mouth. This was not going to be good. They should have been snuffed out quickly in jail. I tried to help them out, really I did, but now it was just going to get worse. Almir was missing, and soon . . .

Elias would find out and, once that happened, his plan for Mama was going to extend to the whole family, me included. My pussy was good, but just not that good to continue manipulating Elias.

Chapter 11

Shanelle

"I'm going to ask you one more time. I got all night. I ain't got shit to do. Nobody knows where you at right now. I got all these toys to play with, too."

Uncle Snap had a sullen look on his face but it was mixed with something else, something akin to calm. He had been methodical in everything he had done and, yet, the man hadn't talked. Uncle didn't seem to be tired or annoyed, though. The place was eerily quiet. Not even the man's whimpers could cut through the silence.

Uncle had pulled a pair of jumper cables from the bag. They were attached to the man's pinkish-brown nuts. Blood, sweat, and piss trickled down the golden attachments as the sharp ends cut into the sensitive skin of his testicles. Snap hadn't even used them to the full extent yet. The sad part about the whole thing was that Uncle

Snap would let the man rest and then, just when he thought it was over, Uncle would start up again. There was something similar to a car battery sitting on the rickety, old table that the other end of the jumper cables were attached to.

"Now, who sent you and why?" Uncle asked again as he circled the man.

Razor blades protruded from the man's back. Sewing needles, big and small, had been stuck into his chest, hundreds of them. A needle prick by itself may have been something to sneeze at, but hundreds of needle pricks was something else altogether.

I was tired, sweaty, and nauseous. Not to mention I wanted to get home and see my brothers. I had so much to tell Javon, too.

"You may as well kill me," the man barely managed to get out, his Brazilian accent heavy.

"Y'all came all the way from Brazil to cut my woman down like a dog in the middle of the fucking street like she was nothing. Killing you would be all too easy."

Mucus-like slobber hung from the man's bottom lip as he spoke. "Maybe, b . . . but ya won't get shit else fra . . . from me."

A sinister smirk overtook Uncle's features. "As you wish," he said then turned to me. "Go home, baby girl. See about your brothers."

"But Ja—"

"Go on home, Shanelle. I'll be fine. Me and the hangman got lots to discuss. And, besides, I don't want a lady to see me deep fry a man's nuts. Go on. Javon and your brothers are going to need you."

For as much as I didn't want to leave Uncle alone, I was no good to him in the state I was in. Not to mention my body was sore and tired. I was hoping like hell I hadn't done too much to put my child in danger. I also noticed that the more the stuff with the Syndicate took over our lives, the less time Javon and I spent together. I missed him and had to wonder if we would ever be the same.

I nodded then hugged the old man. "Call if you need me."

"I got some thieves in the front and out back. Go."

I headed out to a waiting car. I made sure I had ammo and plenty of guns before a lone Thief drove me home. I couldn't wait to get in the house to see my brothers, more specifically Jojo. Since Mama had died, it seemed as if life had hit him the hardest.

I could hear voices inside the house. All the lights were on and I could make out Javon's shadow pacing back and forth in the window.

Thieves were strategically placed around the house. Some pretended to be jogging. Some were even walking dogs, blending in so no one would suspect a thing. The sun had set and cast an orange and reddish glow across the sky. The temperature had dropped a bit more as well.

I had just gotten out the car when Ms. Lily yelled across the street, "You gon' tell Javon to get over here and take out my trash and help me move this stuff out my basement?"

I put on a fake smile, turned, and waved. "Hi, Ms. Lily. I'll remind him," I said.

"You do that, and tell him hurry up, too."

I gave a tight-lipped smile to keep from being disrespectful to the old lady. "Yes, ma'am."

I closed the door of the truck then headed inside. I couldn't front like my paranoia didn't have me looking over my shoulders, even with the added protection around. Before I could push the door open, Navy snatched it wide. My eyes watered and it was as if I hadn't seen him in years as opposed to days. I hugged him so tight I was sure I damn near lifted him from the floor.

"Oh, my God," I whispered. I had more to say but couldn't, not at that moment. I pulled back and looked at Navy. My smile and elation faded. "What the hell happened to your face?" I asked.

He didn't have time to answer because I saw Monty and then I rushed to him. He actually lifted me from the floor with his big, beefy ass. I laughed and cried at the same time. When he finally let me go, I took in the bruises on his face as well. He, too, looked as if he had been in a fight.

"Where's Jojo?" I asked, looking around.

Javon had a despondent look on his face. "He's in his room. Let him be," Javon said.

"Why? What happened? Somebody do something to him?" I asked. There was panic in my voice. If something had happened to Jojo while he was in jail, I wouldn't be able to take it.

"Tried to. But he killed two people before they could," Navy said.

The wild-eyed, doe-in-headlights look told of the sheer horror I felt. "He killed two people?" I asked. "Jojo?"

"He ain't have a choice, sis. I got attacked in the shower. By the time I'd taken those niggas down, I heard a ruckus in the dining hall, so I rushed in. Naked as fuck, but it was whatever. My brothers needed me. We handled business," Monty said.

"It was a setup. Wasn't no guards or nothing," Navy added. "One nigga had a shank but he dropped it. So Jojo picked it up. He put his back against the wall like we told him—"

"Next thing we know, he was screaming and yelling, blood all over him and two bodies bleeding out at his feet. Guards came running then," Monty said.

Javon was shaking his head. "They released him, but he has to wear an ankle monitor. And that's only because Jai was able to call in some favors. He murdered two people on camera, so in reality, he shouldn't even be allowed to piss on his own."

"Didn't Mama have people in the department?" I asked. "Can't we do something to make this go away?"

"Jai's working on it," he said. "But, for now, I'm glad they're home. Glad Jojo's safe."

"Anybody heard from Melissa?" Navy asked.

"Yeah, I tried reaching her, but couldn't. She didn't pick up," Monty said.

"She texted me that she was stuck in traffic when I texted earlier. Told her you needed help. She said she couldn't get to you," Javon said.

I gave Javon a look that told him I didn't believe it, and I wouldn't believe it until we talked to Melissa. Fate must have heard my thoughts because Melissa came rushing into the house. Her hair was wild and her eyes red. She was dressed in red leather pants. A sheer white top with a black bra underneath, thigh-high boots that sat four inches high, and a black leather jacket finished her ensemble.

"I came as quick as I could," she blurted out. "Oh, gosh! Navy! Monty! You're home. Where's Jojo?"

"Where the fuck have you been?" I asked before anyone could answer her.

"I've been . . . I was taking care of the club," she answered.

"Taking care of the club? Did you not know the family was in peril?"

"I did, but I thought it would be a good idea not to let one of the top *legal* moneymaking businesses go to hell while trying to sort the other shit out."

"Are you out of your fucking mind?" I yelled. My anger wasn't really about her not being around. Not all of it. It was more about the nagging voice in the back of my mind telling me my sister couldn't be trusted. To think that hurt like hell. Melissa was my sister. Even though we had no blood relation, I loved her and Inez more than my words could ever tell. I didn't like the feeling that my intuition was giving me.

"Don't talk to me like that, Nelle," she said. She was blinking rapidly, rubbing the back of her neck like she was nervous.

"Calm down, Shanelle," Javon said.

"Calm down my ass. Tell me why and how you disappeared so fast when the Feds got here," I blurted out, completely forgetting that Javon had asked me not to go there.

Melissa cleared her throat then started pacing a bit. "For your information, I was so damn scared when the doors came flying off the hinges that I rushed out of here through one of the secret passages. I figured one of us needed to make it out of here just in case so we could tell what happened."

"So you left the rest of us to fend for ourselves?" I yelled. "No matter what is going down, Melissa, we always, *always* have the family's back. That's the way it's always been."

Her face turned red and she balled her lips. "Yeah, well, shit is different now, Nelle! We ain't those same everyday kids no more. Mama's gone and I'm scared as fuck that somebody is going to come back and finish us off because of who she was. Look at what happened to Cory and Inez," she yelled. "Not everybody is bad ass like you so forgive the fuck out of me for being human."

I got in her face. "You think the rest of us aren't scared? *We* lost Mama, Cory, and Inez in a matter of fucking days! Days, Melissa." I slapped tears away from my eyes. "And we almost lost three more brothers because someone wants to take us out. You think your hurt and pain is more important than ours? Think your fear is more important than our lives? We're all fucking scared."

"Don't get in my face like that, Shanelle," she warned me, then backed away. "I'm not scared of you."

"This ain't about you being scared of me. You abandoned us."

"I looked out for us."

"Girl, bye. You looked out for yourself."

"Like you do?" she asked sassily. "Inez was right," she said, shaking her head. "Her and Cory. If it isn't about you or Javon, you don't give a shit," she spat, stepping closer to me.

Although a part of me knew there was little truth to what she said, being that three of my siblings had voiced that opinion it was starting to weigh on me. Was it possible that I was the selfish, uncaring bitch they saw me as?

"That's enough," Javon said. "Melissa, your absence has been felt. We had a crisis and you were nowhere to be found."

Melissa sighed and shook her head. "Should have known you would side with her, but anyway. Like I said, I was taking care of the club and I was scared. But I knew you and Uncle Snap would take care of it. I didn't know I was needed until you texted me today."

Javon's brows furrowed. "This isn't about me taking anyone's side. I'm worried for all of us and I'm trying like hell to make sure we don't lose nobody else. I know shit has been hectic around here, but we all need to stay close, understand?"

Melissa's face was set in a tight scowl when she mumbled, "Understood."

For a moment, no one said anything, everyone lost in their own thoughts. Navy stood, shifting his weight from one foot to the other. He was dressed in his wheat-colored Tims, some baggy black jeans, and a V-neck tan sweater. Monty had on a thick white T-shirt, some gray sweats, and a fresh pair of white Nike Air Force Ones. He stood with his hands in his pockets, watching me and Javon. His eyes lingered on Melissa like he knew something wasn't right with her, too.

"Tell me what you need me to do," Monty said to Javon.

"Yeah, me too," Navy chimed in. He shrugged. "Shit got me anxious."

"For tonight, just chill. Get some rest. Uncle Snap is working on something right now that will help get us closer to who killed Mama and who's gunning for us now. Tomorrow, we start anew. Start fresh."

"Can I go see my girl?" Monty asked.

Javon shook his head. "No. Have her come here."

"That works," Monty said with a wide grin as he took the stairs two at a time up to his room.

"I'll be in the bunker," Navy said.

"I need to get back to the club," Melissa spat.

She cut her eyes at me before looking back at Javon. I rolled my eyes and moved away from her. Javon nodded, giving her the okay.

Once we were alone, Javon turned to face the wall. His eyes were on Mama's smiling face above the fireplace mantel.

"Uncle Snap is still working on ol' boy. He's fucking him up badly," I said.

"As he should," Javon responded.

"I went to Georgia State today. That's where all the leads led me. Jojo's biggest clientele is out that way," I said.

Javon grunted. "And?"

"Jojo has . . . Javon, Jojo has some grown-ass college bitch pregnant," I blurted out.

Javon got statue still. He turned around so slowly you would have thought he was a mannequin. His eyes were wide and he didn't blink. "Say what?" he said, his voice low and thick with tension.

I repeated my original statement. "And, on top of that, apparently Melissa told her not to talk to me."

"Why?"

"I don't know. And she mentioned some black lady came around asking about Jojo right before he got arrested."

Javon said nothing. He ran a hand down his face then took a seat in the chair across from the fireplace. For a long while, he just sat there, stoic, hands clasped in his lap. I actually thought he had forgotten I was in the room.

"Baby—"

He held up his hand to cut me off. "Not right now, Shanelle. Let me think."

I wanted to tell him that we needed to keep moving. Tell him we didn't have time to think. Tell him that we needed to keep combing the streets because I could guarantee our enemies weren't sleeping. But I didn't. He looked as tired as I felt. So I left him in his thoughts. I headed upstairs to Mama's room.

As soon as I walked into the warmth of her room, it was almost as if Mama were there. I swore I could smell that sweet, flowery scent that she always wore. I took a seat on the side of the bed and held my head in my hands. It seemed as if the hits would never stop coming. I had a good mind to tell Javon to fuck all this shit. We could just take all the money, grab the rest of our siblings, and just run the fuck away.

But I knew we couldn't do that. Now that Javon had taken over the Syndicate, there was nowhere we could run and hide peacefully. I stood so I could take my clothes off, and I felt sick. I rushed into the bathroom and emptied my stomach. Not a lot came up since I hadn't eaten much. After a while, only green bile came up. By the time I was done, I had to sit on the floor to pull my clothes off, then crawl to the tub to get in the shower.

The hot water felt so good against my sore muscles. I sat there for I didn't know how long. So much was on my mind that I wasn't sure if I was going or coming. What the fuck else could come at us? Life was coming like a freight train. There was no more corporate Shanelle and Javon. No more med student Inez. No more law student Cory. I wasn't even sure if Jojo could go back to school. He was still a senior and Mama would cry in her grave if she knew he didn't finish high school.

She went out of her way to make sure we all got good educations. Something had to be done. There was no way we could allow all Mama had worked for to go down the drain.

Chapter 12

Elias

I was pretty much sick of dealing with the fuckups. Melissa was working my fucking nerves, eh. I used to be a part of the São Africana faction out of Brazil. But shit happens, eh? *Sim,* yeah, shit happened. A year ago I met a beautiful white American bitch who had a thing for black cock, no matter what diaspora it came from.

I hadn't been in beautiful pink pussy in so long, *e estou morrendo de saudades.* I was dying of that longing feeling. I chuckled at my own bullshit. Nah. I'd picked her out. She was easy prey. I knew I had no chance with the two black bitches Claudette had for daughters. During my time studying them, they always walked around like the world belonged to them, *sim.* Typical black American bitch shit. Most of the dark-skinned bitches back home knew how to remain humble. Those bitches were at the bottom of the totem pole and they knew it. It was nothing to get them to do shit because of that.

It was opposite with Melissa and her sisters. I mean, don't get me wrong, Melissa was confident, but in the wrong shit. She was confident that as a darker-skinned black man I'd be falling all over myself to have a piece of her. She was right in a sense. *Que lindeza!* What prettiness she was with her big, round ass like a black woman with hips, and tits to match. I guessed growing up around all that color had rubbed off on her.

That was neither here nor there. Getting into her head was easy, especially since she was a little jealous of her sisters and money hungry. So much so that she had gotten herself into debt with me. I smiled while looking at my nakedness in the floor-to-ceiling mirror in my Buckhead mansion. Standing at six foot four inches—I was tall and lean with muscles in places there shouldn't be muscles—I looked like the Afro-Brazilian god I was. My thighs were powerful. I flexed them and watched the muscles coil underneath my skin. Thick black wavy hair fell down to my shoulders. My light brown eyes made most women fall under my spell in no time. My abs constricted as I stroked my thick dick. I loved me. I couldn't help it.

The door to my bedroom suite opened. My love affair with my looks was placed on hold as I turned to face my intruder. "You find Almir?" I asked her.

"I think my uncle has him," Melissa answered.

"How do you know?"

"When I was leaving, I heard Shanelle tell Javon Uncle had someone, working them over."

I gave her a slow blink, a blank look. "He's of no more use to us. Do you know where your uncle is holding him?"

"Not right off the top of my head, no."

I made a move toward her and she jumped back. I smiled. No, chuckled. I had no intention of hitting her. Not now, at least. I moved past her and picked up my boxer briefs off the California king–sized four-poster bed. Dick was too big for sling slot underwear. And too long for regular boxers. I slid my boxer briefs on then picked up my white wife beater to slide it on. I said nothing to her as I pulled on the rest of my attire, some tan tailor-made slacks, and a black button-down dress shirt.

I let my silence speak of my disappointment in her. She hated that shit. I was a master manipulator. My brother, head of the faction back home, found that out too late. By the time he figured it out, I had already taken half his members and was on my way to America, leaving the faction in shambles.

"Aren't you going to say anything?" she blurted out.

"What do you want me to say?"

"Anything. Tell me what the next move is."

I cast a quick glance at her while slipping my feet into my loafers. "You need to find out when the next meeting is for the Syndicate. It's time for me to make my next move," I said as I turned from side to side to study myself in the mirror.

"Why?" she asked.

I stared at her from the mirror. She stood there looking good enough to fuck, but sometimes she was dumber than a bag of bricks. "I'd like to introduce myself the only way I know how," I answered, putting my tie on.

"I . . . I don't understand. Why couldn't you just introduce yourself to Javon and tell him what you could bring to the table instead of going this route? Did we have to steal his shipment?"

"We?" I shook my head with a slow smile forming. "No, you and your team intercepted his shipment."

"Yeah, with your direction."

I tilted my head to the side. I felt my ears itch and sit back, as if I were a breed of wolf. I stalked Melissa until her back was against the golden-colored wall; then I leaned in with my left ear. "Excuse me?" I asked her after licking my thick lips.

"I . . . Nothing. I'm sorry."

I backed away with a smile. "Oh. Just checking." I picked up my designer watch from the nightstand and put it on my wrist. Then I grabbed my father's ring and placed it on my finger. My wallet went into my back pocket.

"I have a very important meeting to attend tonight with some very important people from the Mexican Cartel. If all goes well, the Syndicate will be annihilated. Say good-bye to your brother Javon while you can. That *filho da puta* is on his last life."

"He's not a son of a bitch," she said.

She was so confused. So often she talked shit about her siblings, but any time I did it she balked.

"*Não me venha com essa porra.* Don't give me this bullshit. Get closer to your salad bowl of siblings. They die soon and, this time, I'll make sure it gets done the right way. No fuckups like your last plan. You remember what happened the last time you fucked up, *sim?*" I smiled wide. My perfect white teeth were on display.

She nodded.

"Like always, I have to clean up after you. No biggie, baby. We're a team, right?" I hooked my pointer finger underneath her chin then lifted her face.

"Right," she whispered.

"And you're going to get me the location and time of that meeting, right?"

"Yes, Elias."

"That's my bitch."

I smiled then turned to make my way out the door; then I stopped. My face turned down into a scowl. I snapped my fingers then turned around. "One more thing," I said. I walked back over to Melissa then stared her down. She cowered under my glare. I smiled as I took her hand in mine. I let my fingers massage her fingers while I gazed into her beautiful eyes. Before she could ask what I was doing, I snapped her pinky finger.

Her screams of pain fed me so marvelously, almost as much as her cracking bone did. "Fuck, Elias! Why—"

I towered over her. "The next time you come in here with another nigga's dick on your breath, I'm going to cut your fucking tongue out and pour acid down your throat, *sim?*"

The tears in her eyes pleased me. I loved the shade of red she turned, too. I smiled. Yanked her up enough that I could kiss her forehead then walked out. Her sobs of pain could be heard long after I'd left her in the room.

Chapter 13

Javon

My thoughts were racing a mile a minute. The area around me seemed to roar like running water but I was nowhere but at home. I felt beaten to a pulp, pushed to my limit, and drained of all energy, but I knew that I needed to get my shit together; but I didn't know how. I used the lessons Mama had left me to be a leader to the Syndicate but, now, I felt as if I wasn't living up to the pedigree of that title. This was fucked up. This was hell and, through it all, I just wanted a moment of peace.

I stared at Mama's smiling face. The memory of watching her sit for that painting played in my mind. I recalled her fussing at me for getting in the way of Uncle Snap as he worked on her likeness. On the floor was a scrap in the oak board. Standing up, I walked to that spot; then I dropped down to touch it. This was where Cory was caught playing with his skateboard and ran into Mama's old-fashioned chime clock. He was so scared about breaking it that he worked all afternoon fixing it just for her, and he got caught after the fact. Why? Because that old clock was always stuck two hours behind, and Cory had fixed it to chime on time.

A gentle laugh was in my spirit at that memory. Mama whooped his ass for playing in this room, then cooked him a banging meal of fried catfish, grits, biscuits, and greens after that. She then ended the day with the lesson of "never be a fool who deceives." None of us kids knew what that meant but, as the adult I was now, I slowly thought I was understanding it. See, it's easy to be a smart fool. But a fool who deceives can never be smart enough to stay ahead of that deceit.

Right now, I was thinking of Melissa. Checking on my brothers, I stopped at Jojo's door. I could hear him inside. My brother was in pain, and I wanted to be there for him but he had told me right off the bat that he wanted his privacy. My hand pressed against his closed door and the sign with his name written in spray paint. I listened as I heard muffled slamming and things breaking. I wasn't sure if I could give him that privacy.

"Jojo. We need to talk about a couple of things," I said, knocking and walking in on him.

"Damn, bro! I locked the door so no one could come in here." Jojo sat on his bed with tools in his hand.

His room was a mess. Pictures hanging sideways, papers scattered in disarray, old, empty soda bottles, his PlayStation 4 chilling next to his flat screen in the far right of his room but covered with clothes. I stared at my baby brother then closed the door behind me while standing his trash heap of a room.

"You forget that this was my room before yours. I know how to work the lock." Reflecting on my time in my old room and tucking those thoughts away, I reached out and slid a chair, piled full with clothes, from the corner. I pushed the clothes to the floor. With ease, I flipped it backward then took a seat. "I knew you'd play with the ankle bracelet."

My baby brother gave a shrug then went back to tinkering with it.

"Can you figure out how to break it?" I asked with sincere curiosity.

"Yeah. It's like any other gadget I mess with. But, I might have to ask Navy for help," Jojo nonchalantly replied.

"Good. Figure that out then. But, one thing, I need you not to leave the house unless it's with me."

Jojo sucked his teeth and glanced at me, annoyed. "Nah! I can't do that."

I chuckled low, because my statement wasn't really a question, but I let it ride. "Why? Because you're playing baby daddy to a girl who's too old for you?"

It was then that Jojo's eyes turned cold as ice. I was pissed as fuck at him for being stupid but, on the real, I understood how it went. I wasn't that much older than he was but I was still older, so I could understand feeling like a king when a woman put her all into you. Hell, Shanelle's and my relationship was kind of built on that type of thing. So, I got it. I just was pissed because he wasn't even out of high school yet and now he had three strikes against him.

"You know you fucked up Mama's plan for you," I quickly added before he could act like the teenager he was and get emo. "Three strikes, Jojo. What are you going to do to correct it?"

"First, get this off of me—" he started.

I interrupted. I wasn't done breaking this down. "Nah, first you need to start thinking. You have three strikes that you're about to make four. First, my baby brother is a drug dealer. Two, he has some old, predatory-ass, thirsty college chick pregnant. Three, locked up with a rap for assault and murder attached; and four, you're throwing away your goals. For what? Mama is dead, and you don't have enough money to take care of you or a child while sitting here fiddling with your ankle bracelet. Damn, Mama is probably weeping from wherever she is because you've now jeopardized school and your future. Man, baby brother. What are you going to do to survive this and raise your kid? You know right now that you don't have access to your money except in a little allowance here or there. Not until you hit twenty-one, and the rest you receive at twenty-five. So, what's the business?"

"Don't worry about it. I'll survive. I can take care of this like I have been. None of y'all paid me any attention anyway. That's why I was able to deal and do what I did, because I survive." Jojo glared at me then went back to messing with his ankle.

"You know that I accept my part in not holding down the family as best I should have," I gently explained. "But, naw. I'm not even about to accept that. We love you, Jojo. Everything we did, we did for you and you were spoiled because of it, man. Mama went to the grave spoiling you and protecting you. Then you shit on her and us by not thinking smartly? I mean, shit." Clapping my hands together as I spoke to emphasize my displeasure, I eventually held them out, palms out in contemplation; then I leaned back in my chair. "I get it, but I don't."

I rubbed the back of my neck to stifle the frustration I felt building up while I spoke to my hardheaded brother. "You said that you were doing all this for Mama. Well, baby bro, how are you going to get this right for Mama? Because I need you to start acting smart. We have niggas coming for us as you've experienced. I know why you reacted how you did and I'm not here to judge you on it. I'm just worried for you."

Tossing the screwdriver Jojo held in his hand, he then shifted on his bed and gave me a look of resistance and ego. "Don't be. I said I got it, Von. I got the money I made stashed. I'll use that for me and Dani. Or, for Dani and my kid if I get locked up for life."

"So you good with being locked up?" I asked to see what he'd say.

"No! Fuck that shit, man. Why would I be?" he replied in angry passion.

This little nigga gets his dick wet on the regular then locked up and now he's about being a man? I chuckled to myself and listened while he spoke, just to be fair to my baby brother and all. "Hey, I'm just trying to see where your head is at, Jojo. Because you ended up doing shit that makes it look like you wanted to be locked up, feel me?"

Jojo glared at me then abruptly pushed off his bed with his chest all out. "See, this is why I ain't want to be bothered. How are you gonna come in here and talk all righteous and you doing what you doing, kingpin?"

"Because it's like you said: it's all for survival. Which is why I'm not in here to jump down your throat, Jojo." I gave a deep sigh then stood up to face him. "I don't need to lose another brother. If you're going to continue to create illegal shit, then I need you to be smart with it and not a fool. On my end, I need to make sure your needs are being met, and that I keep you at arm's length for my main shit but in the mix, get me? I'll take care of you until the grave, but you need to think in a bigger scope and remember we're family."

I could see in Jojo's eyes that he was in pain. I knew he wanted to say something but couldn't. Anger had him by the throat, which had me pulling him into a hold.

"I'll help you write a plan for your life. We're working hard in trying to find a way to clear your name to give you some chance out here, all right?" I spoke against his head. "Don't let your anger make you lost to us, please. I can't lose another brother. I'll set you up with pay; just keep it in the house. I don't know what to say about this thing with Dani. Don't tell her *shit* about what you do for me, and I'll pay you like you're working for me at my firm, a'ight? This is your cover now; and keep clear of the cops. Fuckers are watching us hard."

A deep sniffle came from Jojo against my chest. I let him stay in my hold to save face until he was ready to back up, which he did. "A'ight. I'll do whatever. I'm scared, big bro. I . . . I can't go back in there. I won't make it," he said with shaking hands by his side.

"If, by any way, they come and take you from this house, I personally will get you protection on the inside that you control and I control. I mean that. I was blindsided, but not again."

Jojo gave me a nod and then I pulled him back to me in a brotherly hug before letting him go.

"I was hoping that you'd figure out how to get that bracelet off, but you slow as hell, son." I laughed, trying to lighten the situation. "So, I'll see if Navy can help you out with that though."

"I mean, I was trying," Jojo explained. "But, yeah, Navy is good with tech." A chuckle came from him and it put a calmness in my heart.

"Right, which is why I need you and him to be my tech crew with the overall business. Like I said, on some serious shit, we're being gunned. We got a leak in the house, and I know it wasn't you, Navy, or Monty." My hand clasped against Jojo's shoulder and I spoke low. "I need y'all to use your tech smarts with the streets and be my eyes in this house and the neighborhood. Start testing motherfuckers and making up shit, just to see if it goes somewhere and our leak slips up. This is between you and me, a'ight? Can you do that? Start thinking about everything that seemed weird to you in the jail, where you sold, and then some."

"A'ight, I can do that. First thing, though, how'd you know about Dani?"

I smiled and broke it down. When Jojo's eyes got wide about Melissa, I could see that he was putting two and two together about my requests for him.

"This is crazy," he said, plopping down on the couch.

"Yeah, and now I need to check on Uncle Snap. Hit me up if anything feels off, or you need anything. You have right to your own Forty Thief, so I suggest you use it."

I walked out feeling like I did my brotherly duty for the night as I heard the click of his door locking. As I walked in the hall, I saw Shanelle standing outside of Mama's room in a big shirt. She studied me with arms and ankles crossed, her hair shrinking in coils from her washing it. We hadn't had real private time together and I wanted to. There was just too much shit going down back to back. All I could do was wrap my arm around her and kiss her.

"Jojo doing a little better?"

Lips pressed against the crook of her neck, I inhaled her fresh, clean smell and laid my cheek against the top of her head. "For now. Give him privacy. Baby?"

"Okay, I will, and yes?"

I shifted back to study her beautiful dark eyes then I kissed her again, tasting her love. As I looked down at her, my fingers curled around her chin to tilt it up. "I'm about to head out."

"For what?" she sharply said, stepping back. "You need to rest."

"I know, but I'm not going to. You left Uncle Snap."

"Yeah, because he told me to. There was not much I could do," she explained.

A slight note of annoyance hinted in my voice as I ran my hands down my face. "That doesn't matter. I needed you to be my eyes there, especially if our friend spat out some secrets. You needed to watch and study him and learn from him because one day he ain't going be here. I don't have Cory to be my right anymore. I got you. You need to be a queen pin but you not connecting the dots to that reality, Shanelle."

Shanelle's eyes got so wide that I thought her eyes might pop out. Her head tilted and she frowned. "Oh, my God. Really, Javon. I'd walk through fire for you and you know that."

"Baby, I know you would and I'm not even questioning your loyalty or love for me here," I explained. "Everything is happening fast, I know it, but you need to move fast with it. Have you been thinking about my request for you finding out about Ink while I set up this meeting?"

"I mean, it's like you said, everything has been happening fast."

Reaching out, I pulled her by her hip toward me. "I love you, baby, but I just needed you to be with Uncle Snap."

"Von, I'm holding you down," Shanelle said, looking up at me with those beautiful dark eyes of hers. "I found out about Jojo—"

"Yeah, but I didn't ask you to do that. You took it upon yourself to do that. If you're going to be Mama, then be Mama. I need you to not only watch out for the family but also be my right, that's all I'm asking."

Shanelle shook her head and stopped me. "First off, I'm not in any way trying to be Mama. You don't understand the hell I'm going through right now, Von. I have a lot on my shoulders too. You are the head of this family and you should be leading the Syndicate, okay? It's my duty to hold it down when you are working, so I'm doing that. I'll find my place, but you can't just force my place."

"Baby, I'm not trying to force a thing. I'm trying to follow what Mama laid out for us. I have a lot on my shoulders and too much to do. Besides that, baby, I only trust you and Uncle. Jojo and Navy aren't ready for the big time. Monty needs to get his feet settled after jail. Anyway, I just need you to hold it down for real and not run from responsibility. I need to go. I'll be back later tonight."

"Fine," was all she said as she turned her back on me, even though I swore she also muttered, "You just don't understand."

I almost reached for her and asked what she meant, but I let it be. Walking away, I went back to my thoughts. I figured that I was asking too much of Shanelle, but fuck it. I was being asked a lot myself. Had she stayed with Uncle, maybe I wouldn't have had to go back out there and check on him. But, it was what it was.

On my way out, I gave my orders to keep watch of the house and everyone in it. I then walked the block to make sure the cops weren't trailing me, then I slipped away easily, heading to where another car was stashed.

Driving to the storage facility didn't take long at all. I walked in, only to step through a permeating cloud of shit. Our guest was swinging with his innards sagging out, naked like a gutted pig. Blood pooled under him, and at the feet of our guest was my uncle, sitting in a chair, drinking moonshine, and watching the body in silence. I didn't get my payback on the nigga. That was clearly robbed of me. However, my concern was my uncle. I wasn't sure if he would able to function after this. Quietly, I walked up to him and rested my hand on his shoulder. Dead men couldn't talk, and now we were stuck back at square one.

The next day, I woke up early after sleeping next to my angry fiancée. My love was so angry she slept on the edge of the bed. I was upset about it and had upset her, but when I pulled Shanelle to me and played with her juicy kitty and made it purr for me, I simply scooped her from under the bundle of sheets, flipped her over, then caged her, staring in her eyes. Licking my lips, I gave her a silent snarl, curling my lip then dropping down to tear her cotton panties off. When I got a taste of her, she widened her legs, then planted her feet on my shoulders, sliding her curling toes up and down my back as she arched for me.

Head digging in the bed, I cupped her breasts and feasted until it was time to pull off her shirt then sit her on top of me. It was then that I let my love have control and allowed her to ride her anger out on me. Baby girl dug her nails in my chest, leaned down, gave me that same sexy lip curl, then dropped down to lick the side of my neck. Shanelle then bit at my sweet spot, before tracing my ear with her tongue. My dick thumped in her as she showed out and poured her anger out on me. The bed was a classic and sturdy, so no matter how hard we fucked, it didn't shake. Biting my lips, I held her hips was she worked her kitty. I hated upsetting her, but I loved it when we got down like this. Angry fucking was the best especially early in the morning.

I sat on the edge of the bed naked with scratch marks on my back from my feisty queen. My shoulders rose up then rolled to ease the fading tension. She gave a brotha a nice release. I leaned back to kiss the middle of her back and palm her lush ass. After getting my casual feel up, I walked around the bed to pick her up and take her to the shower with me. Comfortable in the steam shower, as the heated water poured over us, I held her with my arms wrapped around her. One around her neck and shoulders, while the other was around her waist. We said nothing as we stood there. I figured we were thinking about everything that we had to do and our obligations.

Which was why I broke our silence. "I'm heading out to meet with the Syndicate. Some already received our SOS and are coming our way."

"Good. Something in the air doesn't feel right about any of this," Shanelle quietly said with her head planted against my chest and heart.

I agreed. Too much just wasn't panning out, and it was time to alert the Syndicate to it.

"Will you be okay here, or do you want to come with me?" I asked just to give her a choice as a show of an olive branch in saying sorry about how I came at her last night.

"I'll stay here to feed everyone, then check in on Melissa," she said, turning to look up at me. There was something in her eyes as if she had something on her mind, and it made me tilt her chin up to kiss her softly, while water ran down the curve of her back and wet, curling hair.

"I love you, Elle," I quietly said, resorting to my old nickname for her.

When she blushed, it made me smile. Especially when she rose up on her toes to kiss me then lean back. "Von, listen. I need to tell you . . ."

As she spoke and I listened intently, both of our cells began ringing our alert line. Turning at the familiar ring, we both quickly moved out of the shower and went to our phones. Answering on my end, I glanced at her. "Speak to me."

"I'm here," Shanelle said on her end.

Gunshots rung in the background like tat-tatta-tat-tat. I could hear shouting and harsh, panicked cursing. Tires squealed, then a loud bang came after.

"Hello?" I shouted.

"We're being attacked," I heard in my ear.

"Creed? Where you all at?" I quickly said in rising panic. "Ride out and get to safety right now, fam!"

I could hear the rush of his breath going in and out as the sound of what I assumed was his feet slamming against asphalt echoed back. "We got ambushed on our way out of Cali. Was heading to you, then . . . Oh, shit."

Gunplay cut off his phone and he went silent. I looked at my phone then at Shanelle, who had her hand to her mouth. Not even a minute after Creed's line went dead, my cell lit up again.

"Who's on your line, baby?" I quickly asked her; then I listened to her as she held her finger up.

"It's Lucky, wait. Hello? Lucky! Hello!" Shanelle gave me look of confusion then hung up. "He said your line was backed up, so he hit my emergency line. Baby, he said he and the Commission were heading to their own meeting to prepare for meeting you when they got hit. He was on the block running from the fitting shop he was at with some of his team. It sounds like they're at war, baby."

My mood dampened. Swiping my cell, I listened to several messages that indicated that the

Syndicate across the board was coming under fire. Immediately, I reached for Shanelle and motioned for her to dress, as I shouted to the family while dressing. Hitting my contacts, I called the Forty Thieves.

"We're under fire. Protect the block, but keep our house up on security right now!" I ordered.

"What do we do, baby?" Shanelle questioned.

"I want you all in the bunker," I stoically responded.

"You need protection, baby," Shanelle said, reaching out and touching my arm.

My gaze settled on her, then I dropped to a knee, reached under Mama's bed and pulled out a Remington shotgun that I knew belonged to Uncle Snap. As I checked it, my mind was going in overdrive. Did I want to take Monty with me or keep him with Shanelle to keep her protected in the bunker? Or leave Uncle with her? He hadn't been right after came home last night, so I knew that protecting them in the bunker would be the best thing, because he was a sleeping lion right now. However, there was nothing like that old man by my side. I had to think on it.

Swinging open the door, I stared at Monty, Navy, and Jojo. Behind Monty was Trinity, who was part of Rize, which was a connect of ours. She wore nothing but lace boy shorts and a tank. Her locs were swaying down her back over her ass and I saw her phone lighting up with messages while she glanced at me with anger in her eyes.

"Trinity, Rize under attack?" I quietly asked.

"Yuh? Fucking bloodclot rassholes came to the restaurant and lit it up, Javon!" Trinity colorfully said in her accented anger.

"Is your brother okay?"

Nodding her head, she wrapped her arms over herself then bit her bottom lip. "Yuh, I think so. He told me to stay with Monty and you. Won't let me come home. Neither will Monty."

My brother glanced at Trinity then at me. "This house need you and shit. I'm not about to be stupid and have you running, blazing out there open and shit."

I sighed then glanced at Jojo, who kept looking over his shoulder at his room. I cursed then I ran a hand down my face while staring up at the ceiling. My fam was going to be the death of me. Head tilted back, I turned it some to stare at my little brother, and simply stated, "Dani is here, isn't she?"

Guilt quickly flashed across my baby brother's features. "Um, yeah. But I told her to stay in the room," Jojo quickly said.

"Fuck!" I growled then glanced at Shanelle. There was a mental thing between us where I was telling her to get his ass before I choked him up.

"Von, me and Jojo can take her to the basement." Navy offered.

I knew he stepped up to calm the anger in me. I appreciated him for that.

Working on short time, because my cell was going off, I moved to the stairway. "All right. Wait. No. I need you all together. Blindfold both of them, then take everyone to the bunker. Board that shit up once you get there. Shanelle knows the way out."

"I thought there was no way out," Navy said, surprised.

"Yeah, Mama always had a contingency plan. It's a tight fit, but there's an exit," I explained. "Monty, I need you to keep everyone else safe. That means go animalistic if you have to."

"Ain't no better way than that, bro. I'll hold the camp down." Monty pounded his fist to his chest and flashed his pearly whites. "Me and Trinity got the house and block."

"Yuh. I'll have Rize walk the streets and be yuh additional eyes and our protection with yuh soldiers out there in the block," Trinity added.

"Respect, baby brother, and thank you, Trinity. You'll be rewarded for that loyalty, fam." Leaning down the stairway I shouted, "Uncle!"

"I'm here, nephew," Uncle said, coming from his room in overalls with his hand scratching over his messy hair. His tone was tired and I understood why.

"I need your eyes, ears, and wisdom with me. Are you up to it? If not, let me know. I'm heading out," I said, walking down the stairs but pausing when he spoke up.

"This is family. I'm always here for ya all. I'll be at'cha side, nephew," he said with a spark of light in his eyes, following me.

I gave him a nod of respect. "Thank you."

"Von," I heard Shanelle ask behind me. Turning, I glanced up at her. "Where are you going?" she asked.

"To get our sister," I said, clutching my Remington.

"Wait." Shanelle ran halfway down the stairs to hug me then whisper in my ear, "I . . . I'm . . ." Curiously, she paused, and with a kiss against my jaw said, "I love you. Come home safely. I'll be your shadow."

Something deep was going on with Shanelle. Something I could read in her eyes, but I wasn't understanding. Whatever it was, it fueled me and gave me additional mental armor to handle business as I told her that I loved her in return. Some bodies were about to drop and I planned on learning who was gunning for us, one way or another.

Chapter 14

Uncle Snap

"Shanelle not coming? Why?" I asked Javon as we walked to the truck.

"Need her to stay here and help protect the house," he said.

I frowned. "And she agreed to that shit?"

He nodded. "Yeah."

"So easily, nephew? Shanelle gave you no lip about making her stay behind? She's your best fucking shooter. Why would you even want to leave her behind?"

Javon stopped walking and looked over at me with a look that said he was turning over the questions in his mind.

"Is she okay?" I asked him. "Shanelle would never let you go into battle alone, nephew. This is the same girl who jumped in your fights in high school. The same girl who picked up a school desk and hit the boy in the head who you were fighting with it. The same woman who has never let you fight alone since you two became an item. The same—"

"A'ight, Unc. I got you. But this was my call. I don't want any of them out here right now."

"I get that, nephew, but I'm saying, though. Check on your woman, a'ight? Make sure she good. And then check Lucky for ringing her line as often as he does. And, while you at it, check Jai for openly lusting after you, too."

Lucky called Shanelle at least three or four times while she was at that storage unit with me. She answered one call to tell him she was busy and then she ignored the other calls. I knew who it was because I asked her and she told me. I asked her what was going on between her and Lucky and she said it was nothing at all. I believed that on her end, but I knew when a man was after another's woman. I knew that from experience. Lucky's apple didn't fall too far from his father's tree.

Javon grimaced and jerked his head back like he had been slapped. "What the fuck, Unc? I don't fucking want Jai."

"Could have fooled me."

"And, wait, Lucky has been calling Shanelle for shit other than business?"

"He ain't got no business with Shanelle. All his business should be with you unless it's an emergency like now."

Nephew glanced around like he was looking for answers as if they would jump out of thin air.

"Look, nephew, I ain't trying to start no shit, especially not now. But something is going on with Shanelle if she let you walk out this house alone with no lip, and you know that. I don't know if it got shit to do with Lucky or if she just noticed some shit with you and Jai—"

"Ain't no shit with me and Jai, Uncle Snap," he barked.

I stopped talking as he stared me down. Maybe I was barking up the wrong tree with this Lucky and Jai thing, but I knew I was right about something being wrong with Shanelle. Wasn't no way she would be okay with Javon going to a fight and not being around to have his back. Anytime Mama had to go to the school because Javon had been in a fight, she had to deal with Shanelle being suspended too. But I let it go. That wasn't my business no how. I hated I said something.

"My bad, nephew. I could be wrong about Lucky and Jai, but I ain't about that other thing and you know it."

With that, both of us hopped in the truck.
Shit was mad tense for a while, but I broke the
tension since I had some info Javon needed to
know.

"Something's going on in Brazil. The faction
down there is imploding and Almir, the dude
I tortured, was a part of the rogues. Before the
piece of shit died, he told me there were many
more in the U.S."

I'd had the Thieves dispose of the man's body.
I had them take him to the Italian butcher Mama
was friends with. That man was the reason I
didn't eat hamburgers unless I saw the cow
being slaughtered myself.

Javon was dressed like he was ready for war,
which meant some shit was going down. Black
combat boots, black cargo-like pants, and a
black turtleneck with a bulletproof vest was
his ensemble. Nephew's eyes danced around,
which told me his mind was working overtime.
When he was a kid, teachers would tell Mama
that something was wrong with him because
he would often zone out while thinking. His
body would be in the room, but his mind was
elsewhere.

I listened as he gave me a rundown on what
Shanelle had told him about Jojo. I didn't even
know what to say. We all knew how Jojo was

when it came to women older than he was. No matter how many his sisters and Mama had beat down, he would go off and find others. That was the psychological effect left on some children who had been introduced to fucking way too damn early. Shit made me sick to my stomach.

"That's something we'll have to discuss as a family later. For now, we got other fish to fry," I said.

"That we do. All the members are being attacked. I was supposed to have this new product and they still haven't received it. Makes me look bad and I'm pissed about that," he spat.

"Be chill, nephew. We still got the samples, right?"

He nodded. "We do."

"Give them fools a hit. Let them see how that shit works and they'll chill out and give you more time to get shit to market."

"That's a good idea, Unc, but my reputation is sullied right now. When I find out who gunned for me, they're dead. And now they've hit every major member in the Syndicate as well?" He shook his head. "Heads are about to roll."

I nodded once, then laid a hand on his shoulder. "As they should. Now let's move."

We made our way to the club, glad there was only minimal traffic. Javon tried calling Melissa from OnStar. She didn't answer. He shook his head and punched the steering wheel. He had the Remington. He was expecting trouble, which wasn't good.

"I sent word to the head of the Africana faction in Brazil. I should be getting word from him soon," Javon said out of the blue.

I knew shit was going to go left as soon as we pulled up to the club to see it wasn't opened. Nah, let me rephrase that. Shit went left as soon as we pulled up to the club to find ourselves outnumbered. Men were lined up in ski masks, ready to rumble. It was as if niggas were there waiting on us to make a move.

"Back that shit up, nephew," I said to Javon as soon as I saw the masked men. How they even knew we would come to the club was beyond me, but we didn't have time to think about that shit.

"No need," Javon said then tapped on the window. "Bulletproof truck."

I gave nephew a sidelong glance. That shit didn't really make me feel any better when bullets started to rain down on us like hail. I still ducked and tried to take cover. They had us surrounded. I wasn't even sure if the niggas dressed in all black and ski masks had figured out their bullets weren't penetrating the truck yet. Didn't matter. Javon put the truck in reverse.

He backed up so swiftly that the bodies behind us fell like dominoes and he rolled over them like speed bumps.

Clearly, no fucks were given in that moment. Javon had just put the truck back in drive when we noticed a nigga with a rocket launcher walking toward us.

"Get the fuck out, Unc," Javon yelled.

He didn't even have to tell me twice. The truck may have been bulletproof, but that shit wouldn't stop a rocket launcher. I bailed out the truck and ran to take cover behind cars on the other side of the street.

I caught a quick glimpse of Javon as he used the Remington 870 with the pistol grip like he wasn't up against automatic weapons. As I got ready to rush across the street to give him backup, a flurry of bullets chased me. I heard nephew yell out as I hit the ground.

"Javon," I called out. He didn't answer. "Talk to me, nephew!"

Being that the club was in one of the most popular areas in Atlanta, I already knew what time it was. We weren't going to have much time to defend ourselves and get the hell out of Dodge.

I knew there was no way in hell I was going to let Javon get caught up. I slid underneath a car just as the truck was hit with the launcher. The explosion rocked the area, causing the people in surrounding buildings to exit and scatter. That was good for us. That gave me and Javon cover. I slid from under the car and quickly blended in with the crowd. I had to get my sights on Javon again. I was getting too old for this shit.

"Javon," I yelled, hoping he was in hearing distance.

I got no answer. The boy was a quick runner. So I was hoping like hell he had gotten the fuck out of Dodge.

All I had was my 9 mm since we had to abandon the truck before we were ready. I spotted two of the shooters searching the crowd. They were more likely looking for Javon than for me. I used their tunnel vision to my advantage. I raced with the running crowd, dipped behind a car that had been abandoned, and came up behind the two shooters. One shot to the back of the head put the one closest to me on his face. I kicked the other one in the back of the leg as he turned around; then I snuffed his lights out with a bullet to the right temple.

I snatched up his AK-47 and went to find my nephew.

Chapter 15

Lucky

I didn't know just what in the hell was going on, but nobody, and I meant nobody, came for me and mine. Even if I didn't have the protection and blood of those who ran the Commission, any man, woman, or child who came for me would regret it until their last dying breaths. We had just been ambushed; in broad daylight, no fucking less! We lost about ten men and barely escaped with our lives. We had some bumps and bruises, but we were alive.

I looked at the Catholic priest, the Jewish mobster, and my uncle. Although I only shared blood with my uncle, who some claimed was actually my father—another story for a different day—the Catholic and the Jew were family to me as well.

"You get to Atlanta and see just what in hell Javon got going on down there," my uncle said.

"You think he would be stupid enough to have something to do with this?" I asked. I was furious. My blood was on lava and I was ready to kill or be killed. Didn't matter to me. Not now. The small underground bunker we were in had men from all walks of life lined up ready to go to war. Javon was a cool dude, but if that fool had been crazy enough to try to snuff me and my people out, son was done.

"No," my uncle said. "This felt personal, but it may link back to Claudette."

"Luci is right," Absolan, the Catholic priest, said. "You need to get to Javon. Make sure he and the rest of the Syndicate are okay first."

They called my uncle Luci, short for Luciano.

Cavriel nodded. "Word just came through the wire. This was a Syndicate-wide attack."

My brows rose. "Say what?"

My uncle nodded. "*Sí,* across the board. Take a private flight and get back to us on what is going on. We cannot make this trip with you. It is too dangerous."

"I'm well aware of that, Uncle. I'll leave my best men here with you."

He shook his head. "And who will be left to travel with you? No. Take your best with you.

I've already called Italy, Absolan has called to our people in Vatican City, and Cavriel has called Jerusalem. We will be fine here. No one knows this place but our most trusted, and even they don't know all the ins and outs."

Uncle Luci had a bruise under his right eye. Most would have looked at the old man and thought him to be frail and too thin, but when it came time to get down to business, Uncle Luci reminded me of the Italian mobsters of old. The old man came from under his trench coat with an Uzi and let it spray. He got the bruise under his eye from falling to the ground to take cover when the Uzi was emptied. The same could be said for the Catholic and Jew. Those old men showed that an OG from any faction was still an OG no matter when the time called for it.

Still, I could tell that the firefight had taken a toll on them. They looked haggard and tired out from all the running and leaping over cars. "You three will rest while I'm away," I stated more than asked.

"We have no time, Lucky. We must get ahead of this thing before it gets out of hand," Cavriel said.

"This is true," Absolan said as he stood. He spoke in his native tongue when he told one of his men to bring in the prisoners. That's right. We kept two of those motherfuckers alive.

I stood with a machete in my hand. I'd seen Mama Claudette use a machete on many occasions. Even from when I was a kid, I remembered the way she handled one while torturing or murdering someone who had dared cross us. I also remembered the look in Uncle Luci's eyes as he watched her. Something akin to love, pride, and lust. I'd never gotten a straight answer when it came to what went on between those two. Not even my mom, who looked uncannily like Mama Claudette, would speak on the subject. I stopped asking after a while.

Two men were dropped, naked, hands tied behind their backs, in the middle of the room. One was black and the other Mexican. I immediately recognized the symbol inside of the black one's wrist and the mark on the other one's chest. I frowned and so did my uncle.

"São Africana and the Mexican Cartel?" Uncle Luci barked out as he jumped up from his chair. "Working together?" The man's face was as red as the shirt he had on.

"What is the meaning of this?" Cavriel spat as he stood over the two men.

Absolan kicked one man in the nuts when he walked over to them. "Speak, you filth!"

"I thought the Africana faction in Brazil was an ally to the Syndicate," I said.

"As did I. This explains why Javon told me he was having problems with shipments out of Brazil," Uncle Luci said. "Make them talk," he ordered me.

I smiled. The black man on the floor held eye contact with me. I knew he wasn't going to open his mouth. He was too calm. He welcomed death and maybe even torture. I let my eyes travel to the Mexican on the floor. He too watched me, but he fucked up. As I stepped closer, I saw the glimmer of fear in his eyes. He tried to hide it, but he was unsuccessful. I yanked the man by his left foot. When I swung my machete, steel cut through tendon and bones.

I tossed the man's foot behind me. His screams and yells fed my need to hurt him some more. It didn't surprise me when he damn near passed out. Uncle Luci didn't let him, though. He placed a small folding chair near the man's head and pulled a small black bag from the table. MAMA C was embroidered on the outside. He pulled out a long needle, jammed it into the man's heart, and woke him back up.

"You only have so many limbs left. Tell us why the Cartel is working with the Africana faction," he asked the man.

Water leaked from the man's eyes just as piss and shit leaked from his penis and asshole. The man's answer was to yell unintelligible Spanish and to spit at Uncle Luci. The old man jumped back with swiftness but not quick enough so the spit wouldn't land on one of his hands. He grunted, stared the man down for a long while, then stood. He grabbed a Clorox wipe from the bag then wiped the back of his hand. Once he was done, he went back to the bag and pulled out another needle then held it out to me.

I grinned wide. Mozambique cobra venom. Mama Claudette had a whole arsenal of shit to make people talk, but this was my favorite. I laid my machete down then put on the thick gloves. I grabbed the needle from Uncle then straddled the man. Two of my men held the man down, one at his feet—well, foot—and the other holding his head.

"This is going to hurt like fuck," I told him just before forcing his eyelids wide with one hand then injecting the venom with the other.

The cocktail of toxins consisted of nerve poisons harmful to the sensitive cornea. The stinging pain often sent men and women into convulsions. There was no doubt the shit would leave them blind since it was directly injected into the eye. I stood then looked down at the man as he bucked and squealed like a pig.

Thick puss started to form around his eye while he foamed at the mouth. I looked at the black man then smiled my best smile.

"You're next," I threatened.

He simply gave a slow blink then turned his head. The Africana faction often trained their men to withstand torture when they trained. I knew it would be hard to get him to talk, but not impossible. My attention was turned back to the Mexican. He started speaking Spanish rapidly. He was telling us something.

"Slow down. Slow down," I said. I spoke Spanish very well, but the man was speaking so fast that I was having a hard time comprehending.

"*Tratando de adquisición.*"

"Who's trying to take over?" I asked.

A movement behind him caught my attention. The black man had used his legs to take one of my men down. He did some kind of ninja move. Jumped from the floor and the next thing I knew, he had brought his tied hands underneath his feet so that they were now in front of him. He'd grabbed the gun from my man's belt so fast that all I could do was grab my uncle and take cover.

"*Trader porra,*" he yelled at the Mexican before placing a bullet in the man's head.

I jumped up and tackled the man just as he tried to shoot himself in the head. Even with his hands tied the man was quicker than lightning. He tried to us his legs to flip me off of him, but I was quicker. I flipped him over my head, got to my feet then kicked him in the head, rendering him unconscious.

Cavriel and Absolan had been guarded by my men. Uncle Luci slowly got to his feet. As he dusted off his clothes, he said, "Keep him alive. Leave him here. Get to Atlanta. If this is some kind of hostile takeover, Javon's in trouble and so are the rest of you."

Chapter 16

Javon

I was shaking. Too much adrenaline, anger, and low-key fear was racing though me. Bullets blazed past me. For the life of me, I wasn't sure how or why none of them hit me, but I had to think that it was Mama protecting me. Shit, I mean if the old lady ended up in heaven, after everything she had done, including the mayhem she had put on others and the blood on her hands, then Mama could protect me anytime. Hell, I'd start to believe that some people in heaven might have owed her some things, if she made it to the pearly gates. But that's neither here nor there, as Mama would say.

For now, her grace was protecting me. Because my armored truck was in a blaze, in the chaos of it all me and Uncle were split up. It worried me, but I was good with it. Shanelle had the best aim in the house, but Uncle was a beast with tactile maneuvering. That was why I was happy he was here regardless of what he had said, which was a hell of a lot. I didn't want to think on it, so I pushed it outside of my mind and checked my surroundings. I had a key to the club, so I knew that I could roll inside unnoticed if our enemies stayed distracted.

But for now, because I was waiting it out, I crouched low then sprinted away from the battle around us. Ahead of me was a large Dumpster. I decided to use it as my shield until I could make it to the front of the club. At that point, I was biding my time. We were in Buckhead. The rich folks in the area were not about to let their property drop down and become devalued because of some shooting going down. Therefore, I knew that it was only a matter of time before the cops showed up.

Whoever these fucktards were, they clearly weren't thinking about those odds. Or, they didn't give a damn about it. Taking a quick glance, I decided that they really didn't give a damn. Unfortunately, I did. I needed insurance just in case. So, I dug in my pocket and sent a text to Shanelle. The message simple stated, Emergency. AT lawyer.

AT was code for "Alert Trey." He was our in with the police for now. The positive was that if he could set me up with protection if I got caught, then I needed that set up immediately. Mentioning our lawyer was to say call her as well.

Checking my Remington, I reached in my pants, pulled out the small box that held more rounds, and reloaded. Everything was feeling like the last fight in the parking lot when we saved Shanelle. That's when it clicked in my mind who these niggas were. The pattern was glaring. These dudes had to run with the same ex–São Africana crew. Quickly peering beyond the side of the Dumpster, I did a mental count. Who was the nigga running them? Why were they parked out in front of Melissa's? Where was she at, as well? Nothing was sitting well with me.

As I crouched, pressed, nearby the pounding of boots came my way. In one fluid move, I stood up, flipped my Remington in my hand, then sent the handle of my gun against the underside of my enemy's chin. I watched his head crack back. He stumbled in surprise trying to right his balance and come at me. As he did so, I flipped my gun again then pumped several rounds in his body. Glancing down at him, I snatched his gun and tucked it behind my back. I then patted him down, noting the burned-out São-A branding, and I found a hunting knife.

Taking it, I looked around, pulled him behind the trashcan, then noticed Uncle. I flagged him down. The old man came my way with a slight shuffle and it bothered me. It was clear he had been hit because, any other time, the old man moved as if he were in his early thirties with no major issues. Now, he was clearly tired out.

While he made his way to me, several men chased after Uncle. He turned to shoot off rounds and, as he did so, the bodies fell behind him without him squeezing off any bullets. Uncle's face turned to look around then above us. He was as surprised as I was. More bodies dropped, leaving a clear way for Uncle; and I helped with it. I used my shotgun effectively then turned to see who was helping. Sunlight glinted momentarily in my eyes, keeping me from seeing who it was.

As Uncle slid to my side, I glanced up again to where he pointed across from us on a roof of a building close to the club, but I saw nothing. Yet, more men were being taken out. Heads were imploding. Arms and legs were being blasted off. Blood was everwhere. Yet, I saw no one on the roof. It was as if there were a ghost, and it baffled me. Whoever it was, I was grateful. Returning my attention to the body at my feet, I took a knee and hoisted it over my shoulder.

"Any way out of this, nephew?" I heard Uncle ask while panting.

We had to move out and quickly. Flashing lights were coming our way and I didn't want either of us caught up. "Yeah, in the club."

"Through the tunnel exit," Uncle said while he glanced around. He moved out of my way as I dropped the body in the Dumpster. "You knew about that?"

I shrugged while looking down at him, then wiped the sweat from my forehead with my arm. "If I didn't, I do now. Got anything that I can light?"

"Push it, and I got you, nephew," he said, digging in his vest.

With a sharp grunt, I pushed the Dumpster in a roll then let off several rounds. Uncle, from behind me, tossed something circular in it and pulled me backward.

"Run, boy!" he said, heading to the back of the club.

Following him, we ran as fast as we could as a large bang went off. I glanced at him with wide eyes and covered my ears then fell to my knees. "The fuck! You had a grenade!"

"A Molotov cocktail, nephew. A little moonshine can go a long way."

With that, we managed by the grace of God or Mama Claudette to make it into the club. Locking the door behind us, we caught our breath then quickly moved on. I followed Uncle as he shuffled and pointed for me to go in the back. Lights were flickering off and on, streaming their beams around the massive club. It seemed empty in here and I appreciated the quiet. I needed to think.

"You get any inkling of an idea of who is guiding these people?" I heard Uncle ask, rubbing his leg.

I watched him move to the bar, pull a bottle down, then slide his hand against the side of a shelf. Behind me, near a tall supporting beam, appeared a door. The old man leaped my way. I made sure that he wasn't leaving a trail of blood and I glanced around. I felt eyes on us. It was fleeting and for a second I thought it was Melissa. However, her car wasn't anywhere around, and the place was locked up tight. I only was able to get in because of my key and access code. So, Melissa being here didn't make sense to me. Which meant she was here.

Leaning in to my uncle I whispered, "Go down. I'll be behind you."

"That's not smart of you, nephew," he muttered back, also watching his surroundings.

"I know, but you feel it, don't you?"

Uncle gave a slight nod, then reached up to thumb his nose. "Yeah. We got a traitor in the midst."

"So, I'm not tripping then. It's M?"

"Mm hmm," Uncle said, affirming my thoughts.

"Go ahead. I got this," I said, ushering Uncle down the tight corridor then turning around. As I did so, I looked around again.

"So, you just going to play hide-and-seek with a brotha? You want me dead, so don't be a lame and hide. Face me." I stood there talking to air. There was nothing but silence and the flashing lights.

Pounding started on the doors of the club. I could hear a large commotion and it made me antsy. Maybe she wasn't here. Maybe Uncle and I were tripping. Either way it went, I didn't have time to wait around.

"Lissa. Whatever the hell is going on with you right now that has you hiding and ignoring your family, especially with us almost being killed out there, it's going to come to light and I'd rather you come to me on some real shit and talk this out." I looked around then slowly backed up to the door. "We're family. No matter the good, the bad, we're here. We may whoop that ass, but in the end we're family and we're your home. Come talk and leave the bullshit behind you."

With that I went down the corridor, hearing the door shut behind me. Everything I said was a bald-faced lie. If she did have something to do whatever the hell was going on outside with us being ambushed, best believe I planned on feeding her the same bullets that came for me and mine. You don't gun down your family and expect a housewarming. We ain't the Huxtables.

By the time I caught up with Uncle, he was sitting on an old plastic bottle crate, drinking from his bottle of vodka and pouring it over his bare leg. "'Bout time you showed up. Thought I'd have to wobble my old ass back to you," he said in a tired huff. "As the old negro American saying goes, I'm getting too old for this shit."

I gave a weary chuckle and took a look at his leg. It wasn't bad at all. Just a flesh wound and one that went through his calf cleanly. If Inez were here, I was sure she'd patch him up with no issue. I exhaled and glanced up at my uncle at the thought of Inez.

"We need a medic backup. We need people in the prison on our side, we need a fucking car, and we need to get the hell up outta here." Tossing my uncle's arm over my shoulder, I helped him stand up. "So, don't die on me, old man. You need to live forever. Lead us out."

As he pointed ahead of us, we headed down the dark tunnel. "All that going on in your head, huh? Well, I'm not going anywhere. Watch my old ass become immortal, okay? Y'all need me," he said with light humor in his voice. "What'cha going to do about that child Melissa? It was her, huh?"

"Seems like it, and I'm not sure." I exhaled slowly and kept it moving. "Feels like all of us kids are screwing up and have secrets."

"Yeah. That's the nature of close families. Throw it up in the mob scheme of things and shit gets every more complicated," Uncle explained as if this was nothing to him.

"True that. Still, we need to find out if that was her, and what her angle is here and why. It better not be about some petty shit. I don't think I can take another jealous sibling."

Uncle let out a deep laugh then groaned. "Damn my leg. It's just not hitting me, and so what if it is? Clean her up straight or end her. It's all up to you, boss."

I gave my uncle a look, then we kept it pushing until we made it across a block. The only reason I knew that was because of where the entry ended: near the highway. In front of us was an empty lot with a SUV waiting.

"Called for pickup while you were talking to ya sister," Uncle explained.

The door of the black SUV swung open and out came Shanelle with Monty. They quickly ran over to us in a frenzy. Shanelle was in dark clothes: jeans, boots, jacket, and a handkerchief over her face. Her hair was pulled up in a bun. Monty was in a matching outfit and the same mask. My brother threw a black blanket over Uncle's shoulders and head, as if he were James Brown. Shanelle gave me a handkerchief and I tied it while she glanced behind us in the tunnel, making sure that it was clear.

Walking to the SUV, we all quickly climbed in, where I noticed a sniper rifle. It was Shanelle's and I realized she was the one on the roof.

"Take us to the Westin and get a medic in the building," I ordered, leaning back, closing my eyes. If I had paid attention, I would have seen that the cops surrounded the club, which was also now on fire.

Once at the Westin and after having our room secured, we entered through the back, masks off, faces downcast. Plastic with towels were laid out for Uncle to lie on as his leg was examined by our Syndicate medic.

Two hours passed with me pacing the room. I glanced outside at the view of the city, in thought and on my cell. "Has everyone in the Syndicate been accounted for?"

I listened to the voice on the other end give me the lineup about the status of the Syndicate table. According to Jai—who was laying low because of Trey along with several other of our staff who were employed by the Syndicate—we had several injuries and a death. One family head from the Commission was injured and Miguel, our Mexican head, was killed while he was at a family function. Ming Lee was currently in critical damage, with her eldest daughter Song Lee stepping in as the new head for now. The rest, for now, were in hiding and working on coming to Atlanta.

Anger had me punching the window. Everything I worked for was now back to one. Whoever had come for my family had also single-handedly put the Syndicate on pause with one swift, effective move and that put a pit in my stomach. Who was this asshole?

"Do we have any idea who this ex–São Africana is? I need to reach Delanna's son, Amen, and his wife, Cintia."

Jai shuffled on the other end of her phone then spoke up. "Okay, I'm sending that SOS out to them now. If Cintia is busy with her filming and musicals on Brazilian Broadway then keep her protected in that, but get me Amen."

Since ending Delanna and putting her son in her place on the Syndicate, the South American pipeline had been going well until civil unrest occurred and our product Ink was taken.

"I did speak to Cintia about our product's whereabouts and who was kicked out of the São-A's."

Rubbing my temples, my eyes were half closed while I glanced at everyone in the room. "And?"

"No one knows. Delanna had an issue with one of her family members several years back. The result ended in a shootout by a rival gang that severely cut the ranks of that family, but that's it. No one was kicked out of the São-A's. Many of the members are very loyal and only go out by death."

Frustration had me running my palm over my waves. "Find out who the hell exited them by death then! None of this shit is adding up!"

"Calm down, Javon. I'll handle it. The Ink, from what I understand, was taken by a new gang, but no one knows who they are; and the areas they are supposedly located at has turned up empty or as traps," Jai explained.

My head started to spin. Shit was sounding too set up, too cleanly done. I didn't get it, but I needed to. "Just find out more. If I need to fly down to Brazil I'll do that," I said, hanging up in Jai's ear.

From how Shanelle watched me, she didn't like what she heard on Jai's end as well. "Lucky is in town. He made it down and wants to meet up," she quietly spoke up.

Her cell was at her side on the bed and Uncle Snap was near her feet, snoring. I stared at her for a long-ass time, remembering how we used to be with one another, remembering the times she fucked niggas and came to me like nothing had happened. Don't get me wrong, I'd done some messed up shit too, but nothing hurt a man more than when he could smell another man on his woman. Nothing.

"Why does he keep hitting you up on your line and not mine?" I asked calmly.

Shanelle watched me quietly before speaking up. "I asked him the same and—"

"And he continues to call you on your line." I felt like saying some sarcastic shit but I kept it chill. "Do we have an issue?"

When her eye twitched, I knew she knew what I was asking. "No, Von. Don't even do me like that," she said, then cast her eyes away from my glare.

"Why shouldn't I? We got a history, right?"

My baby gave me a sharp look. Her face contorted then she looked me up and down where she sat. "This isn't the time, Von. We have too much—"

"Nah. This is the perfect time. See, if we're all about to die over some other crap then it's time we spoke. What is going on with you? Why'd you easily stay behind but be here now? Why is Lucky overstepping his role and contacting you over me?"

"You feel threatened, huh?" Shanelle stood then came up to me. "Because if you are then I guess I should be about Jai."

I kept my chill and looked down at my heart. "Why? Jai is beautiful, but I'm not after her. I haven't stepped out on you in years."

"Then I can say the same thing. Lucky is fine, but I'm not after him. I haven't stepped out on you in years," Shanelle countered, repeating me verbatim.

A scowl spread across my face, then I moved out of the way. "Since he loves hearing your voice, let him know to meet me at the address I'll text him."

"Von, don't walk out. It's too dangerous," Shanelle said behind me.

I ignored her. Too much shit was on my mind.

"Wait! I'm pregnant! That's what's going on with me."

I stopped midway to the door, then turned around. At first, my main thought was whether it was Lucky's, because of our conversation.

"It's yours. I've only been with you, Von. Can't believe you'd look at me that way."

"He's been calling, and you've been acting distant, Elle," I said quickly, trying to explain myself.

"So have you! But I'm not going into thinking you've fucked Jai! You've been distant too! Been talking to her a lot, too. Calling and texting," she shouted at me.

"She's our attorney and Mama trusted her even in death. On top of that, I'm trying to bring in more women for the Syndicate to balance our bullshit. It's not on some dick crap, baby!"

"I can't believe you. Fuck you, Von!" she added, turning away from me. "You always think the worst about me."

Embarrassment along with shame had me moving to her side to pull her to me. "I'm sorry, baby. I'm sorry. For real. I shouldn't have been thinking crazy, but you do the same to me."

When Shanelle pulled away from me, I felt like shit. "Don't touch me right now. You know we've been trying, and I can't believe your stupid ass."

Out of respect for her space, I backed up. It gave me time to realize what she had shared. Everything was making sense on her changed behavior. It also had me reflecting on her being here. "You need to either stay here or get out of ATL, Shanelle," I immediately said.

"What? Why!" She turned in surprise.

"Because if you lose this child too it will break you and hurt me. We need to be careful, clearly."

"No. You need me out here. I'll protect our child at all costs, but I'm also going to protect you," she disputed. "I'm calling an audible before you can even demand I leave you."

A frown set deep across my face. I wanted to curse her out, but I didn't. I just stared at her then headed to the door. "Let's go then."

"Where?" she quickly asked, following me.

"To handle some mob shit and get my men in line," I said sharply.

Leaving the Westin, we ended up only a few blocks away in a private garage. We waited in silence. Shanelle stood against the side of the car, arms crossed in a slight pout, and I stood beside her, keeping her partially blocked just in case.

While we waited, I spoke to her without looking at her. "The fact that you're pregnant again has me proud, baby. I'm no doubt happy to be a father soon." The feel of her hand against my arm had me briefly glance at her.

"Me too, Von. I wanted nothing but this for you and me. I promise, I'll take care of myself and be careful," she softly said.

I loved how her voice lightened the way it did. It was a mixture of love and a warmth only she could give. I was about to turn and kiss her, but I kept my gaze on the car that pulled up. As it parked, out stepped Lucky. With him were several men at his back. I watched him stare at me then glance at Shanelle while keeping his distance.

"We're alone," I calmly said.

Relaxing a bit, Lucky glanced back at me. "Tell me what's going on, boss?"

I swore there was some sarcasm in his tone when he called me boss. It had me fist my hands as I broke down what was going on.

After, Lucky came up to me then exhaled. "I didn't know what to think. So, you think this is some old shit linked to the OGs of the Syndicate?"

"Yeah," was all I said before walking up to Lucky, then slamming my fist into the side of his face.

My blows were swift and purposeful. I watched as he slid back against the hood of his car. With that, I followed and used my hand to slam his head against the hood. Smashing his face, I pulled out my Glock, and I heard Shanelle behind me.

"Keep back!" she spat out and I knew that she was pointing steel at his men.

"Now, we cool and all, Lucky, but that cama-
raderie doesn't extend to you doing two things:
one, disrespecting my authority; and two, thou
shalt not covet what isn't yours." Pressing hard
on his face, I laid my pistol against his temple
and continued speaking. "Meaning finding
yourself trying to get between the thighs of
my woman. Last I checked, her pussy comes
willingly to me and only me. There's no swaying
at all. Understood?"

When Lucky stayed quiet, I took the safety
off my gun. "Can't hear you, fam. I call you that
because my mother trusted you. Now, if you
can't give that same trust and respect, then I'll
have to pull your seat."

"It's cool. Just playing around, fam," Lucky
said between clenched teeth.

"Good. I recognize that you're not a pushover,
and I don't see you as one. You, the Commission, and I need to keep cool—" I started to say.

As I spoke, Lucky pushed me back then sliced
my arm with a blade I didn't even see in his
hand. Shit was so quick, most niggas would have
thought it was magic. That mess cut clean like a
hot knife in butter. Bright red seeped from my
wound in my arm. I thought I was in shock for
mere moments when I stared at Lucky like "this
motherfucker," then shot that nigga in his arm.
Fair exchange.

"Oh, shit!" Lucky spat out, holding his bicep. He cursed in Italian and bared his teeth. Ruby liquid seeped from between his fingers. He glanced between Shanelle and me, then grinned wide. He grinned like he knew something we didn't or grinned like a madman. Either way, shit didn't stop the pain in my arm from the cut he gave me.

I was about to shoot that fool again until he said, "We're even. Now what are we going to do about whoever is after our family?"

Chapter 17

Melissa

Tears fell down the apples of my cheeks as I sat hidden in the upstairs VIP area of the club. I had come here after Elias and I met back at the hotel to empty the drawers and safe of the club. I had no idea that he was going to use my place as meeting ground for his killers. Once I saw that, my heart broke into a million pieces because on the monitors I saw Uncle and Javon. I didn't plan this or expect them to come here.

It showed that Elias was a million steps ahead of me on his plan and it pissed me off. He didn't tell me anything of it, but now I was getting the brunt of it. My family was doomed. Smoke was pluming from where I had lit the bar on fire as glass shattered all around. I was scared. Javon's words played back in my mind. If I told them what I did, how I stupidly planned Mama's death, then how Elias took the reins and made me go through with it, maybe they'd forgive me somewhat. I wasn't sure. A part of me wanted to believe him, but the street mentality I learned from my siblings and my time between foster homes just wasn't allowing that trust. He'd kill me if he knew the truth.

Standing, I gathered my things, and quickly exited. Shades on, hair smoothed back in a bun, I strolled out in my white and baby blue striped shorts, with a white baby-top lace shirt and matching heels. Diamonds sparkled on my wrists and in my ear. I looked like money and I felt like money. All I could do was take the earnings from the club, cash in on the insurance, and pay for a ticket to the Philippines, or France, where one of my sugar daddies lived.

There was nothing here for me. Elias was becoming dangerous on a level I didn't want to deal with. I loved me some strong men, but Elias was a weak man acting strong. The moment he started putting his hands on me, I saw it clear as day. He was crazy and deliciously sexy. But in all of that, he was a malicious man who was weak.

I enjoyed our time in the sheets, but I really didn't like him. There were some people with whom it takes time to see who they really are. Elias was one of them. A part of me felt that he could elevate me to where I wanted, but all he ever did was sex me, then manipulate me. I was deeply lost in his sauce and I let him lead me on a path I never thought I'd take. I hurt my family. I took out the one woman I loved above everything and now I was going to lose it all.

Chalk it up to the game. I was deeply sorry. I just needed out of the poverty and streets. Being a part of a crime family wasn't want I wanted. But, being a killer wasn't what I sought to become, either. I blamed myself and Elias. I hoped that he got his karma. It was too bad that I wouldn't be around long enough to see it.

On my exit, all I could do was leave Von and the family some seeds pointing to Elias and the black cocaine he was dealing in. I had money, and I was stealing the rest of what I needed that would make me a self-made millionaire. I wasn't as stupid as Elias felt I was and I intended to show him that. Mama Claudette's plans for me had strengthened me. Me killing her had put me on the path where I needed to be to believe in myself. I just now had to act on it. I just had to be smart.

I'm sorry, Von.

Chapter 18

Shanelle

A week later and Javon was still dealing with the fallout behind someone trying to take out the Syndicate. Melissa had disappeared, confirming the family's suspicion that she had turned on us. There was nothing worse than a fucking coward. I hated fucking cowards with a passion that couldn't be explained. I was an advocate for owning your bullshit. If somewhere along the line a person fucked up, they should own it and deal with the consequences.

The fact that she'd done some fuck shit and disappeared made me hate my sister. And I hated that I hated her. I'd lost two fucking sisters and Mama. It was just me and my brothers now. I had no woman to bond with. No one I could run to when I needed it, nothing. That shit hurt me so badly. I couldn't explain the pain I felt day in and day out. I kept looking at

Inez's pictures, wishing I could have a do-over that wasn't coming. Then I looked at Melissa's pictures, wondering why she did it. What had we done to her? What was so bad that she would turn on us?

We never made her feel like an outsider. In a family full of black and brown people, we loved her. Her race didn't matter to us. *Why, Melissa? What did we do?* As I looked at old photos of us at parties, in clubs, out and about, pictures we had posted to Instagram, Facebook, and Twitter, I kept wondering and asking myself why.

Tears fell down my face as I sat at the dining room table in Mama's kitchen. It was where I'd last seen Inez. I'd tripped my sister to keep her from going after Javon while he was fighting with Cory. God, how I'd give anything, anything, to have them back. For as crazy as Cory was, he always had my back. No matter what. I felt as if I'd let him down too. How had we not seen the drug use and the change in habits? Yeah, he was good at hiding it, but still.

"I miss y'all so much, Cory and Inez. I do. I wish . . . I wish I could do all this shit over. Wish Jojo would have picked Mama up. Wish we could have spoken to you two better when we found out y'all were having problems. I'm so, so sorry," I spoke quietly to myself.

"You okay, sis?"

I jumped then turned to see Trin behind me. I quickly wiped my eyes with the paper towel in my hand. I stood and walked over to the stove to stir the spaghetti sauce. I'd been crying so much that my nose was stuffy. I couldn't even smell what I was cooking. Gotdamn baby had me all emotional. "Yes, I'm fine," I lied. "How are you? Everything okay? Monty treating you well?" I asked her, trying to deflect.

"Yeah, I'm cool. We're chilling. Shit's been crazy as fuck around here, though."

I sighed then put the spoon I'd been stirring with on the counter. "I know. Would you believe, before all of this, our family was pretty normal?" I asked then laughed.

She smiled then nodded. "I always think the same thing about me and mine before shit popped off."

I nodded. "Your brother and his crew okay?"

"Yeah. Javon got them on some kind of mission. So they're in these streets doing what they do."

"That's good to know. I've been trying to figure out how and where our product was taken."

"Oh, yeah. The Ink, right?"

"Yeah. Traced it to a warehouse in Florida if my notes are correct. I need to make Javon aware of this as soon as he comes in."

"Damn, you're good," she said.

"When I need to be. If you look here," I said, pointing at the world map, "it left Brazil on time. Arrived in Cuba when it was supposed to, but that's where shit got muddy. After it left the water at the port of Miami, we were robbed. Ink hasn't been seen since. My cousin, Trey, says some of his boys in vice down that way have been hearing about some new shit that's about to hit the street. Supposedly some black cocaine. We're the only ones in the state who had access to that shit. That tells me that's our product they have."

She turned her lips down with raised brows. "So when do we go get that shit back?"

I looked at Trin and smiled. She was always ready to go. She reminded me of Inez in a sense with that personality trait. "When my fiancé says move, we move," I said.

"Fa'sho. I'm ready."

We were quiet a minute while she looked through all the papers I had on the table. "You know Monty's pretty shook up about what y'all's sister did. He said he didn't ever think Melissa would play family like this. He doesn't get it," she said.

"Shit, none of us gets it. We never saw this coming."

"Right."

"But we can't cry over spilled milk. We have to figure this shit out before we lose everything and everybody. Our family can't take another hit."

"Tell me about it. With the way Javon just put Rize on, we can't do shit but help out, and look out for y'all, too. Rize coming up in ways we couldn't imagine and, if all goes well, my bro is still trying to get a seat at the table. He understands he gotta work for that shit, though, you feel me? We ain't looking for handouts. We don't mind working like hell for that seat."

I smiled at her tenacity and I knew she was the right woman for Monty. I was about to tell her that when Dani walked in. My smile faded and so did Trin's. She looked at me then glanced at Dani.

"Hey," Dani said. Her voice came out like she was a little girl instead of a grown woman.

"Hello," I said, then turned back around. I opened the package of ground turkey so I could cook it.

"Whaddup," Trin spoke.

"Is it okay if I have some of the apple juice in the fridge? Jojo said it was yours and I had to ask you," Dani said.

"I don't care," I answered.

I heard when she walked over to the fridge and opened it. Heard when she closed it. I was hoping she got the fuck up out the kitchen as I didn't like being close to her. I didn't even like her being in the house. I hated that she slept in the room with Jojo. I was going to have a word with Uncle and Javon about that shit. No way they would have let a grown-ass nigga lie up with me, Inez, or Melissa. No fucking way.

"I know you don't like me, Shanelle, but I love Jojo," she muttered.

"He's a kid."

"I'm only four years older than he is."

"He's a minor."

"Not in the state of Georgia. He's seventeen so he's considered an adult."

I turned to face that bitch so fast, a piece of the meat I was putting in the skillet flew across the room. If Trin hadn't stepped in front of me, I'd have laid hands on her.

"Even if that is the case, by the same law he was a minor when you started giving him pussy. He was sixteen freaking years old, Dani," I yelled.

I heard feet scrambling upstairs and then heard them running downstairs. I knew Jojo would show any minute. As if on cue, my younger brother, who was taller than I was, came rushing into the kitchen. Dressed in baggy jeans and a black sweatshirt that read NERD IS THE NEW SEXY, he may have been tall and stocky enough to look like a grown man, but he had a baby face that made you remember he was just a kid. Yes, his voice was deep and he was wise beyond his years but, to me, he would always be my kid brother, Jojo. My heart damn near broke in three when he stood in front of Dani.

"Leave her alone, Shanelle, please," he said.

Behind his black-framed glasses, his eyes told me he meant it. That angered me more. The thought of Dani turning my brother against me, the thought of losing another sibling for any reason, made me see red, the blood kind.

"Fuck this child-molesting bitch, Jojo. Fuck her. Don't send her to ask me for shit," I yelled.

Jojo cast a glance down then turned to Dani. He took the apple juice from her hand and placed it on the table. "Okay," was all he said; then he took Dani's hand and walked out of the kitchen.

I was so angry that all I could do was shake my head. I went back to the oven to stir the sauce and turn the meat on. Once done with that, I walked back over to the table. By then, my anger had overtaken rationality and, before I knew it, I flipped the whole fucking table over. Papers went flying and the dishes on the table crashed on the floor.

"Whoa, sis!" Trin said.

I'd forgotten she was there. I stood by the window. My anger wouldn't allow me to explain to Trin why I was so angry. There was not one of us kids who hadn't been touched inappropriately at some point in our lives. None of us; and to know that shit had effected Jojo to the point he purposely sought out older women sickened me right along with the anger I felt. I knew he couldn't help it in a sense, but that made it no better.

Yes, Dani was only four years older than Jojo. To some, they wouldn't see it as a big deal, but because this was a pattern with Jojo, it was a big deal to me. I opened my mouth to say something, but a movement in the backyard stopped me. A cloaked figure was standing in the bushes staring at me. At first I thought I was tripping. I grabbed my gun from the kitchen drawer. Trin was right on my ass.

"Something popping off?" she asked.

I didn't answer. I got to the back door just in time to see the figure running away. I shoved the screen door open and hopped off the porch.

"Turn the food off. Tell Monty to lock the house down. Get Navy to call Javon and get everybody in the bunker," I yelled over my shoulder.

I took off running full speed ahead. Whoever was in the cloak had a head start on me. He, or she, was running so fast through one of the neighbors' backyards, their shoes were kicking up dust.

"Hey!" I yelled.

I didn't know why I was yelling. It wasn't as if they were going to stop and talk to me. I chased the person down the street, then realized he had zigzagged through a yard and was heading toward Ms. Lily's again.

"Yo, Shanelle," I heard Navy calling behind me. I knew he was running too, judging by how close he was to me. "What the fuck? Shanelle, why you running?" he asked again.

"Somebody was watching the house," I said.

The person jumped over a car then ran through a group of kids who were playing. They were all bundled up, which reminded me it was cold outside. A woman was coming from her house with a trash bag yelped and tried to move out of the way a second too late. The figure damn near ran through the woman and into her house.

"I see him," Navy yelled. "Go left. I'll go right."

I did as he suggested. He went one way and I went the other. By the time we met up at the end of the street, the person had all but disappeared.

"Fuck," Navy spat. "The nigga was just right there!"

I huffed and puffed as I hid my gun behind me in the waist of my jeans then pulled my shirt over it. I turned left then turned right. It was as if the person had disappeared into thin air. "Damn it," I breathed out. It was only then that I realized some of the Thieves had been running with me too.

"If you had given us a heads up, we probably could have cut him off when he darted across the street," one of them said.

"Y'all didn't see him in the yard?" I asked.

"You told us we could break for lunch. We were in the front of the house."

He was right. Shit had been quiet on the home front so I'd had pizza and Chinese delivered for the men. They had been on duty nonstop until that moment.

I took a deep breath then said, "No more breaks. If you get hungry, you eat at your post. If you need to piss, do so outside and make sure someone is watching your back. The only time you leave your post is to shit and even then make sure it's covered until you get back."

All the men nodded and a collective, "Yes, ma'am" rippled throughout them.

By the time we made it back to the house, I was tired and my chest hurt because I had been running in the cold with no protection. Monty came storming up from the basement.

"We good, sis?" he asked me.

I shook my head. I was a bit confused. "I don't know. I . . . I think . . ." I paced around the front room. "It's weird is all."

"What, Shanelle?" Navy asked me.

I kept moving my mouth but nothing came out. I looked at Navy, Monty, and Jojo, who had a blank look on his face. I knew he was mad at me, but I was glad he came to check on me. All three looked concerned. And I felt as if I was losing it.

"Don't think I'm crazy, a'ight? And this stays between us for now, but it was almost as if I was staring at . . . Cory."

Chapter 19

Uncle Snap

"I'm telling you right now, the who's who in the Mexican Cartel have no fucking idea who organized their people to be a part of this," Montego adamantly said. "They wouldn't intentionally start a war they know they can't win."

"Something has to be done about this, Javon! It's been seven damn days and we have nothing," Creed shouted. He was angry. He had taken a huge loss. Ten of his men had been gunned down. They all had families, wives and children.

"We've been here seven damn days. We've traced every lead and we got shit, bro," Lucky added.

Javon looked haggard, worn out. He'd gone above and beyond trying to find any lead he could and we still came up short.

Lucky said, "I don't like us being a target not knowing where the shit is coming from."

Javon glanced at me then back at the five people surrounding the table. "I have one more possible lead and then I think"—he sighed—"I'll know exactly who's gunning for us, or at least who had something to do with it."

Creed leaned forward. Miguel's son, Montego, put his glass of tequila down and sat straight up. Lucky leaned to the side to study Javon. Ming's daughter's eyes narrowed as she zoned in on Javon. Nighthawk folded his arms across his massive chest then tilted his head.

"You got something?" Lucky asked.

"I do," Javon said.

I knew it was a knock to his pride for nephew to admit what he was about to, but he said it had to be done. Said he needed to show his hand to also show the Syndicate he could be trusted.

"Talk to us," Nighthawk's booming voice said. Luckily, he hadn't lost anyone or had any injuries. His security at the Reservation was Fort Knox tight.

I didn't agree with what Javon was about to do, but it was his call. "I think my sister, Melissa, is connected to this in some way," he said.

Lucky quirked a brow. Creed sat back like he had been punched. Nobody else moved a muscle.

"I don't know how or why. Just going with my gut instinct. She's disappeared. She took all the money from the club and cashed her part of

Mama's insurance check. Luckily I had a good mind to change all the pin numbers and authorizations on the other accounts a week after Mama died or I'm sure she would have cleaned me out."

"So what are you going to do about it?" Song asked. She was a spitfire. I could tell she was deadlier than her mother just by the way her eyes shot venom Javon's way.

"I'm with Song," Montego echoed. "How you gone handle this, holmes?"

"First, I need to find her. I need to make sure she hasn't been kidnapped or forced to do anything against her will. Once I make sure of that, I'll know how to proceed," Javon answered.

Montego, who looked like a darker version of his father, frowned. "As the man taking my father's place, I need to know if I got a right to search for your sister. My *papi* is dead, *sí?* And I need a little revenge for that affront."

"My mother is barely hanging on, still needs a machine to breathe. I need—and when I say need, I mean like I need oxygen—to find out who did this," Song's baby soft voice said.

"I lost ten men," Creed said.

Lucky cut in. "They came for the Commission. That cannot, in any way, go unpunished."

"While the Rez suffered no losses, the fact is it was a united front against the Syndicate. It must be dealt with accordingly," Blackhawk said.

Javon clasped his hands together on the table, his lips pressed together in a hard line. Nephew's eyes watered a bit. I knew that was more out of frustration than anything. "All right, but if you find her, bring her here to me so I can get the truth from her myself. I'm asking that you don't kill her before I get to say my piece to her," he said.

Montego stood. He was only five ten, but he stood like he was tallest man in the room. The black suit with the white collarless dress shirt underneath fit him perfectly.

"I can't make you that promise, Javon, and I'm just being honest. *Papi* was gunned down while he was holding my son, his grandson. That could have been my boy who got hit, too, but *Papi* died shielding him. I want you to understand the pain in that for me."

"My mother was shopping for my little sister's graduation. She was doing family shit. I know that being a part of a criminal enterprise comes with this kind of fanfare, but to know a member of the Syndicate's family has a possible connection to this makes it personal for me because she trusted you. She spoke so highly of you from the moment she left the meeting in which you took over. She believed in you, Javon, just as she believed in Mama."

"Mama was good to me. Always had been. That was why I respected you so much. I still respect you and I appreciate your honesty in telling us about your sister, I do. But I lost some of my best men. They died protecting me. I have ten families with over twenty kids to take care of for eternity. This is not an affront to your authority, brother. I'd never do that. As Song said, this is personal. Forgive me if she doesn't make it to you alive," Creed said before standing.

I could see the vein throbbing on the side of nephew's face. "I understand," he said so low we barely heard him.

Creed nodded once then headed out. Montego and Song followed close behind him.

"I have to run this by the Commission. Not sure how they will respond," Lucky said while standing. "I'll get back to you."

We remained silent while he made his exit. Once it was only Nighthawk and me left, Javon looked at the Seminole, waiting for his words.

"If the rest of your family needs protection for any reason, the Rez is available," he said.

Javon nodded. "Thank you, Nighthawk. I appreciate that more than you know."

"May the Great Spirit be with you, my brother."

Once Nighthawk walked out, Javon stood and kicked the chair he had been sitting in across the room. "I'm down three siblings, Unc. I'm about to lose my shit," he roared.

"I know, son. I know. Gotta let nature take its course, though. I think they respect you more for being honest about it. It probably would have looked bad had they found out on their own," I said. "I know that's no comfort to you right now."

Javon looked at me. For the first time I saw something in his eyes I hadn't seen before. There was fear and that puzzled me a bit. I hadn't seen that look in his eyes since he had taken over the Syndicate.

"What you scared of, nephew? If she gets killed, she brought it on herself," I said.

"I'm kind of okay with that, Unc. I am. But . . ." He dropped his head then gazed back up at me. "My gut, something deep inside me is having me believe Melissa had something . . ." Javon shook his head.

"What, son? Talk to me," I asked him. My head told me where this was going, but my heart, that motherfucker was holding me hostage.

"Unc, I think she had something to do with Mama's death," he said. "If the same men who attacked Mama are working in tandem with her then she was who was in the video. The reason Mama stopped fighting that day. That person she knew."

Before what he said could take root in me, he had tears rolling down his face that he quickly slapped away. His eyes were so red you would have thought he was drunk or high. He sent me a long, pained look before his shoulders slumped a bit. His words made my stomach harden. Spots flashed before my eyes. At first my heartbeat seemed to slow then, as if the world around me were caving in, that shit seemed to stop altogether.

I needed to grieve, but couldn't. Not at that moment. Not when nephew looked as if he was on the verge of a mental breakdown. I was quite sure if I lost my shit in the moment, it wouldn't help him any. No. I'd do what I'd been doing since my woman had been gunned down. In my room, late at night when and where none of the kids could see me, I'd let my emotions take me away. I'd let my memories of the only woman who'd ever had my heart drown me in my sorrows.

This shit was personal for me for reasons I couldn't explain to nephew at the moment. One thing was for sure: God knew that if I found Melissa before Javon did, she was a dead woman walking.

Chapter 20

Elias

How I loved it when a plan came together so fucking well. Going at the Syndicate had been easier than thought. Getting the Mexican Cartel—well, the rogues—to go along with my plan was like manna from up above. It was amazing what hard work and determination could pull off.

Now all I had to do was find that bitch Melissa, and I would find her. Believe that. Sending me texts telling me how weak she thought I was had to be the most comical shit I'd come across. That funky white bitch had the gall to call me weak? Wasn't she the one who wanted to snuff her dear old Mama out for dough? Then her weak ass chickened out at the last minute. So I had to make sure she got me my money.

Wasn't no backing out of nothing once I got going. Once I set my sights on something, I didn't stop until the endgame. A hostile takeover was what I was aiming for. If I crumbled the Syndicate from the inside out, then I could run North America with an iron fist.

"Ay, boss. Got some fodder on the wire," one of my men said as he rushed in.

Camilo was one of my best. I nodded at the Brazilian brother. "Say what you gotta say."

"That cat we went at in New York, word is members of the Commission were with him. They're telling me the Commission has a seat at the table of the Syndicate," he said.

I frowned and jerked my head back. "That's absurd. Why would the Commission take a seat at the table of the Syndicate when they are pretty much the godfathers of all this shit? Who told you that?"

Camilo chuckled. "Our connects on the street."

I flipped my hand. "Kill them. They're useless."

He nodded. "As you wish."

"You find that bitch yet?"

"No, but she left a trail. We have her on camera getting her hair cut at a salon in Riverdale on Highway 85. She's looking like a redheaded Amber Rose right now."

I grunted low then smacked the woman between my legs. She flinched then whimpered while looking up at me. "Watch those gotdamn beaver teeth, bitch," I fussed.

She blinked back tears then said, "I'm sorry."

"I know. Now suck my dick and shut up."

"Of course," she said.

"Where did she go after?" I asked Camilo.

"We lost her trail at a Quick Trip on Upper Riverdale Road."

"When was this?"

"About four days ago."

That alone proved to me Melissa was indeed dumber than she looked. A smart woman would have been long gone. She robbed me of the money I'd left in a safe at a hotel room we shared. She had to know I'd have her head for that.

As I spoke to Camilo about what the next move should be, a commotion outside the house caught our attention. Rapid Portuguese was being spoken as my men pointed in the distance, which told me something was wrong. I stood; my dick had all but lost its rigidness. The chick's saliva left a trail from her mouth to my dick as it slapped her in the eye, but I'd worry about that later. I shoved it back in my slacks, then zipped up. I rushed from the front room to the outside where all the commotion was.

My men were pointing to a building across from us. It was an empty warehouse. One I'd planned on using in the future. Up top was someone in a cloak. From my vantage point, I couldn't really tell if it was a man or a woman, but I sure as fuck knew what a rocket launcher looked like.

"*Puta merda!* Holy shit," I yelled.

I damn near tripped over my own feet running. One of my men screamed for everybody to run just before the missile from the launcher hit the house. The explosion knocked me from the front yard to the middle of the street. Debris cut into my arms, elbows, and back. Swore it felt as if I broke something when I hit the ground. I couldn't stop moving, though. I looked over my shoulder to see half the mansion up in flames.

Camilo grabbed my forearm and pulled me up. "Come on, *familia,*" he yelled.

Has that nigga Javon found me already? Shit, he moves quick, were my thoughts as another missile hit the house. Just as I and some of my men crossed the street, an engine revving caught our attention at the end of the street. Somebody in a ski mask on a yellow Ducati picked the front of the bike up as they sped down the narrow street. I knew what the fuck was coming next so when the AK-47 came out, I took a swan dive behind a truck in one of my neighbor's yard.

Whoever was on the bike lit the path after me up like the Fourth of July. Once they had done all the damage they could, they sped off toward the exit of the exclusive neighborhood. There was no doubt that once they hit the street they were heading for the expressway.

Once the heat died down, I looked behind me hoping to find Camilo, only to find he had been shot down in the front of my neighbor's yard along with the rest of my men.

"Okay, motherfucker," I yelled to no one in particular. "You want to play, Javon? Let's play, *caralho*. Prick!"

Chapter 21

Javon

I was supposed to return to work. To step into the role of what my life used to be just to keep up pretenses, but I couldn't bring myself to do that. Instead, I sat in my car, listening to the engine hum. My gaze was fixated on three grave markers. Trio monoliths dedicated to the family I lost since becoming a part of the Syndicate and doing my damnedest to uphold a legacy I wasn't sure I was right for. Too much was on my mind.

The carefully etched names of CLAUDETTE VIOLA MCPHEARSON, CORY BAYANI WILLIAMS-MCPHEARSON, and INEZ JANISA BATISTA-MCPHEARSON latched on to my psyche.

Along with the words: EMBRACED AS FAMILY AND UNITED IN HEART, MIND, AND SOUL.

Too much had been lost.

Too much had been compromised.

I sat there, hand on my steering wheel. Music on a low timbre. While aware that the Forty Thieves were somewhere keeping me protected. Shanelle had given me the rundown on the intel she had gathered. I was impressed but not surprised at her tenacity and ability to get the information she needed. The fact that she had come up with anything was helpful in what I needed to do. Now, what had me shook was the ghost she had seen. Naveen had come to me, worried Shanelle may have been losing it. So he told me what, rather who, she thought she'd seen.

I didn't know what to make of that. Grief. Angst. Disillusionment of what we lost. However, the fact that I was staring at fresh flowers at Mama's side of the grave, two sets, let me know something wasn't right. Why? None of us at the house had time to visit the grave, and if we had, we weren't leaving yellow roses and white lilies. Two sets of flowers directly from Mama's garden in the back.

Uncle Snap always left sunflowers from the garden with a mason jar of moonshine, while the rest of us would leave her orchids. Flowers she could never grow but loved to have in her house on Sundays next to her sunflowers. The importance of the yellow roses and lilies was simple. When we were kids and first came to Mama's house, it was Mama's yellow roses Cory accidently trampled in while running from her. After that, he'd always made sure to take care of them and bring her fresh roses on her birthday.

Whereas, white lilies were Inez's favorite flowers. I recalled Inez telling me that they reminded her of spring with Mama. Mama would make a big thing out of taking Inez and the girls to the science museum. Mama would stop near the park by a row of lilies and buy ice cream from a vendor for the girls. As she did so, Mama would always make sure Inez would share what she learned from visiting the museum. After, she'd pluck the lilies and put them in my sister's hair, and they'd go have lunch at Pascal's soul food. I knew this because they'd always come home and brag about it to their big brothers. We'd used to be salty about it, but eventually we got over it. We boys would spend our time cooking with Uncle Snap. I could still smell his cigars and pipe smoke while hearing Mama fuss about how dirty her kitchen was, while smashing fried salmon cro-quets, rib tips, grits, corn, and honey biscuits.

The memories were bittersweet.

Climbing out of my car, I walked to the grave then stopped. There was a packet wrapped in plastic against Mama's grave, marked SEED. I looked around then picked it up. Ripping it open, I poured the contents out and my jaw clenched in anger.

Melissa.

Fuck her, really. She broke everyone's heart and this family. Her disappearance wasn't just a coincidence, especially with going through the accounts. She had a hand in this, and the fact that she left this specific package on Mama's grave solidified that fact for me. She helped kill Mama, or she planned it. And at the end of the day, the poignant fact was this: Melissa deserved to die by family hands. Not the Syndicate.

Rubbing the stubble at my jaw, I stared at what fell at my feet. I wasn't sure if this was a trap. But the idea that Lissa thought that she could trip me up amused the darkness in my soul. Scanning the papers, I saw an address, a map, pictures of my product Ink in shipyards I assumed were in Miami from what Shanelle had found, and with it was a picture of Melissa with some suave-looking motherfucker. Immediately, I snatched everything up and went back to my car, grabbing my cell in the process. I needed to move quickly.

"Shanelle?" I asked in a hurry.

"Yeah, Von? Are you okay? Why aren't you at work?"

I slammed the door to my ride then started the engine. "No doubt I'm good, and we have other work to do. I need you to grab me some clothes. Black everything. Hoodie jacket, jeans, boots. Then meet me with Uncle Snap. I'll text the address. How are you feeling? If you can't ride with me, and you know what I mean, stay where you are, but I might need your sharp-shooting," I explained.

Shanelle shuffled around the house and I heard it through the phone. "I want that grown-ass woman out of this house; then I can focus on being okay."

"Well, baby, unless you want to go dark and push her ass down some steps, I doubt Jojo is going to be accommodating to your needs in her leaving." Getting to the highway didn't take long. I rode as low-key as I could in my Lexus, then took a ramp that led to an empty parking lot near an old strip club. "Where she goes, he'll go and we don't need him doing that, especially with the ankle bracelet. We keep bitching, he'll want and defend her more. That's how it is."

"And that's why you're accepting of that . . . that . . . pedo-thot in our house?" Shanelle incredulously asked.

"Pretty much, baby," was my response. "Anyway, let me hit you back. Meet me where I texted."

"Wait. Just tell me yes or no. Does it at least piss you off?"

Silent for a second, I sighed. "We all know what went down with Jojo, so yes, it pisses me off and I want to harm her in the most fucked-up way imaginable until she gets some intelligence in her dumb-ass brain. But, I figured you'd handle that eventually, baby. Mother of our child. Sometimes, these things are left to women, handling other women. I'm sure you'll make me damn proud once you figure out what you want to do or not do. I'll see you soon."

"Yes, you will. I love you," Shanelle softly replied.

"I love you too." Hanging up, I quickly dialed my cell.

"*Alô,* my ally and boss," answered in my ear.

"*Alô,* Amen. I'm sending you a picture via text. I need you to tell me if you and your wife know who this is, immediately. Tell me when you get it." Driving with one hand, I took a picture of the image lying on my passenger seat of Melissa with the unknown man.

I smoothly maneuvered through traffic and took an off-ramp, slowing down at a yield sign, then merging into the car lane.

"*Sim,* I have it." Amen's deep voice bellowed out for his wife. "FaceTime us, my friend."

"Will do. Give me five minutes," Hastily, I hung up then sped on until I got to my destination, which was the empty parking lot next to a sushi and steak house.

Tapping into my secured Wi-Fi, I pulled up FaceTime and a monitor popped up on my dashboard. Immediately the faces of Amen and his wife Cintia appeared before me. Both were very good-looking people. Both were proud of their African features and ancestry. Amen and Cintia were the color of russet brown. Amen's large afro was pulled back into a wavy ponytail that puffed in the back, while Cintia had twisted locs that adorned her oval face like a crown, wrapped in African-pattern head wrapping.

"Any idea who that man is?" I asked immediately, not wasting time.

It was Cintia who spoke up. "*Sim*. His name is Elias and we thought him dead."

"He is my elder brother and he had a right to our mother's seat had he not gotten himself killed several years ago out of recklessness and greed," Amen eventually said with sadness in his voice.

My mind blew up. Here we were with another family who had internal issues. What the hell? "Explain," I said, keeping my cool.

"Elias wanted to be at the Commission table. He wanted to take over Mama's shares and he began doing background work to push her out," Amen detailed. "He linked up with rogues around Brazil, and began building his own empire and team. Quietly causing street wars as a means to attack us São-A's. His goal was to cause discord and distract us by leaving our mother open for attack. It didn't work."

"You see," Cintia cut in, "Mama always was ahead of us with regard to family drama and underhanded dealings. So, when she found out, she ended him, as Amen was told."

Anger caused Amen's brown eyes to shift to the color gray as he slammed his fists down in front of him. "We all saw him put into the ground. I do not understand how he survived."

"You all have a traitor in your ranks as well and it leeched over like a virus into the Commission. Your family drama has affected us, as well as my own." Pain caused my temples to throb and I rubbed them. "He was a perfect fit for my sister then."

"What? I do not understand," Amen said with wide eyes.

I quickly explained everything and, as I spoke on, I watched the anger rise in Amen. In the middle of our discussion, he broke off and I watched him order men around then turn back to the screen.

"You are dealing with a dangerous monster, Javon," he stated with heat in his gaze. "He is not someone to take lightly. You kill him on sight when you see him. This is our approval. All I ask is his head delivered by you. My men in the States will be sent to assist you."

"If there is any more information we can share we will. As for now our faction will help you seize our product from Florida and distribute it appropriately," Cintia said for her husband. She had her palm resting on his shoulder. There was clear love between them. Both were young, around my and Shanelle's age, and it made me respect their adjustment to power in the Commission even more.

"Indeed. We will touch base again soon. Until then keep your ears on the Syndicate circuit. They are hunting my sister," I explained.

"Of course—" Cintia started but was interrupted by her husband. Quietly, she folded her hands in her lap and watched the screen.

"Javon. I, of all, understand the loss of a mother. What you did, it was necessary. My mother was a harsh woman who turned my brother into the monster he was. *Sim,* it hurt, *pero,* going after my brother. I wish my family could take that weight

for you, but we can't. In exchange, if we find your
sister first, we will give her the same honor that I
ask of you."

"I don't want her head. Her body would be
enough," I quickly made clear.

"But of course. Peace be still, my friend." With
that, Amen gave me a respectful nod then hung
up.

A soulful sigh came from me. I dropped my
head back against my seat then took a second
to compose myself. It was then that a familiar
SUV rolled up. Some ways behind it was another
car I knew to be the Forty Thieves. The door of
the SUV swung open and out dropped Shanelle,
clad in all black: leggings, a long, conformed top,
bulletproof vest, her hair pulled back, a cap, and
a mask. Shanelle looked my way then waved her
gloved hand at me.

I quickly got out of my ride, jogged to her,
then pulled her into an embrace. "Here. This
was left at Mama's grave."

Shanelle took the packet and I moved to the
back of the ride to dress, while nodding to Uncle
Snap, who was in the passenger seat readying
his weapons.

"Really, Melissa? This is some foul shit. You've
got to be fucking joking!" Shanelle quipped,
shuffling through the papers and showing Uncle
Snap. "Melissa did this?"

Adjusting my dick in my pants, I zipped up my jeans, then sat to lace up my boots. "That she did, babe."

"Never in my life has anything gotten so hard for me or ya mother that we'd gun for each other. Nothing! Y'all understand me? Nothing?" Uncle was so livid that he was shouting. "We didn't raise y'all to be this way. To kill the hand that loved, cared for, and fed you when they did nothing to you? No!" Spitting on the ground, Uncle Snap shook his head. "Disrespectful. But I bet you one thing, all of this is coming back on that child. She's not of us anymore."

I stood back listening in agreement. I then grabbed the map with the address. "I need everyone to cover me. I'm checking out this address. If it's a trap, I need you all to hold it down."

"That's what this is about?" Shanelle asked then climbed back in the SUV. "I hope Melissa is stupid and shows up."

Shanelle's smart comment made me laugh. I got in my car and took it to the address. All around was nothing but abandoned warehouses and buildings, except for a few houses. It was the one house that was nothing but cinders that pissed me the hell off. Climbing out of the car, I angrily strode to the house and looked around.

There were scorch marks all around the house, including the street.

"Son of a bitch!" I shouted, looking around at all angles. The sharp smell of fading gas was all around. Shattered glass. Damaged cars and furniture.

"Hey," I heard Shanelle behind me. "This wasn't the Commission, right?"

"Nah, they'd call and let me know," I said, kneeling while inspecting the house.

Uncle walked around then clicked his teeth. "Looks like straight Baghdad."

"As if a missile ran through it," Shanelle muttered.

Exhaling, I signaled to them. "Let's go."

It was as we were leaving that my cell rang. Picking up, I listened. "Talk to me."

"Hello, Javon. It's me, Jai. I was contacted by the Feds to speak to Jojo and you about the club burning down today. No one is answering at the house and they are coming within the hour. Some kind of way I got them to agree to come to the house as opposed to having to bring Jojo in."

Shaking my head, I sat back in my car, then sighed. "We're on our way. Wait outside for us." With that, I hung up and drove off, making it home quickly. Disappointment had us riled up.

"Jojo!" I shouted once we got inside. Shanelle came to my side as Jojo came downstairs. "We'll be having a meeting with the agents. They want to talk to you," I explained.

Uncle took guns and moved to hide them.

"I don't have to go back to jail, do I?" The panic in Jojo's voice was gut wrenching.

It made me step up and rest a hand on his shoulder. "No. They supposedly want to talk to us about the club burning down and then your case."

"Damn," was all he said before he disappeared upstairs.

My gaze went to Shanelle; then we both went upstairs to change. By the time we were done and we came back down, Uncle was showing in Jai, and Agents Monroe and Stillwaters. A huge part of me didn't want to allow them in the house, which was why I stepped up and held a hand up.

"Step into the sunroom. Our living room is cluttered right now," I coolly stated.

Both men followed me then took their seats. I pulled out a wicker chair for Shanelle and Jai; then I took my seat. "How can we be of help today? Jai stated that you wanted to speak to us about the club. Was there a problem?"

Old, sour hate shone in Stillwaters's eyes as he addressed me. "I find it kind of ironic that your club burned down, is the problem. Right in the middle of an investigation, too."

"I'm curious as to why." I clasped my hands in front of me once I leaned on my knees. "I'm baffled and dismayed about the club burning down. It was a business that our sister chose to take on as a means to help a family friend and then we lose it? I find nothing ironic about it. Have you checked to make sure he had had nothing to do with it burning down?"

Stillwaters and my eyes locked on each other. I had enough of being challenged today. I wasn't about to let this asshole disrespect any of us in this house.

"Gentlemen," Jai smartly said as a means to interrupt us. "You both wanted to speak to Jojo about his case. The club is being inspected, and we filed the necessary paperwork with the police. Is there an issue?"

"Ahem." Stillwaters cleared his throat as Jojo walked into the sunroom and sat down with an attitude. "The inspectors came back to us and reported there was no foul play. The seemingly random act of violence against the club is still being investigated but won't hinder your claim."

I said nothing at first. I just nodded. "I'm glad to hear that."

"Mr. Jo-nathan Atkins—" Stillwaters said with glee and a rock of his solid body.

"McPhearson," Jojo stated sternly.

Shifting through papers, Stillwaters smirked. "Mr. Atkins. Your little incident in lockup has proven to be a difficult one, hasn't it?"

"My last name is McPhearson!" Jojo started.

"Are you here to interrogate my client? Otherwise, your reasons for wanting to meet with us were misleading, and if that's the case, my client will remain silent and you need to go now," Jai jumped in with anger flashing in her eyes.

I bristled with how Stillwaters was being an asshole toward Jojo and I felt Shanelle rest a hand over mine then stand to grab a jar of water.

"This is part of our meeting. Mr. Atkins—"

"McPhearson," Shanelle, me, Jojo, and Jai said all at once.

Stillwaters ignored us and kept talking. "Made it a point to act in a disruptive state."

"Stillwaters, we already spoke that it was unclear if he provoked," Monroe interjected. He gave a light chuckle and gave a shrug, taking the glass of water Shanelle poured for them. Monroe was oddly calm around us. He'd always been. "That's why we're here right, Stillwaters? We don't want to spread strife among brothers and sisters, but I personally hate a false witness

who utters lies. We need to be clear on what
happened, is all, before we go accusing the kid of
senseless murder."

Shanelle stopped pouring then glanced at me.
Like her, my senses were alert. Did he just specifically quote a phrase Mama always would say?
I knew that I had to have misheard him. Mama
would always say two things that she always
hated like God: "a false witness who utters lies,
and one who spreads strife among brothers."

I always remembered her adding, whenever I
got caught in a mishap, "In due time, all truths
come to the light and, when they do, this belt
will always whoop your little lying behind, boy!"
So, I was incredulous that Monroe would state
that particular phrase. I glanced at Uncle, who
was lighting his pipe. He stopped his flicking of
his lighter then studied Monroe.

Even Jai became quiet, until she softly spoke.
"What exactly did you need again?"

Monroe said, "We wanted to be sure that your
family has no specific enemies or people who've
made threats your way. In our investigation,
we've come across some glaring issues."

"Such as?" I asked, finally finding my voice.
"Because your partner seems to believe we are
the ones at fault here."

I watched Stillwaters glare at me then look at Jojo. "Your brother has a serious issue that has come to the point where we've had to be involved. A drug charge is a serious situation to be in, not to mention, he killed two men while locked up."

"Yes, and he has no priors. He was also defending himself in lockup, which the video will clearly depict. Furthermore, are you even sure the drugs you found were his?" Jai interjected. "Your boys in blue came into a home of a woman who was known in the community for her social work and activism. Anyone could have had a vendetta against her and chosen to use her children as a means to harm her. Hence, persuading Jojo to unknowingly be a mule."

Monroe calmly nodded and took a sip of water. "This is true. There were some discrepancies that have occurred and investigating that was not done correctly, to be sure, to know whether what we found was young Jo-nathan's. Even to the point that he may have not been read his rights, and may have been violated by being placed with adults at seventeen. Isn't that what you told the judge this morning?"

Stillwaters grunted and leaned back. "This is why we were asked to come and speak with you. We might have been overzealous in our actions."

The man looked as if he had swallowed a pile of sour shit. I knew it bothered him to know that we had friends in high places; friends of Mama's who Jai had called on to get JoJo out of lockup even with the serious charges leveled at him.

Stillwaters added, "I just want it to be known that if it were left up to me, that little piece of shit would be locked up until the hairs in the crack of his ass turned gray."

Monroe frowned. "Stillwaters," he called out to his partner sharply. "This isn't up to us," he said then leveled Stillwaters with a gaze that chilled even me.

Something unspoken had passed between them.

Monroe stood and handed Jai a form. "These are court-ordered forms to remove Mr. Atkins-McPhearson from house arrest. He still has to relegate his movement to the community, and has a regulated court-ordered curfew until we finish our investigation; but, for now, he does not need the bracelet."

Jojo sat up so fast I thought he might have been hit by an invisible hand. "Really?" he said, excitement filling his voice. He smiled for the first time since his arrest.

"Yes, but if you break your court-ordered curfew and are found with contraband of any kind, we have the right to take you in," Stillwaters gruffly stated.

"I'll do whatever, just take this crap off me, man," Jojo said, moving toward them.

Both Shanelle and I glanced at Jai. She looked as confused as we did for a brief second, then she lightly smiled as if something clicked in her head.

We all waited as Jojo was released. Stillwaters stormed from the house like he was pissed the fuck off that Jojo was getting any semblance of freedom.

"Just so you know," Agent Monroe said once his partner was gone, "the tip about Jojo's little illegal enterprise came from within."

There was no need for me to question what or who he meant. By now we all knew Melissa had turned on us. What none of us could figure out was why.

Both agents eventually left, and I stood, talking to Jai. "This your doing?" I asked with my arms over my chest.

Jai glanced up at me. "I did put in a favor to clear him of charges, as you so angrily ordered me to do."

"But is this you?" Shanelle repeated by my side.

"It might be. I have to talk to my people and find out specifically. But for now I'm so excited that he's at least got that darn ankle monitor off. Mama Claudette wouldn't have wanted this for Jojo and—"

"Hey! Hey, it's you. That's the black lady I told you about, Shanelle," someone shouted, abruptly cutting off Jai's words.

We all turned to see Dani coming from the kitchen. She had a wild look in her eyes, almost as if she was panicking. She stared at Jai and pointed, then jetted for the stairs.

"Yo, Dani, hold up," Jojo yelled after her, then rushed to stop her from running up the stairs. "What black lady? What's going on?"

"It's her. She's the black lady who came to my school that day! Why is she here?"

Confused, I turned to look a Jai, ready to give her the third degree about what Dani had revealed, but Shanelle beat me to it.

"Hold the hell up," she said, pulling out her Glock and aiming it at Jai.

Jai's hands shot up in the air like she was being held up. "What the hell? Get that gun off me, Shanelle."

When Shanelle hit one hundred on her anger, there was hardly anything anyone could do. So I just stood back to let it play out.

"Why were you running around the school questioning Dani? You set Jojo up?" Shanelle asked Jai.

Jai backed up a bit. Her eyes darted around the room as if she was trying to find an escape route, but that wasn't going to happen. Uncle Snap and I had the doorway blocked. I guessed Jai wasn't answering quick enough. Shanelle reached out and yanked her by her hair. This caused both women to tumble around, knocking pictures on the wall around, and bumping into a side table. Both grunted like wild animals and snatched at each other. Jai tried to take Shanelle's Glock but she was at a twisted angle where she couldn't pull a smooth move to disarm Shanelle.

Shanelle had pissed me off just that quickly. I didn't give a damn about her whupping Jai's ass, but she must have forgotten she had our kid inside of her.

I marched across the room. I grabbed Shanelle around her waist. "Chill out. What the hell is wrong with you?" I asked her, knowing she knew why I was asking.

"Get your fucking hands off of me, Shanelle!" Jai snapped.

"You sneaky bitch," Shanelle snapped, completely ignoring me. She moved out of my grasp and went back at Jai. "And then you run your manipulative ass in here trying to pretend you have our best interests at heart," Shanelle shouted, and then swung Jai around by her hair.

Jai landed with a hard thud on her hip when she hit the floor. Part of me knew Shanelle was probably adding into the fight the fact that she thought Jai was after me or that I liked Jai in some romantic capacity. I finally snatched Shanelle off Jai and pulled her back.

Jai stood there, looking nothing like the polished attorney she was. Her eyes were red and her shirt had been torn. She was breathing erratically. She huffed before saying, "I went to the school to find the girl Jojo knocked up. Mama knew about his drug dealing and had been protecting him from law enforcement's eyes around town. She also knew about the baby, but she didn't leave me any instructions on what to do if she died in regard to the baby and the drugs. So I had to find that girl. In order to keep protecting Jojo, I needed to know who he knew at the school and who he had been dealing to. I'm not a damn threat. I loved Mama and never would be a turncoat to her or her family! How dare you come at me like I'm some random bitch on the streets!"

"For my family, I'd go at God the same way," Shanelle spat.

The two women stared one another down for the longest and I swore Jai wanted to jump at Shanelle again. But my girl still had her gun in her hand. Jai knew Shanelle could shoot quicker than she could run.

"I don't have time for this ghetto shit," Jai snapped then snatched up her briefcase. She hightailed it to the front door with fire in her eyes. Jojo followed her, more than likely so he could question her about what Mama knew.

Uncle Snap chuckled. "Well, that was interesting," he said.

I stared Shanelle down while shaking my head. A few seconds later, Jojo returned with a box in his hand then handed it to Uncle Snap.

"What's that?" I asked, walking up to him.

Jojo shrugged. "Don't know. One of the Thieves said the mailman dropped it off."

I watched as Unc opened the box. Inside was a black cell phone. It rang as soon as the box opened. Uncle and I eyed it skeptically then I hit answer and put it on speaker.

The accented voice on the other end of the phone said, "Javon McPhearson."

I had no idea who the voice belonged to on the other end of the phone, but my gut told me only one man would be so anxious to talk to me that he would have a phone delivered this way.

"Elias Gallo, I presume."

"Ah, you come to my home and set it ablaze, but you speak to me as if you don't know who I am. Cunning."

A scowl spread across my face. I didn't know what the hell he was talking about but I played along. "Of course I would come for you. What did you expect? You set this game in play; therefore, I aim to end it. For my mother, bitch."

Elias gave a guttural chuckle; then came a sharp scream like that of a child in the background. "Good. Killing her was just a taste of what I have in store for you, Javon."

Elias had just confirmed my thoughts and stepped into my game. I glanced at my uncle and he fisted his hands.

"It's time we do this with no more false pretenses between us. Now it's my move." When the line went dead, my eyes narrowed and I threw the phone.

Anger blazed through me. My fist connected against the wall and I stormed through the house. It was war time and I planned to cleanly take that bastard's head from his shoulders.

Chapter 22

Melissa

I couldn't breathe. My body hurt and tears stung my eyes. Everything around me was murky and dark. There was a constant drip, then the sound of something like a washing machine nearby. The scent of mothballs and mildew made me sneeze while I struggled for freedom. I had stupidly let my guard down and I went to Mama's grave to leave my form of an apology to the family, when I was snatched from behind.

Now I was in pain, shaking in fear. Piss slid down my thighs, wetting my jeans, and I didn't know who had taken me or why.

I had royally fucked up and all I could was scream.

"Let me go!"

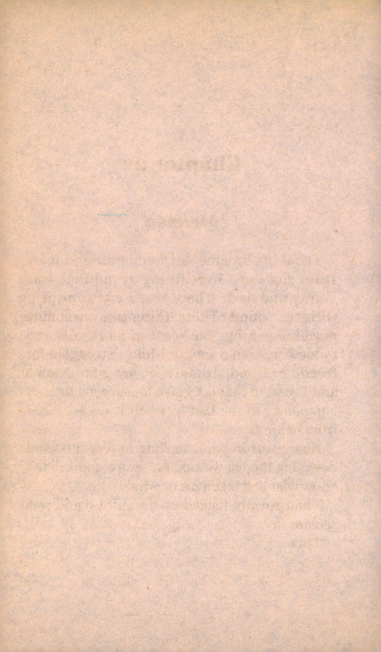

Chapter 23

Shanelle

There was a knock at the front door. It was hours after the phone incident and it was as if we had been sitting on pins and needles, waiting for the sociopath, Elias, to make his next move. At least I felt that way. Javon had left the house with Uncle Snap. His plan was to attack before being attacked. I couldn't be mad at him for that. Never mind the fact that I kept thinking about how so much had changed for my family in so little time. So much so that I handed over my resignation of my regular job. It would be quite awhile before we would be regular again.

I opened the door to find an angry Ms. Lily. Her face was red and she was bundled up. It was colder than a polar bear's twat outside.

"Now, I asked that boy over and over to come help me take these things out my basement and he never did and now they gone. I can't find them. Don't know where they at. I asked you and all your brothers to tell him to help me as well and nobody made a move. Now I don't know where it's at," she fussed.

Know where what was at? Wasn't no telling with Ms. Lily. She was a damn hoarder. I already had a headache from previous injuries when I'd thrown my head into the window of a vehicle and then into the vehicle itself. I'd killed three men in a parking garage who had come after me because one of Javon's other enemies needed him to be sent a message. So in order to make it look like someone else had killed them, I used my own body as a deflection. Those pains were ailing me now. Not to mention, I'd tussled with Jai. I really wasn't in the mood to deal with an ornery old woman.

"I'm sorry, Ms. Lily, but things have been crazy around here," I said.

"Oh, don't I know it," she huffed, and she rolled her beady eyes. "Who was you and that Indian child chasing through the streets the other day?"

"He's Bangladeshi and his name is Naveen."

"I know his name," she snapped. "Who was you chasing?"

I took a deep breath, trying to keep my cool. "A stray dog is all."

"Humph. I'd say. Stray dogs wear capes and thangs?"

I tilted my head, about to ask her if she wanted to come in or go back home. I didn't have time for her fussing. I really didn't. Ms. Lily was too damn nosey for me and, like Uncle Snap, I didn't know why Mama was so nice to the woman.

"Ms. Lily, would you like to come in for hot cider or cocoa?" I asked. "It's a bit chilly out here."

She peeked inside the house then turned her nose up. "Naw. Don't like the smell of that ethnic food y'all always cooking over here."

"Would you like a bowl of chicken pumpkin soup, Ms. Lily? Mama told me that's your favorite." I smiled. Ms. Lily was lying. Every time we or Mama cooked something, Mama took her a plate. That old German white woman would eat every bit.

Ms. Lily's eyes widened as if I'd just offended her. She balled her lips and turned in a huff to strut back across the street. I watched as she crossed to make sure she got to her home safely; then I closed the door.

Just as I did so, Monty and Trin came in from the closet under the stairs. She was in tight-fitting jeans, some Polo combat boots, and a BLACK LIVES MATTER sweatshirt. Her locs swung, brushing her shoulders. Monty was dressed like a lumberjack all the way from the big brown boots up to the oversized coat and flannel red and black checkered button-down shirt.

"You find anything?" I asked Monty.

He shook his head, his long, silky black hair curtaining his face. "Nothing. She wiped her apartment clean."

"There was no trace of nothing, sis. Not even a stray hair."

"Damn," I said. So Melissa was long gone. We wouldn't get the chance to confront her. I thought that angered me more than anything. "Thank you," I told them.

I held my tongue as Jojo and Dani came from the kitchen. He had a big bowl of the soup that I knew was mostly for Dani. He didn't eat that much. Dani kept her eyes away from me as Jojo led her upstairs.

"You know Mama wouldn't allow you to eat in your room, Jojo," Monty said.

Jojo stopped, pushed his glasses up on his nose, then looked from me back to Monty. "Kind of hostile down here, though," he said.

I rolled my eyes.

"Even so, little bro. You know the rules," Monty said.

"Fine." Jojo took Dani's hand then headed to the dining room.

My nerves were just about on E. "I'm going to head out. I told Javon I would take care of something for him. Somebody tell Naveen to meet me in the car," I said.

I grabbed my coat, purse, and my keys then headed outside. By the time the truck was warmed up, Naveen came jogging out the front door. In a blue bubble coat, he pulled up his baggy jeans while his Tims thumped against the pavement. He hopped in the truck and slammed the door behind him. There was aggression in his movements and tension rode him like a cowboy.

"You okay?" I asked.

"Yeah. Broke up with my girl. Shit's stressful," he said, staring straight ahead.

"Why, Navy? She was a cool chick, I thought."

"She wants time I can't give her right now. She doesn't understand that."

"She can't come to you?"

"I've asked her several times and she doesn't want to, so fuck it." He shrugged then let his seat back a bit.

"Navy—"

"Nah. I ain't got time, Nelle. I don't. So, save it. No lectures, sis. She's safer away from me right now anyway."

I looked at my younger brother. Normally I'd say something snide about the brutish way he was behaving, but in a sense he was right. Maybe his girl was safer on the other side of town away from all the madness.

I put the truck in reverse and pulled out of the driveway. I saw Ms. Lily peeking out her front window. She was starting to creep me out. Something about her wanting Javon and only Javon to come get whatever it was out of her basement was starting to seem strange to me.

Headlights in my rearview didn't readily alarm me. A group of Forty Thieves were at my beck and call. They were my shadows.

"Where we headed, sis?" Navy asked as we headed for 75 North.

"To Cory and Inez's old place in midtown," I answered.

I felt Navy look at me. I knew what he was thinking. I saw the way they all looked at me when I told them I thought the person in the cloak we were chasing was Cory. They all thought I was losing it, even Javon and Uncle Snap. Javon shook his head. I knew bringing up our dead siblings was a sore spot for him, but I knew what I saw . . . or what I thought I saw.

Whoever it was had Cory's eyes. I knew it.

"Sis, they're dead. Why you gotta make the pain worse?" Navy asked.

I glanced at him, my hands gripping the steering wheel. "Make the pain worse?"

"Yes, Nelle. Worse. We had to bury them with no bodies. Don't give us false hope that they're out here somewhere, running around in our back yards. All that blood in that car and the fact the Irish wouldn't even give us their bodies back."

"I know, but we never got their bodies. How do we know they're dead?"

"Stop," he snapped at me, making me narrow my eyes at him. "And even if the Irish did have them alive somewhere, you think after Javon did what he did to the Irish that Cory and Inez are still alive now?"

I sighed. Navy was right. Even if the Irish did have Cory and Inez stashed somewhere as leverage against Javon, surely after Javon had them all blown up, our siblings were dead now. However, I was still going to their apartment. I just needed to feel their energy once more. With everything going on, it had been hard for me to feel any kind of normalcy.

Those were my thoughts while I drove until my mind started to kick my ass. *Let it go; better yet, let them go, Shanelle. Let them rest in peace,* it screamed at me. I felt my eyes burn, but I refused to let the tears fall. I handled the wheel with one hand then grabbed a tissue from the armrest. This mess was stressful.

Instead of getting off at the exit where Cory and Inez's apartment used to be, I took exit 248B and headed to Jesse Hill Jr. Drive. The man who had been driving the car when Mama was killed was stilled holed up in Grady, according to our sources there.

Before going to check for information on Jojo while he was locked up, I'd put word on the street that I was willing to pay for information to anyone who could tell me about a man who had been shot around the time Mama had been gunned down. No matter how secretive people tried to be, the streets always talked when there was money involved.

Instead of chasing ghosts, I decided to chase something tangible: one of the men who had helped to kill Mama. Once we got to Grady, I paid to park—cash. Navy and I hopped out of my truck and headed inside. We emptied our pockets and headed through the metal detector. The waiting room was beyond full. Squeaky tires from a stretcher rolled down the narrow hallway on the gray and tan marble flooring.

Someone was hacking up their lungs while sitting in one of the gray cushioned chairs in the waiting room. Another man was holding a bloody shirt up to his head. His eye was swollen and his lips were busted. A kid vomited all over the floor while the mother yelled for "some-motherfucking-body to hurry up" and see her child. Shit, she had been sitting there for three hours, she yelled. The little white boy did look pale, like death was knocking on his door.

I walked up to the Plexiglas registration window and smiled at the nurse there. She had on blue scrubs with latex gloves on. Her hair was braided and she looked like Rachel Dolezal.

I slid an envelope through the hole in the window then said, "Is it possible you can tell me which room Diablo is in?" Diablo was the street name that had gotten back to me. My source had told me to go to Grady and look for the white girl who looked black with blond faux locs.

She took the envelope and slid it her pocket. "Seventh floor. The men who are normally there left to get food. Fifth door on the right," was all she said as she quickly went back to writing on her chart.

I nodded. Navy and I made our way to the elevators. Didn't take us that long to reach the seventh floor. Navy and I smiled at women at the nurse's station. They paid us little mind as a man in one of the other rooms was yelling and screaming about his dick burning.

"Oh, my freaking God, Joanne. He's pissing on the damn floor," a white nurse yelled.

"Fucking Grady," a black nurse, who reminded me of a "Big Mama," quipped before rushing to the room with other nurses behind her.

I looked at Navy when we made it to the fifth door on the right. He glanced around to make sure nobody was paying attention to us. I pushed the door open and walked in. Machines beeped. The man was in bed, sleeping. His head was leaning to the left; slobber was slowly leaking from the corner of his mouth. He had been bandaged from his torso to his shoulder. His right hand was heavily bandaged as well.

I nodded to Navy. He walked to the right side of the bed while I walked to the left. For mere moments, I stared at the man. I'd never seen him before, but he was the man who had to be driving the car when Mama shot at it. He had jet-black wavy, thick hair on his head. His skin was the smoothest of light brown I'd ever seen. Although his face looked a bit swollen, clearly he was a handsome man. I easily cuffed his left hand to the bed without waking him. He couldn't do shit with the right one since it was obviously injured.

My brows furrowed. I drew back. My hand seemed to be frozen in midair for a second before slamming down on the man's right cheek.

He awoke with a start. His wide gray eyes shot open and looked at me. Before he could get any words out, Navy punched him in the stomach then threw his weight over the injured man's torso while taping his mouth shut. We only had a few minutes to do what we needed to do.

I pulled out a picture of Melissa. "You know this girl?" I asked.

The man's eyes widened, but he didn't respond. Navy grabbed the man's right hand and beat it as hard as he could. The man's screams and yells were muted. I knew he was in pain, but I guessed, like the other man who Uncle Snap had tortured, this one wouldn't talk either.

"That's enough," I told Navy, who stopped immediately.

Navy had a sinister look in his eyes that told me shit was just as personal for him as it was for me.

"Tell me where your boss is. I know you know. We took out his mansion over near the warehouses," I lied. "So tell us where he would go next."

The man's eyes roamed around wildly. I could see fear there, something I didn't see in the other man. Since he was the driver, he must have been a newbie to the rogue faction that Elias was running. Even so, the man didn't answer.

Navy said, "Look, homie, I'm annoyed as fuck. My sister is being nice. I don't have time. I just broke up with my girl. I want to get back home and send her some fucking passive-aggressive texts to make her feel like shit and then leave snide comments on all her social media posts, you feel me?"

Navy pulled out this black stick then snapped it so it elongated. He pressed a button and blue electricity shot from the end. "So this is what's going to happen. There is enough electricity in here to fry your brain, fam. I mean, this shit can burn your skin smooth off. Wanna try it?" Navy asked.

Before the man could blink, Navy put the end of the stick against the man's dick and, sure enough, skin peeled away. The smell reminded me of burning rust. The veins in the man's eyes turned a blood shade of red. His back lifted off the bed and his whole body trembled.

"You want to talk now or do I have to go for your balls next?" he asked the man.

The man nodded vigorously. I slowly pulled the tape from one side of his mouth.

"Stone Mountain," he stammered out with a thick accent. It sounded more like, "Stunned Muntin."

"Where in Stone Mountain?" I asked.

Before the man could answer, the door swung open. Two men dressed in all black with bags of food in their hands gave me and Naveen murderous glares before dropping the food and rushing us.

"Hey, hey!" I heard one of the nurses yelling. "Somebody call security!"

The man who came at me shoved me into the machines. I went tumbling back, hard. He tried to punch me in my stomach, but I was too quick. I picked up a bedpan and knocked him back. I saw Navy wrestling with the other man. Navy threw a punch just as I scrambled to my feet only to have the man I was fighting with grab my ankle and almost send me face first into the marble floor. I caught myself using my hands to break the fall right before I landed on my stomach. I heard the zap of Navy's black stick and heard the other man cry out as they tussled. Just as the man behind me grabbed my ponytail, Navy rushed over, and zapped him with the stick, making him fall back.

Blood rushed to my ears. My heart slammed into my ribcage as my breath caught in my throat. Either being pregnant was tiring me out, or I was losing my fight. Either way, Navy grabbed my arm.

"Come on." He rushed out as we ran for cover.

We could hear the men chasing us. We knew we couldn't make it to the elevators so Navy pulled me toward the stairs. He shoved the door open and we both took flight down those stairs like we had rocket propellers on our shoes. We were almost down the first set of stairs when one of the men grabbed my ponytail. I yelled out as I fell back. When I fell, the stair seemed to slice the middle of my back. It hurt so badly. I quickly got my footing while Navy dodged a kick from the other man, then yanked him down the stairs by his ankles.

I grabbed the man, who I had by the nuts. He howled out and tried to punch me. I stepped sideways, causing him to punch the wall. If I made him injure his hand, he couldn't swing at me anymore. I heard to zap-zap-zzzzzz-zap of whatever Navy called that instrument he had made. The man he had been fighting with yelped and hollered. The smell of burning rust lit the small area. I glanced back to see Navy had the electric end of his weapon on the man's neck. His flesh was peeling away. It reminded me of how we used to let glue dry on our hands and then peel it off.

The man who I'd been fighting with tried to launch at me. I still had a grip on his nuts. I twisted and turned. Lips snarled and teeth bared, I tried to twist those motherfuckers off. As I did so, I took my left hand and punched him, repeatedly, in the face. My blows were rapid and all landed on his nose. Strikes to the nose disoriented a man the same as it would a dog. My left hand had rings, too, and each time I struck, I made sure to go in an upward motion.

Soon, he fell to his knees. I picked up the heel of my boot and kicked him dead center in the head. At the same time, I heard Navy breathing hard. I turned around to find he was stomping the man's hand into the ground. He remembered a lesson from Uncle Snap just like I had. If you took out an opponent's hands they couldn't swing on you, or grab a gun to shoot you or a knife to stab you . . . or pick up a phone to call the police. Just like he'd told me about punching a man in the nose in an upward motion.

It was crazy and probably stupid in hindsight that we went to that hospital, but we raced down the rest of the stairs, which didn't take that much time at all. Luckily, security wasn't there waiting for us. We headed straight for the parking deck to the car. I told Navy to drive. I just couldn't. I was disoriented. Navy got in and we peeled out like hell was after us.

Chapter 24

Javon

It seemed that too much was going on in my days. Back to back to back there was something. No lie, my hands were shaking because I wasn't sleeping well or enough. Bags hung under my eyes, and I was moving sluggishly.

After the call with Elias, I had left with Uncle to give orders to the Forty Thieves. I then headed out to our zones to make sure Elias wasn't sniffing around, which had me in Rize's zone, sitting at a wobbly oak table.

When Uncle Snap and I walked into Rize's restaurant, my head began to spin in stress. My boots crunched on sprinkles of broken glass. Boards acted as barriers over shattered windows, and tables lay on their side in disarray. We glanced around the popular restaurant and made notes of the holes in the painted walls. I could smell bleach, and I could see where they were cleaning and patching up holes.

Elias had given us a taste of the type of attention he was seeking. I now sat in thought, eyes closed and head throbbing at what his type of war was going to look like. The bastard was ahead of us in his tactics and my mind immediately went to Melissa's treacherous ass. *How could you do it, sis?*

"Nephew, are you able to handle this?" I heard Uncle ask of me.

A big part of me wanted to go off. If I wasn't able to handle this, I'd walk away. What type of fuck shit was that? But I kept my thoughts to myself. Those were the whispers of anxiety, exhaustion, and frustration, not logic. The old man was just checking in on my mental state. I didn't have Cory here to be that voice anymore, so all I could do was rely on Uncle in that.

Reaching for a glass of ice water, I took a comforting sip then checked my cell phone. "I'm tired is all, but I can handle this." There was a text from my employee Danny. I quietly read over my work I had sent to the office. I needed some normalcy and I needed to keep an unassuming cover, which was why I sent in a request to be of help from home. It was rare that my bosses would allow something like that, but they understood from my current situation, and responsibilities, as well as from the damn good work I did that I could leave at any moment and take the crew I trained with me. Yes, I had threatened to leave and start my own security technology company, but for now it was just an idea I shared with my coworkers.

So, there I was, approving codes that I had created, allowing them to rise up, while I sat back being a criminal kingpin. I scrolled through the information, then checked with Danny that my connect with his boss, Sato Ayame, was strong, considering everything. I needed something that I had brought to the table at the Syndicate, thanks to Mama's notes, to stay steady. If I could keep it steady, with no threat from Elias, then I could pull them in as another power move, as I did with the Commission. Revealing that Sato Ayame's Japanese ties link to an old family mafia syndicate, the Yakuza, could help bring a sense of stable power back in my hands after everything with Melissa.

I needed this.

Holding up a finger to my uncle, I listened to Danny: "The attack didn't affect us, I assume, because we are so new to the table."

"That would make sense. Have you connected with São Africana?"

Danny affirmed that he had and that their crew in Brazil would be of protection to the

São Africana family while some of their crew was busy in Miami.

"My thanks. You have the information of who Elias is and his old connects. His power here is too strong for me, so whatever you find out in addition to what I do, relay it immediately. As for work, keep me abreast of everything occurring there."

"I will." Danny chuckled.

"What?" I curiously asked.

"You still stay several steps ahead; it is a good thing. If you do choose to stake out on your own, I'll follow. I'm tired of working for the Klan," he said in response to how ruthless our bosses could be to anyone of color.

I felt light laughter in my chest at what he said, and I welcomed it with a slight chuckle. "Of course. When I rise, I always make sure family rises with me."

"We all appreciate that, too, man. I'll keep you abreast of all going on here and send those weapons you requested."

A beep sounded on my cell, indicating another call. "Good. I'll be in touch." Flipping over, I answered, "Speak to me."

"The shipment of ammunition is now resting in your private warehouse." It was Nighthawk.

"Great. The Japanese connect is sending more weapons for us to stock."

"That is a good thing," Nighthawk responded.

"Definitely. Now, I have a request for you. Have you found out anything new, first of all?"

A light shuffling sounded, then liquid pouring with a clink of something I assumed was ice. "My people are sifting through the streets. As of now I know you're with Rize."

My nose twitched at that, but I wasn't mad at it. Nighthawk and his crew were no joke when it came to security. They were right there with the Forty Thieves, which was why a few of them worked with the Thieves as well. "Indeed," I calmly stated.

"With all things and in all things, we are relatives. My brothers and sisters the Sioux say that and I believe in it as I see your actions follow the same path. I'm here to help in any way and right now I'm helping you, my brother," Nighthawk explained.

"So, I take that as you saying you've found out some new information," I said.

"More like it found me. But, I will inform you about that once I gather more information. For now, your hunch was right about Elias keeping a second location near your sister's favorite hotel, the W."

A flash of a smirk slid across my face. I glanced at my uncle, who watched me in curiosity. As we sat, food was brought out to us. Large plates of oxtails, plantains, rice and peas, steamed cabbage, Festival, and escoveitch fish. Several empty plates with utensils were set out, along with glasses of ice water, and bottles of ginger beer. Nodding my thanks to the older beauty, who I knew to be the aunt of the leaders of Rize, I then returned my attention to the call.

"If they were deeply involved, I figured that he'd stay near her favorite haunts, and the W is one of them."

Nighthawk gave a light chuckle at my comment. "Very smart. For now, we are watching him and trailing him to see where he'd move his base, now that it's gone. The rest I will report to you as it comes to me. You have my word."

Reaching in my black jacket, I handed my uncle a thick envelope. He dutifully took it, then stood as Khalil stepped out. His face seemed to contort in pain. His arm was in a sling, and the side of his neck had a large bandage as well. My friend and his people had been aggressively attacked and hurt. It angered me, but I contained it. I owed them better protection.

"Thank you, my man. Before I hang up, I ask if you can connect with the table and have them send two of their best. Rize is owed protection for the work they've done in protecting us in the

Syndicate. I'm also giving them access to the Forty Thieves."

"Of course, boss. I'll send my own immediately," Nighthawk stated.

"We'll speak again, one." I then hung up, and stood.

Moving around the table I walked up to Khalil as Uncle Snap handed him the thick envelope. The evening sun started to drop and its shining light cascaded in the restaurant. Khalil handed the envelope to his aunt then walked toward me.

"Take a seat, man. At this table we're all equals," I said, helping him sit down.

"No doubt, fam. We thank yuh for this contribution of yours. As yuh see, we were hit hard," Khalil said in his accented voice.

"I'm seeing. I also noticed that the whole block was kill zoned as well?" I asked but really it was a statement.

"Ah, yuh. Several businesses were hit by strays, and some homes," he explained while tiredly taking his glass then lifting it to his lips for a sip of water. "How's mi sister?"

Leaning back some, our plates were filled by one of Khalil's crew, a pretty golden brown girl with kinky long hair that fell to the middle of her back. She sported high tops, tight jeans, and a simple tank. From the contour of her face, I could tell that she was family of some sort as well. She had the look of Trinity to her. With a matching plump ass.

I told her thank you, as Uncle watched the girl walk away. I wanted to chuckle but right now we were conducting business so I had to keep it professional. "Outside of her blasting anger at you being hurt and not letting her come home?" I chuckled with Khalil and made a face; then I continued. "Trinity is doing well and is protected. Monty is making sure of that."

Khalil gave a deep sigh then began to eat, while speaking with his hands. "What is going on, brah? What do you need me and my crew to do fah yuh?"

"For now, I need you all to rebuild, and reinforce your place and block. I appreciate you and your family sending soldiers out in the street," I said.

"It's irie." Khalil gave a smile. "It was nothing for the overall objective. We were able to find out that that Elias nigga is working to collect surviving Irish. They helped point out our digs."

"Did they?" Immediately my mind went to Cory and Inez. My jaw clenched and I kept my cool.

"Yuh. We took out as many as we could, though. You know? Fair exchange," Khalil said with a light laugh. He licked sauce from his fingers, then wiped his mouth. Homie looked as tired and battle worn as I was, but it was good that he felt comfortable enough to eat with us like family. It made me dig into my food and enjoy the spices and flavors that took me on a mental trip to the Caribbean.

Uncle Snap was next to me tearing into his oxtails, nodding at the conversation, before he spoke up. "Good deal. Have one of your leads give me a rundown on the remaining Irish wipeout. You think they might be ready for something new?" Uncle said, looking my way.

"But of course. Khalil, I want you to take some people you trust and expand Rize." A slick smile spread over my face as I watched Khalil's eyes widen in joy. "Take over the Irish territory. If you have some members of the pale side in your crew, or Asian, it's my suggestion that you use them to secure the old Irish pub and take it over as a yuppie Caribbean spot."

I paused in thought, thinking about the business end of what I was suggesting. It was Shanelle who gave me a deeper understanding on how we could profit from this exchange. She broke down the business logistics and I formulated the rest. I had to thank her again, when I saw her next.

Returning my attention to the present, I lifted a piece of fresh cocoa bread, ripped it apart, and then dipped it in my oxtail sauce. "It'll give you a cover, and generate legit cash flow, where they would have no idea, except possibly the true Irish mob that is lingering. Any who step to you, erase them. We need to micromanage that zone. The only Irish allowed to grow will be the ones we control and trust. But, on the real, I don't trust those motherfuckers worth a penny. If you need more white faces, hit me up and I'll send Creed and his people to back you. All startup funds will come from us. You good with this?"

Khalil sat back, then wiped his mouth. He extended his free hand toward me then nodded. "Hell yeah, I'm good with this, brah!"

Taking his hand, I shook it proudly. "Then heal up, and keep yourself low. You as a boss need to be protected from Elias and people who are like him. So be smarter in how you protect yourself. Bulletproof this place."

"Yes, add steel security doors, no bars. Build your security basement better. I'll send some of my people who are construction workers here," Uncle added while looking around as if he were appraising the place. "Shouldn't cost a mint at all."

"Trin said that to me." Khalil laughed then sat back. "I'll do that. It ain't my thing to hide, though. But, I'll be smarter in how Trinity and I protect my base. Nigga opened my eyes, as did you two," he added.

"He opened ours as well," I quietly said, then held up my hand.

My cell was buzzing, as was Uncle's. I knew when that happened that there had to be a family emergency. I saw that it was Navy, and I quickly answered, "What's happened?" It was late in the evening now, meaning it was dark out. The fact that Navy was calling worried me. Had Elias come through on his word or what? I still needed to hit him before he hit us.

"Shanelle's hurt, bro," Navy spat out.

The terror in his voice had me on edge. I pointed for Uncle to move from where he sat so that I could get out. He did so, while looking at his cell.

"What happened, Navy?"

His car roared in the background. I could hear him telling Shanelle to wake up. "She won't wake up!"

I glanced at the men at the table, and Khalil gave me a reassuring nod. "Gawn, brotha. We are good here. I'll contact you later."

"Uncle, make sure he's squared away with the final details. I'll be near the car. We need to move out now," I said, glancing at the two men and one women who were the Forty Thieves I brought with me.

"Young Khalil . . ." was all I heard Uncle say as I walked to the back of the restaurant instead of the front and made my way through the kitchens to the back.

"Navy, take her to our house since it's closer." I told him to go the back way. "I'll have the medics waiting with the Thieves."

"A'ight. I'm on the highway heading there now. I'm sorry, Von," Navy said into the phone.

"Take a deep breath, and tell me if you feel her pulse then tell me what happened." I tried to keep my voice calm and even as I asked that, although my heart was pumping a mile a minute.

Everything we were doing was catching up on us. None of us had time to grieve. None of us had time to process the fact that we agreed to be a part of the crime world, and none of us had time to shift our everyday lives to cover our asses while building up our criminal backdrop. It all was piling up on us. The car chases, the battles, the running, everything.

My head started to spin. The cool breeze of the night wasn't helping against the heat I was feeling. A light compression was centering on my heart and I had to focus on my car just to keep it together. I couldn't lose Shanelle and I knew that she couldn't handle another child lost just because we were committed to living out Mama's dreams. I was bred by the streets, raised in the streets; but how could a brotha like myself transform all of that and balance it out with a family?

How did you do it, Mama? I felt myself mentally whisper in the heavens.

I stood there racking my brain trying to pull it together as I listened to Navy explain how they went to Grady. What they did, I respected. It was a good idea to step back and go to the beginning of how this all started. It was just the fact that they now were running from more of Elias's goons, with Shanelle passed out, that wasn't working for me.

Suddenly, the scent of fried catfish and okra wafted across my nostrils. I felt the light touch of a palm at my shoulder that slid to the side of my neck and gently squeezed. I knew that I was having a panic attack, but I didn't expect to turn and see Mama standing behind Uncle Snap.

She stood there with her apron on, looking like a Big Mama, with a knife in one hand and a mason jar of something clear in the other. Mama smiled lovingly at me when our eyes locked; then I heard her say, "I heard that Maya Angelou lady say something that I knew growing up, but never could put in pretty words like her. 'N' right now, Von, you need these words."

I thought I asked, "What is that, Mama?" but my mouth didn't move.

"Von, baby, sometimes it is necessary to go through defeats so that you can know what it is and who you are in that lesson." Mama gave me a stern look then took a sip from her glass. She stepped closer to Uncle Snap and appraised him in love before continuing. "It's necessary, baby, but what also matters is that you don't be defeated. That's how I made it. All of this will pass and you'll find your footing, boy. You are a leader; and don't feel like you can't do this."

Mama's hand gently caressed Uncle Snap, then my jaw, before she hauled off and slapped me hard. Shaking her finger at me, she scowled. "Now, get your butt up before I shoot ya pinky toe off, boy."

A light chuckle came from me at that tone of hers; then I muttered what I always did when Mama was giving me a lecture. I quoted Winston Churchill, a man from history I had no respect for.

"If you're going through hell, keep going."
Mama nodded in pride with a smile then faded away.

I stood there looking at Uncle Snap, who had taken my cell from me. He pulled me into a tight hold then whispered in my ear, "I miss her too, nephew. She wouldn't want you to break because of none of this, so take a minute, and pick yourself up. This family needs you and so does Shanelle. Let's get to her, nephew. I'll be by your side until I can't be anymore."

Gripping him by his shoulder, I took a moment to get my thoughts together. Taking a deep breath, I shook off my emotions and got to work doing as both he and Mama had told me. It didn't take long for us to make it to the house. Once there, both Uncle and I sprinted inside.

Everyone was hovering in the room. Navy stood by Mama's bed staring down at a resting Shanelle with worry in his eyes. Clear tubing ran from her arm to the clear bag of liquid hanging by her bed. Several medics were around them but they moved to the side to allow me through.

Without any hesitation, I took her hand then kissed it. When Shanelle gave my hand a grip, everything in me relaxed and I gave a sigh of relief. I wasn't feeling her laid out like this. It hurt my heart. Watching her, quietly, I looked up when Navy came to my side.

"They said she just needs some rest. Her electrolytes are off, and she didn't heal up right from her time in the hospital. Oh, and she's pregnant!" Navy gave me a look of surprise.

I couldn't help but give a quick grin while looking at Shanelle. "Yeah, Elle and I are going to be parents," I said. "We just gotta keep her safe and let her run everything behind the scenes and not in the streets. I have to remember that," I muttered to myself.

We all stood there listening to the orders of the medics. Once I had them leave the room for a moment, I spoke to my family about what was going on. We all had to protect Shanelle at this point because if Elias got a whiff of this news, he'd use it against me. Shit, if it were Elias in this situation, I would do the same just to break him. Which was why I doubled up security, then sent word to go to Grady and kidnap the shooting survivor. He, his friends, and I needed to have some words.

Later that night, because I couldn't sleep, I pulled on my jeans, laced up my kicks, pulled on a sensible shirt, and grabbed my jacket. I then made sure I was strapped, grabbed a set of extra keys, then walked up the block, stopping by Ms. Lily's to take her trash to the front of her house.

Chapter 25

Ms. Lily

"It's 'bout time you brought your fool ass over here like I asked ya," I said to the boy— well, he was a full-grown man now, but still a boy compared to my old age—who had come to finally move my trash. "Ya mama always said you was a stubborn child."

Javon turned to look at me with a frown on his face, but it softened when he remembered the manners Claudette had taught him, I was sure. "I'm sorry it took so long. Been a little busy at the house," he said.

"No need to tell me that. I can see and hear."

The night was chilly. I was in my housecoat. My bones ached. Old age hadn't been kind to me. Fate was probably coming around to kick my ass sooner rather than later. That was fine. I'd deserved no less. I'd done a lot of evil shit in my day. I welcomed my karma. But until that crotchety old sum'bitch came for me, I was gonna keep doing what I been doing.

"Still need that stuff out of your basement?" he asked.

"Naw, but I need you for summin' else." I tightened my housecoat then pushed the screen door open for him to come in. "Come on in for a minute, will ya?"

He looked hesitant for a moment. I knew he had a weapon on him. He was paranoid as hell, too. Could tell by the way he kept looking over his shoulder, even with all the protection around him. I was old, but I wasn't damn stupid. Sure wasn't.

Javon finally walked in. I closed the door behind us. Locked all seven locks on my door. Yeah, I was paranoid too. When you had done as much evil as me, paranoia was a friend. No lights were on in my house, just candles lit everywhere. The smell of the ethnic food I'd ordered earlier, some Caribbean food, could still be smelled in my home. Didn't matter. The place was warm. The apple-cinnamon candles I burned made it smell inviting, too.

"Come up to my attic. Got something for you," I said.

The boy seemed larger than life in my house. He was way taller than me. I was only about five foot two in heels. Javon was a strapping young lad, broad shoulders, lean muscles all over. And he strutted with a gait that had many a young girl crazy about him. He looked tired and stressed.

"When's last time you got some shut-eye, Javon?" I asked him as we walked through my hall. Pictures of family and friends hung on either side of the wall. Some in black and white. Some in color. The coloreds sat on one side of the wall, the black and white on the other. I got in the middle of the hall, just under my attic door and pulled the long, thick string there. The door to the attic creaked open, revealing a brown set of wooden stairs.

"Can't sleep, Ms. Lily. Too much going on," he answered.

"I see. I don't 'spect you think you can handle it on E, do ya? Shanelle and that baby okay?"

When I asked that, he took a step back and glared at me. He probably wondered how I knew what I knew. I stood my full height and glared up at him.

"You know who ya Mama really was by now. You think I lived across from y'all this long and know nothing? Nothing and nobody 'round here what they seem, boy."

He grunted, but remained quiet. I didn't want to push it. There was no doubt in my mind Javon would shoot me if I pushed him too far or said the wrong thing.

"What's in your attic, Ms. Lily?" he asked.

I rolled my eyes then climbed up. Once I was in the attic, he came up behind me. Gun was in his hand when he stepped into the small space. I watched as he glanced at the CCTV monitors around the room. There was a long bar that went all the way around the way. Ten flat-screen TVs sat mounted above it on the wall. On the bar were laptops and computers. GPS monitors beeped and flashed with different locations around the city.

Javon stood slack-jawed. I gave him a few seconds to take in what he was seeing.

I said, "Claudette always stayed one step ahead of all of her enemies. That's how she stayed untouched all those years. She built a foundation around her. In order for her to have been gunned down like that, it had to have been someone she knew, understand me, son?"

His face was unmoved, so I couldn't tell if I'd gotten through to him until he nodded and said, "You're right. It was someone she knew. Someone she would have never saw coming."

He had my attention now. I wanted to know who killed a good friend of mine more so than they did. I was anxious for revenge. I grabbed his arm to turn him to look at me. "Who was it?" I asked merely above a whisper. I waited with bated breath for him to tell me.

"Melissa," he answered solemnly.

I jumped back and clutched the top of my housecoat like they were the pearls I wore to Mass. "You lie," I said to him.

"No."

I was quiet for a long while. My lips were so thin, it looked as if I had none. I moved around the room, cleaning things that didn't need cleaning. Tears burned my eyelids. I couldn't grasp it. Not one of them damn mangy kids had turned on her, had they? No! My mind wouldn't allow me to believe it. I shook my head over and over.

"No, no. No. No," I kept murmuring. "Taking in strays. Told her. I told her. Wish King were still here. King wouldn't have allowed it. He helped kids, but he ain't let none live with them. Gotdamn Raphael!"

I mumbled and talked to myself, forgetting Javon was even in the attic with me. Lost my damn best friend. *Lord, you had to take her from me? Now? Like this?* I knew it was coming, but not like this. Wished King were here. King wouldn't have allowed her to roam no streets like that by herself. I was hurting, aching. Felt like something was constricting my heart.

"What did Uncle Snap do?" Javon asked.

I snapped my head around at him, once I stopped slamming things down on tables.

"Brought that gotdamned child to Claudette. He brung Melissa to her, he did! Found her in a whorehouse with her no-good mama. The mama offered Raphael her daughter for drugs. Raphael brought her to Claudette, you see? He brung Mama her killer," I roared. "King wouldn't have allowed it!"

I couldn't even see Javon through my tears. He was just a blurry shadow.

"Luci wouldn't have allowed it, either," I shouted. "Crazy-ass Italian old man wouldn't have let her take in strays."

I caught myself then looked at Javon. Deep down, a part of me hoped he knew I was in pain. He didn't know how much Claudette had done for me. Met her back in Harlem with King. I was sent to kill King, but they ended up saving me. Long, long, long story. I was sobbing loudly by now. I missed her so much.

I walked over to the file cabinet. Took something out and put it in my robe pocket. When I turned, Javon was there. It scared me. That damn gun was still in his hand, but when he put his arms around me, I laid my head on his chest and cried like a baby. I let it all out.

Once I was tired of standing, I asked Javon to help me back downstairs. He did. I needed to get in the bed. My soul was tired. Once he helped me to sit on the bed and handed me tissues to clean my face and nose, he kneeled down to help me take my slippers off.

"Thank you, son," I whispered.

"You're welcome, Ms. Lily," he said.

I petted his shoulder. "She loved you like you was her own, you know that, right?"

He nodded. "I know."

"She tell me lots of times she wish you had come from her womb, you know?"

He smiled.

"She knew you was a leader. If we had known the killer came from within . . ." I shook my head. "Listen, I need to tell ya something, all right?"

He stopped smiling, got serious. A studious look spread across his face. Yes, yes, Mama loved this boy. I smiled. His eyes were weary. Broad shoulders kind of slumped because his body was tired.

"You listen good, you hear?" I said.

"Yes, Ms. Lily, I'm liste—"

Before he could finish, I jabbed a needle in his neck. He fell back. He tried to aim his gun at me, but it fell from his limp hand. I stood and looked down at him as the light dimmed in his eyes.

"Mama always said, 'Trust, but verify.' You didn't verify, Javon."

Chapter 26

Elias

Nothing was more gratifying than seeing your plan of action come to life. The plan all along was to initiate a hostile takeover of the Syndicate. That was the only plan. I knew I had to get rid of the leader and it proved to be easier done than said. There was always, always a crack in the foundation. I found it, exploited it. Shit felt so fucking good, it made my dick hard.

I looked at all my men as we stood, stoic, in an abandoned air field. We were ready for war. I intended to crumble the Syndicate, take it down to its bare minimum and then take over. I already put one member in the ground. Got one on her deathbed and got the others scattering like roaches.

"Men, as we stand here tonight, we have officially given notice to the Syndicate. We have them running! They attacked us haphazardly.

Showed us their hand. Now we know they're not as 'official' as they would like us to believe. We hit every ally they had and yet there's no real retaliation. They even had infighting while we planned to attacked. They no longer have the Irish in their corner. This is ours for the taking," I yelled emphatically.

My men roared with me. Shit was powerful. I had rogue Mexican Cartel members along with rogue members from my parents' faction. *Mamãe* and *Papai* would be proud of me. I looked out at all my men dressed in black fatigues, combat boots. Bulletproof vests were underneath their clothing, scowls now on their faces. *Mamãe* never did right by *Papai*'s seat at the table and, now, I would rectify that. He was forced out by *Mamãe*. She was a crude bitch, but she was deadly. I appreciated her for what she was.

Javon had her murdered before our plan could come to fruition. Yes, *Mamãe* had been in on the plan. She told me the inner workings of the Syndicate. That was why I was confident I would run it with an iron fist. Had Claudette not set it up so her mutt son could take over, we wouldn't have had to go this route. Stupid son of a bitch didn't even know that he had already done eye for an eye. I killed his slut mother and he in turn took mine out by default.

I smirked, then slid my hands in my pocket as I walked away, my men behind me in the fields still yelling and ready for war. I headed into the old warehouse, whistling along the way.

"She's gone, boss. No sign of her," one of my men said when I walked inside.

I grunted. So Melissa had gotten away from me. That annoyed me. Made my asshole constrict. Oh, well. The fact that I took out her whole family would eat that bitch alive until I found her again.

"The Irish are willing to play ball with this plan, but said they need to be sure you can pull through. They sent soldiers, but expendable ones. They won't send the true players in until you win this fight," he said while we walked down the dimly lit hall.

"Tell me something I don't know," I snapped.

"All the members of the Syndicate have gone under. No sign of them anyway. I think Mr. McPhearson may be on his own."

I pushed open the door of the room at the end of the hall. Before stepping into the room, I turned with a sinister smile and said, "We move soon. In a few hours, we take the fight to the Syndicate."

I changed out of my fatigues into one of my signature tailored suits. I slipped my feet into a pair of black designer loafers. My men would soon follow suit. Before a fight, I always got some pussy. I needed some pussy before a fight. That was how I'd always been. Even as a teenager, if destiny had set it for me to fight, fate made it so I got pussy beforehand. This would be no different.

Once outside, I signaled for the twenty men I always had follow me around. We all piled into black-on-black SUVs. We were headed to the best pussy palace in Atlanta, Magic fucking City. I knew what I'd said about black women earlier, but if any man had any sense about him, he'd get the best piece of black pussy he could find before he went to prison, before he got into a fight, before getting married, before any got damned thing that was going to cause him stress.

Dark-skinned black women, they fucking hated me. I didn't know why. *Fuck those bitches,* I thought. But gotdamn it if those bitches didn't have the best pussy in life. Never had a piece of dark-skinned pussy I didn't like. Never. Wouldn't ever marry one of those bitches, though. Couldn't live with a bitch as dark as me or darker, and I was a pretty black motherfucker.

I laughed. My men looked at me. They were used to me laughing out loud at odd times. They went back to laughing and talking about whatever they had been talking about. I resumed my thoughts as we rode through the streets of Atlanta. They had so many damn Peachtree Streets. Shit annoyed the fuck out of me.

The nightlife was alive. I knew the club would be crowded before we got there. It was Monday night. Monday nights at Magic City were like winning the lottery of beautiful pussies. Black women, the best of the best, of all shades and hues lined the stages. I could have had some whores come to us, but I liked chasing my pussy.

I cursed when we pulled up to the small black, white, and gray building. Cursive blue neon letters spelling MAGIC CITY glowed in the night. All the parking spots in the front of the club were already taken by Maseratis, Bugattis, and other high-end cars. We were late, but oh, well. We still had money to blow. My men paid to park as I exited the truck. All of us dressed like we owned Atlanta. One of my men carried a duffle bag filled with money.

Just as we were making our way to the door, a homeless cunt pushing a cart bumped into one of my men. He shoved her down while others laughed. She hit one of the trucks, hard. Her face was heavily patched on one side. An eye patch on her left eye. She was the cleanest dirtiest homeless woman I'd ever seen, even down to the wine-colored boots.

"So sorry," she cried, then threw her arm up like she was afraid of being struck.

My men got a kick out of that. I grunted. "Leave her," I yelled.

I turned and continued my stroll to the club. The big black bouncers at the door gave us no issues. They knew me by name. When they opened the doors to the club, that lame-ass nigger rapper named Future—or was it 2 Chainz?—was yelling about how all his niggas looked rich as fuck. I swore it was like walking into the Garden of Eden. Money was flying, lights flashing. A DJ who needed to learn how to speak the proper English shouted over the loud speakers about ass and titties. All around me were the most beautiful whores on God's green earth. My eyes automatically trained on the darkest ones in the club. Asses a-jiggling. Pussies a-popping. Yes, first I'd get some pussy and then, then, I'd go kill Javon McPhearson and take down the Syndicate while at it.

Chapter 27

Lucky

"I've sent in the cavalry," my uncle said on the other end of my phone. "They've touched down in Atlanta. All they need is a location."

"Waiting on Javon for that," I said. I looked at the white gauze still wrapped around my arm. I didn't tell my uncle what had happened between Javon and me. There was no need. We handled it. That didn't mean I wasn't still salty about it. I looked out over the Atlanta skyline. The clouds were hanging low, which meant rain was coming.

"How is he handling this? Is he being the leader we thought him to be?" he asked.

"It's hard to call right now. He did tell us that he thinks his sister is behind all of this in some way."

There was silence on the other end of the phone. Uncle Luci grunted before demanding, "Explain."

I did. I told him everything Javon had told us; then I waited.

"And what is he doing about these . . . thoughts?"

"Said he had to find her. Wanted to get her account of what happened," I said.

"And then what? How does he plan he handle it once he has her?"

"He didn't say. Just asked that if we found her first to bring her to him."

I was met with more silence. I could hear the Jew and the priest murmuring in the background. They were discussing it among themselves.

"Do you trust him?" Absolan asked.

I nodded once then looked out over the Atlanta skyline again from the penthouse suite I was in. Just as I thought, it had started to sprinkle. I said, "I do. He hasn't given me reason not to."

Cavriel asked, "And the girl?"

I thought about Shanelle. Thought about the ways she brushed me off. Javon had marked his territory and I had no chance in hell of encroaching on it. It was funny with them. I never saw them showing affection. It always seemed business with them, which was probably why she seemed so available before. I probably owed her an apology, especially after the way I saw she kept my men at bay while Javon and I had "words."

"She's loyal to him. I never had a chance."

"Claudette was loyal to King, but King had his issues. She was loyal to Raphael, but he had his demons. No man is without fault. There will come an opening."

"Why do you encourage him to do such things, Luciano?" Absolan asked his friend. "It didn't work out well for you and Claudette."

"Probably why he wishes to live vicariously through his so . . ." Cavriel stopped, then cleared his throat. "Nephew."

I ran a hand over the waves in my head as I listened to the old men. "I have no intentions of seeking her out again, Uncle Luci. She made it loud and clear where she wants to be," I said. "I was only initially supposed to see if she could be swayed so we would know if Javon would let his heart render him unable to lead proficiently."

"And did he come after you?" Uncle Luci asked.

I looked at the wound on my arm again. "No. Well, he did, but not in a manner that would suggest it would cloud his judgment. We talked like men and left it where it was."

The Jew and the priest laughed.

"What's so funny?" I asked.

"Your uncle's nose is crooked thanks to King's fists," Cavriel said.

"And he walks with a limp thanks to Raphael," Absolan added.

Both men let out boisterous laughs at the expense of Uncle Luci. He cursed them in Italian; verbally assaulted them with words that would get him killed otherwise, had they not been friends, of course.

After a while, I hung up the phone. Called Javon's cell, anxious about what the next move would be, but I got no answer. After another two hours passed with no answer from him, I decided to try Shanelle. I knew she wouldn't answer, but I tried anyway. I left her a voice mail telling her Javon was supposed to hook up with me hours ago and had yet to call or send any correspondence. I also sent a text just in case.

I grabbed my holster and pulled my bulletproof vest on. Then I grabbed my two SIG Sauers, placing them in the holsters. If Javon hadn't come to me, I was going to him. At least that had been the plan, until I opened my suite room door and found a woman there.

Her face was heavily bandaged on one side. When she pushed back the hood of the jacket she wore, I could see one side of her head had been shaved and she had stitches. Her left eye had a patch, too.

"How'd you get past my men?" I asked.

"Don't worry, I didn't kill them. Just rendered them unconscious for a few moments."

"Who the fuck are you?"

"Put the gun away. I have something for you," she said, calm in her voice with an eerie look in her eye.

For some reason, she looked familiar to me, but I couldn't place her. She had on all black, something that reminded me of a cat suit, and wine-colored combat boots.

"I ain't putting shit away. You have ten seconds to state your business or you're dead. Ten," I started counting.

"I have an address for you," she said, then held up a picture. The man had dark skin. Long, thick, wavy hair cascaded down to his shoulders. He was tall, about six four in height. Broad shouldered with light brown eyes.

"Eight."

"Magic City."

"Six."

"The man you're looking for, Elias, was there."

"Was?" I questioned. "Four."

"He had about twenty or thirty men at the strip club with him. More scattered throughout the area. He left."

"Two."

"In a few hours, he plans to attack the Syndicate by going after Javon first. We know where he went when he left."

I cocked the handle. "One."

As soon as the last number left my mouth, somebody, who I assumed was male by the stature, rounded the corner. He had a Desert Eagle aimed at my left temple. I couldn't see his face because of the hood of the heavy cloak he had on. The girl took my gun away from me. I raised my hands like I was being robbed. Didn't want to make any sudden movements.

"Don't do it, fam," he said. "We come in peace. We're not the enemy. You heard what she said. That address on that picture is where you can find Elias."

"Why are you bringing this to me?"

"Aren't you a member of the Syndicate?"

"Yeah, but why not Javon? You trying to set us up? Set me up?"

"Fam, if we wanted you dead, you would be dead by now."

"How did you find me?"

"That's a 'need to know' thing and you don't need to know. Turn and face the wall. Wait thirty seconds before leaving. If you leave before thirty seconds, I'll blow up the whole place."

"You're lying. You'll still be in the building. You'll kill yourself."

The man chuckled. "I'm already dead, fam."

"Where's Javon?"

"Wish we knew," was all he said before I heard him and the woman running down the hall.

Chapter 28

Ms. Lily

I heard moving around in the room upstairs. I knew that meant hell had awakened. I made my way upstairs. I pushed open the door of the room where Javon had been sleeping. His gun was placed in the center of my head before I could walk in the room.

"Old woman," he spat through clenched teeth, "give me one reason this bullet shouldn't slow dance with your brain matter."

I stood unmoved. I was a trained assassin. Javon's gun didn't scare me. I didn't care how big it was. It was light outside now. The morning had come. Javon had slept for a full eight hours.

"You're mad, as you have all right to be," I said coolly. "But you should be mad at yourself for trusting so easily in this game. I simply put you to sleep, stubborn-ass boy. If I'd wanted to cause ya ill will, would I let ya keep a loaded gun, eh?"

He frowned.

"You been running around here like you in this fight alone. Like you ain't got people who will go to war for you. The reason you ain't got nowhere is because you think you Superman. You trying to figure it out all on ya own, and you don't have to. You ain't eating. Ain't sleeping. Who you gone lead on low fuel, boy?" I said.

"What the fuck did you do to me?" he asked.

I sighed. "I just told you. I put you to sleep. You needed it. I put a little extra in the needle, too. You should feel livelier than ever. Be mad at me all you want, but Claudette was my best friend and she, too, started off shaky. She went through the same shit as you. Something similar. I ain't having my best friend's favorite son and best son die on my watch."

"You couldn't find another way to do all this?" he questioned.

"Would ya have listened to me if I had tried to talk rationally to ya? Ya stubborn like a jackass, like Claudette said you was. I been asking for days for you to come by here."

"I had shit to do, old woman!"

"And? Ya missed pivotal information—"

"I ain't got time to sleep!"

"But ya did. Nothing happened while ya slept, now did it? Shanelle was calling ya. Some fool named Lucky did, too. Called back to back."

Javon growled low in his throat then paced the room like a caged animal. "I have to go, Ms. Lily," was all he said before storming down the stairs.

I stood at the top of the stairs, watching him. "Fine by me, but, Javon?"

He took a deep breath, then turned back around with a frown.

"Ya Mama has peoples everywhere. All you gotta do is pay attention. You ain't gotta go at it alone, ya hear? You ain't gotta. But they need to trust ya, you see. They needs to know if you gon' protect them and takes care of they families like Claudette did. Put out what she would call a bat signal, baby. See who all responds. All them bank accounts she had, the money needs to keep flowing into 'charities.' Got me, baby?"

He gave a look that said he understood, but wasn't too sure. "Okay," he said.

"When it's time and you can sit and think awhile, it'll come to you."

He nodded once. "I have to go now."

I said, "Because I loved her, I love all you strays, too. But you best kill that bitch, Melissa."

"I'll handle it," he said on his way out the door.

"Javon," I yelled. "Don't you want to know what's in the basement?"

He didn't answer me or didn't hear me. Either way, ghosts were still in my basement.

Chapter 29

Uncle Snap

A loud, shrill yell jerked me out of my sleep. Shit sounded like a banshee. For a second my mind was foggy. Flashes of the night before replayed in my mind. I'd gone to a place I hadn't been in a while. Had Trey ride with me to find someone. Javon had gone missing. I wasn't worried since the Thieves told me he had gone to talk to the old lady across the street.

I needed a woman. Couldn't just be any woman, though. It had to be a woman who could give me what I needed, one who looked like Mama. Trey took me to the Den. To make a long story short, the Den was where women gave you the time of your life for a price. I had never paid for pussy a day before in my life. But the Den had a woman there who looked like Claudette. I knew this because Mama kept the owner safe for a fee. The working woman was younger, but she looked like my woman. And, for a few hours last night, I was with my woman.

Pathetic, I knew. Trey didn't ask me any questions, just let me be free for a few hours. I couldn't ask Javon to take me there. Didn't want to embarrass myself that way in front of him. Didn't want him to see me become so weakened without my woman that I had to seek out a working woman. I paid my share. The woman pretended to love me and only me for as long as I'd paid for it. And that was fine by me. Just needed to hold a warm body. Needed to drown myself between a pair of thighs, thick thighs, that reminded me of Claudette McPhearson.

I asked her to wash in the soap Mama used to wash in. Asked her to spray herself with perfume Mama used to wear. She didn't mind. The working woman didn't mind at all. She saw men like me all the time, I bet. When she came from the bathroom, her hair was wet and wavy like Mama's used to be when water hit it. Not that mixed silky shit. I meant the kinky kind of wet and wavy. The kind that caught a man's fingers when he yanked and pulled on it.

The steam and the dim lighting from the bathroom made it seem like she was an angel in disguise. She didn't see me as an old man, either.

I wasn't an old man who felt aches and chills every now and again when he was out there in the streets. No, I was just a man needing a woman. She was thick like my woman used to be, too. She even smiled like Claudette. I didn't know the working woman's name. Didn't even think to ask. She was Claudette to me.

For about four hours I apologized to my woman for bringing her killer into her home.

All those thoughts faded as I heard that woman crying again. I jumped from the bed, pulled on my slacks, and grabbed my gun. I rushed into the hall to find Shanelle, banging on Jojo's door. Monty and Navy came running up the stairs.

"What's going on, Shanelle?" I asked.

She shrugged. Niece had on nothing but a sports bra and shorts. She must have been scared; otherwise, she would never have shown herself in front of us that way. She banged on Jojo's door like she was the Feds.

"Jojo! Jojo, open the door," she yelled.

The door flung open and Dani ran out, holding a bloody lip, wailing at the top of her lungs.

"What the hell?" Navy said then rushed into the room. I was right behind him.

"What happened?" Shanelle wanted to know as she grabbed Dani to keep her from running down the stairs.

Jojo sat up in bed looking like a deer stuck in headlights. His room was clean. Dani must have cleaned it. Jojo was messy. He had a wild look behind his glasses. "I ain't mean to. I . . . she . . . I didn't know it was her," he said.

Navy walked over then looked at Jojo. "Calm down, bro. Tell me what she did."

Jojo shut his eyes tight, squeezing them before opening them again. "She . . . she snatched the covers off me. I thought I was dreaming. She snatched the covers away. I thought she was them. I didn't mean it. I don't hit girls," he pleaded.

"Damn, nephew," I said. We'd been through this before. There was certain shit you couldn't do to Jojo or it would trigger a reaction. The same thing for Navy. You couldn't say and do certain shit to them. Navy had damn near split a boy's head open in high school. They were in the shower and the boy made the mistake of taking a joke too far. Told Navy to suck his dick. Claudette ended up having to pay for the boy's medical and dental bills.

Dani snatched the covers off Jojo, probably triggering him back to the most traumatic times of his life. The woman his mama had sold him to, Jojo told us, she used to snatch the covers off him at night when she was about to do something she shouldn't have. Add that with the fighting he had to do in jail and Jojo probably woke up swinging.

"I got it, y'all," Navy said as he sat down on the bed beside his little brother. "Let me handle it. I got it," he said.

I didn't have it in me to handle it anyway so I nodded. I backed Shanelle up out of the room. The front door opened downstairs and Monty rushed down to see who it was. I heard Javon asking where everyone was.

"Up here, nephew," I said while Shanelle took Dani into Mama's old room to help her with her busted lip.

He came bolting up the stairs two at a time. "The hell you been?" we both asked one another at the same time. I was the elder so he had to answer me before I did him. He knew this.

"That old lady kidnapped me," he said.

"What old lady?" me and Monty asked at the same time.

"Ms. Lily."

"What?" I asked.

"Tell you about it later. We need to meet with Lucky. Strap up. We end this with Elias today."

I could tell nephew had a lot on his mind. I nodded. Went back to my room and dressed quickly. I could hear Javon telling Dani she had to leave the room for a minute. He and Shanelle argued about her staying behind. Javon yelled at her. Something he rarely did. He yelled at her, told her to sit the fuck down and listen to him for a change. For a second, I thought I was about hear furniture moving. I stepped out my room and saw Navy stick his head out Jojo's door. Monty was looking upstairs. Dani had run downstairs. But the rest of us were waiting to make sure Shanelle and Javon didn't revert to their old selves.

"Gotdamn, Shanelle, why you always fighting me on some shit?" he snapped. "Listen to me, a'ight? Listen to me. I know you love me. I know you have my back. I don't doubt that, but I got this, baby. I got it, okay? Stay here. Lock the house down. Protect our child. You owe me that. Remember? You owe me this child. You promised me. Keep your promise because I've kept every last one I made to you."

There was silence. No one was more shocked than me when I heard a light, "Okay," from Shanelle. There was silence for a long while. I didn't know what that "you owe me" stuff was about, but I figured it had to be deep for Shanelle to agree without a fight.

Javon snatched the room door open. He nodded at me then looked at Navy.

"Tell Jojo we'll speak when I get back. Navy, I need you to be on your tech shit right now, okay? Get to the bunker, all right? Pull up the bank accounts. I'm going to give you a code. I want you to figure out which one of those accounts has the most charitable donations. See when Mama made the last donations. If they stopped right after she died, make double the donation. Melissa figured out who Mama had been paying and for what. That's one of the reasons why our allies in the police department didn't move faster getting Jojo out. That was how she was able to put a hit out on the three of you while in there. Get those payments sent out to all those 'charities.'"

I gave something akin to a smile as I watched nephew's mind work. He then turned his attention to Monty. "The leaders of Rize will be here soon. Lock this place down. And I don't care what Shanelle says, she is not to leave this house."

Monty quirked a brow then ran a hand through his long hair. I knew what he was thinking.

I said, "Nephew, nobody trying to wrangle Shanelle's ass but you."

Javon scoffed. "Y'all let her bully you too easily," he said.

"I heard that," Shanelle yelled from the room.

"Quiet, woman. Monty, she doesn't leave this house," Javon said, rushing down the stairs. He stopped abruptly then turned back to look at Monty. "For your safety, don't give her a gun unless it's absolutely necessary." Javon gave a quick smirk then glanced at me. "Come on, Unc."

That boy had a fire under his ass. I didn't know where it had come from, but I liked it.

"Lucky got some info for us. Said some people came to his hotel room and delivered the location of Elias and his team," Javon said.

I strapped my seat belt on while looking at Javon, who was pulling out of our driveway. "How do we know this ain't a setup?" I asked.

"Lucky said the man was in a cloak."

"Like the man Shanelle said she chased through the neighborhood?"

He nodded. "Allies?"

"I believe so."

"Lucky sent some of his men to scope the location."

"And?"

"Elias and all his men are there just like the people said."

I asked, "So what now?"

"We end this."

It was silent in the truck until we got on the expressway until Javon told me what happened to him the night before. Told me about Ms. Lily, an ally I didn't know Mama had. That was how Claudette worked, though. She never told everybody everything, not even me. Javon told me about how Ms. Lily had said Mama had allies everywhere. They were just waiting on him to reach out. It made sense, especially since things had been so touch and go. Shit wasn't working like the well-oiled machine it should have been and now we knew why. Melissa had fucked us good. I still couldn't believe it. Javon didn't know how much that shit ate away at me. To know I'd brought Mama's killer to her.

"What about Melissa?" I asked.

Javon said, "Haven't been able to find her, but we will. I'm confident we will."

Chapter 30

Melissa

Pussy-ass men can't do a damn thing for the enlightenment and elevation of women. Let me say that again. Pussy-ass men can't do a damn thing for the enlightenment and elevation of women. Pussy-ass men are only good for two things: dick, and always finding ways to break a woman down. When a man shows himself to be a pussy-ass man, there's only one thing a woman can do. Milk him for what he's worth and use his dick game, only if it's good, until you're ready to move on.

I lived by that code for years. Throughout those years, it kept me safe until I met Elias. He fooled me into thinking that he wasn't a pussy-ass male. I thought that maybe he would be worthy of being one of my high-esteemed lovers, but sure enough, his true colors came out. He twisted me by my own game. He took my petty jealousies and cosigned them to the point that I began to believe the house that once saved me was really holding me back from greatness. Elias, smart as he was, led me to being dumb right along with him. I called him dumb now, because I now knew who Elias was and I was disgusted to my soul. I was also frightened.

When I was at Mama's grave, I left my tears and regret there. I left my pain and anger there as well. I yelled, and blamed her for not saving me fast enough. For Uncle Snap not coming sooner to get me out of the brothel. I slapped my hands against her stone, mad at myself for killing her and starting this war that was going to wipe out her legacy. I really didn't want that, but I did. I mean, if it could keep everyone else out of harm's way then so be it.

The tears that fell from my swollen eyes as I was bound to my chair were the evidence of my grief. Yes, I had turned on my family in the worst way. Set them up for failure. At the end of the day, I didn't know how to save them, or redeem myself, until I heard voices. My struggles with my captors kept me calm. I listened hard, learning that they were Elias's men. Relief hit me in finding that out because I knew that I could survive this if I played it smart. Which was what I did.

I played the scared mouse. I struggled against my bindings as a means of a show for them. I let them believe that they had won the upper hand, every day becoming cocky. And, everyone knows, cocky mouths make easy marks. Every day little slips of information came my way. Elias was the son of the former chair of the Syndicate, Delanna Gallo. That woman was dead now and he was aiming to take her spot. More little pieces revealed allowed me to deduce that Elias's quest for vengeance was just another power play. I gathered that he wanted the Syndicate for himself.

It was then that I realized how much of a pawn I really had been in the whole situation. I knew he had pissed me off and that I didn't like being manipulated by him, but to realize that it was all just to get the Syndicate? Anger had me riled up. It had me thinking back to the lessons Mama gave me. Lesson one: keep a blade on you at all times. Be it your shoes, your hair, your earrings, your nails, even your pussy or mouth. Keep a weapon on you at all times.

Mine happened to be my ring, which popped out a blade that I used to cut myself with. I used that as a deterrent. Once the men saw me sobbing and crying and bleeding too much, they had no choice but to untie me. Once they did, I used that moment to take one's gun and take down my two captives, all blindfolded. Shit seemed impossible, but it happened.

I grew up living in the dark of a brothel. Watching women give their bodies, and taking money. Those skills of survival had been in me before Mama. The ability to fight I learned from Shanelle, studying her and modeling my fighting style from her. My family had taught me a lot, which I was able to be grateful to now. I had messed up. I gave a seed of truth about Elias to Javon, and now I wanted my payback. I too knew people in interesting places and, if I knew Elias, those places were where he was going to head.

After escaping, I cleaned myself up and made some calls while laying low for some days. I knew that Elias would be looking for me; however, if he really was going to war, I figured that it would distract him in hunting me down. So, I decided to send trustworthy eyes to watch him: one of my dancer friends. It was her duty to tell me everything he was doing, from afar. I needed this time so that if Elias caught me again, I had something to contribute in the event of my possible death.

So, while I made my will and gave my living testament on my phone, the plan was to have it time sealed to send to Jai if I wasn't around to put in the code. Everything I stole would return right to the family, plus what I made on my own. I guessed that was the right thing to do, considering. However, I planned to live, so as long as that happened, they weren't getting shit.

While I put my life in order, it wasn't until several days later that I received a call. "Hello?" I answered.

"Sis, guess who's at Magic City!"

"Venus," I started. Immediately my girl Venus started bumping her gums, during which I quickly shut her down. "Venus, kill the noise really quick. I don't have time for that just yet. Thank you for calling me and relaying that good tea but I need to cash in on a favor from you, Breezy, Kitten, Lush, and Cookie."

"Oh, a'ight. Girl, whatever you want we got you always. What do you need?" Venus asked with a pop of her gum in my ear.

"First off, you need to go black. Second, this favor isn't simple, this is a code D. I'm cashing in, I told you." The door of my ride slammed and the sound of my heels on pavement clicked with the swish of my ass.

Venus made a tapping sound, then all playfulness switched from her tone. "Tell me that nigga's name."

A smirk spread across my face as I told her want I wanted and needed to have happen. While we spoke, I used the card of one my friends to enter through the locked back door. This was risky because this was a well-known establishment, but the money I dropped into the owner's account would make up for whatever uncomfortable situations may occur after.

I knew that this plan wouldn't take long to happen. Once I made it into the changing area, I was surrounded by my girls. We went over what I needed, and I watched five girls turn into twenty. Each girl stood in either nothing but string and heels, or topless, bottomless, or in full attire. As for me, I slipped on a black wig, slid on a flesh-toned laced-open bodysuit, with my tits pushed up to my throat. Flesh-toned stilettos were my friend, and I counted the hours for my plan to go into motion.

Music had the club thumping. Girls slid down poles, gracefully gliding into nasty pussy-petting splits. Others undulated their bodies in sensual, nasty ways that made every male and female in the club who watched them find ways to adjust themselves, while others danced and kept the place entertained in various sexy ways. All while the party was going on, I walked around serving people.

My face was partially covered in a mask. Any identifying tattoos on my body were covered in body paint and the lace bodysuit I wore. Tonight I was an enigma ready for my revenge, and my gaze settled on the one I intended to kill. Elias.

Elias sat back with his men. I counted them out, and I knew my girls could handle them. While I kept my distance, I signaled them to drape themselves over Elias's men. A slick smile spread over my face in glee. Pussy-ass men always had a weakness for that they are: pussy.

The music changed accordingly. 2 Chainz was rumbling and shouting about some shit that had every dancer's ass clapping and wobbling for cash. My girls were no exception. They grinned against Elias's men. Spreading their thighs so whoever was in front of them had a peep show of their goodies while winding against hard dick.

Heat in the room had me taking an ice cube and running it over my lip while I sauntered close to Elias's party. His eyes lustfully came my way. No smile was in my eyes, or upon my face when I stopped in front of him, then aimed my Glock. Behind them the room emptied on cue, except for a few stragglers.

"*Olá, amante.* Hello, lover," was all I said in Portuguese when my girls locked those same thighs and held his men down.

Everything began to happen quickly. Blades slid across the throats of every male my girls were draped on. Some were ass up leaning in close while warm blood dripped over their hands onto the couches. Other of my crew came forward and let out rounds on soldiers who tried to gun me down. Their bodies shook with each impacting bullet. My girls stood wide-legged in heels with their breasts jiggling with the power, their hair flipped over their shoulders, and masks on their faces. Bitches were bad. I loved that I knew them.

In the midst of it all, Elias and I never let our eyes off each other. I pulled off my mask, then finally smiled, ready to squeeze my Glock. "Instead of running, my dear, I thought I'd come back and finish out your plan. The Syndicate isn't dying tonight, but you are."

Hatred and something like amusement flashed across Elias's handsome face as he stayed calm, legs wide, his arms stretched back against the couch he sat on. Elias gave a sexy, throaty chuckle then winked and said, "*Você cadela estúpida.* You stupid bitch."

Lights flashed and dazzled around us. My pouty lips turned into a frown and I gave a sad sigh. "This world isn't yours."

People screamed and I watched Elias kick his table toward me with lightning speed. I stumbled back, and let out rounds at the air. My aim was never as good as Shanelle's but I for damn sure tried. I fell with a hard grunt, and turned to shoot at him again. Glass shattered, liquid spilled, and people ran as I tried to push up and go after Elias.

"Elias!" I shouted.

Never in my life had I seen someone run as fast as Elias did. His disjointed laughter irritated me while I scanned the club. I could hear him saying, "You stupid white whore! I'm still going to kill them, but first me and you must dance!"

Several of his men flanked him. My girls brandishing weapons took them out as best they could while I followed. From his quick moves, I could see that he realized he was now at a disadvantage, and it made me smile. Never again would I listen to him call me his whore. Never would I see my mother's blank, cold eyes as she allowed men to take her every kind of way for drugs.

I'd never be the little girl hiding in her closet, being forcefully pulled out, screaming for the grown men not to touch me while they made me down strange blue pills that made me woozy and tired as my mother snorted her coke. Never would I have to be her. Elias was all of those men for me. Elias allowed me to hurt the only family I had. Mama saved me and I turned traitor on her. I blamed myself but, above all, I blamed Elias.

I did my best to follow him but came up empty. It was only when a cloaked figure ran into me that my fall from grace began. The shoulder slam hurt me so bad that it knocked the wind from me, while slamming me to the side as I aimed my gun at Elias. I stumbled and missed that sick bastard.

A ringing in my ears started and I tried to right myself. Wiping spilled liquor from my face, I slipped as I tried to get up. Anger had my face contorted and I motioned to point my gun at whoever of Elias's goons had hit me, but it slipped from my hand. When I glanced at my attacker, shock caused the blood to drain from my face. The whites of my eyes grew big and I stared into the face of a person who made my stomach bunch in knots. A gun was pointed at me and all I wanted to do was scream.

"Wait, please. I need to kill him," I pleaded, slipping and crawling back on the floor. "He's going to kill everyone!" The quick touch of light from one of the colorful dance projections made my hands cover my mouth as I realized that this was not my imagination.

"Tell me one thing. Why'd you do it?" the person asked.

Staring into familiar eyes, I opened my mouth, but a bullet pierced my thigh. Pain sliced through me. This wasn't happening! I wasn't supposed to go out like this. Hot tears ran down my face, and the pain had me crawling faster, trying to get away as my thoughts spilled from my lips.

"Don't lie," the ghost said in constrained anger.

How did they even know? "I . . . I wanted a better life than Mama could ever give me," I stammered. "I . . . I wanted to be more than where I came from the streets, the brothel, the ho in school. I wanted freedom. She couldn't give me that. Elias said that he could. He said if I did this, you all wouldn't be hurt but better from this. I believed him. I wanted that. I was stupid. Please. Let me kill him. I'm so sorry."

The sound of another bullet exiting its chamber hit me, this time in the other thigh, and I screamed bloody murder. Another hit me in my stomach as my ghost stepped over me and pressed the heated steel of a gun against my forehead. I stopped my crawling. I stopped my crying and I realized the situation that I was in. It was the same one that Mama had been in the day Elias and I gunned her down. I realized that, in some way, this was poetic justice. Who better to kill me than ghosts?

"Naw. You need to focus on your own atonement. That nigga over there is long gone and his is coming next," my ghost said. There was a deep sadness in that voice. One I was familiar with. One that made those tears of pain from the gunshot changed to ones of remorse.

"Before you kill me, please let me help one last time," I pleaded, showing my cell with my confession, notes, and Elias's plans.

"I think that it's a little too late for help."

I heard that said to me as the blood rushed from me. My gaze turned to the face of another ghost and I trembled in fear. "You're alive."

"Maybe."

The sound of a bullet exiting its chamber was the last thing that I heard as darkness took over. In my last breath my cell fell from me and I whispered, "Mama. . . ."

Chapter 31

Jai

Contingency plans were my thing. As the descendant of Stephanie St. Clair, I learned to always document and learn how to use information to your advantage in taking down the enemy. That was why I was chosen by Claudette McPhearson and I adored her and her lessons. She allowed me to be me. Allowed me to flourish in my own way to satisfy the bigger picture in working with Syndicate, and that was self-preservation. Mama knew that there were enemies. She knew she would have to be the hand that took them down if she lived that long.

But as any good kingpin or queen pin, she didn't foresee her death happening so soon or at the hands of someone she trusted. That was where I came in. I was the authority of her contingency plan. I helped her make out a will, I set up her insurance, protected her real assets, and made sure it all got into the hands of her children. Except, really, it was only a few of her assets. I was given a code, one only a few others knew. I was given numbers and names to all of Mama's secret allies, including an old lady across from her house.

I sat at my desk, crossing off names from Mama's list who should be taken out. Javon did good in that. He just needed some fine tuning in not going at it alone and he'd be okay. After learning about Elias's real connect to everyone, I made it my point to use my gift of sorting out intel and use my own resources to snuff out Elias's home crew in South America. I made it my priority to do some background checks and street work to find out if Elias's brother and wife could be trusted.

Since I was good at my work in researching people, under my order my crew was able to discern that they could be trusted. My crew had uncovered a lot of intel for me and had taken to the streets and the barrios of Brazil, washing the street in blood. The end result of that purging was ending everyone associated with Elias's faction while leaving his brother and his brother's wife alone. They were only associated by blood and not by factions. Mama Claudette's family and everything she built was my priority.

Everyone needed to be protected, including the Syndicate.

After making sure that my orders were in motion, an alert from Javon to secure the Syndicate compound had me rushing around the room grabbing my things. On my professional game, I made two calls leaving coded messages with a slight smile. I hated that a part of me would immediately go into action at Javon's command. I hadn't expected that I would behave in such a way just because he said it. I knew it wasn't because our business tie, that he was my boss. No, see, at one point, I was somewhat attracted to Javon. But, since getting to know him more, I knew that there was nothing in it.

I didn't want Javon in a romantic way and clearly he didn't want me in that same manner. I didn't even want to fuck him at this point. The initial bout of lust for him was now long gone. And any fool could see Shanelle had him on lock. I was about business and not bed play with my clients, unless it was to get intel for Mama Claudette and the Syndicate.

However, there was something from Javon that I did want. I wanted, no, needed to be respected by him and the family. I had earned Mama Claudette's respect and now I needed to do the same for the new generation. See, my work was always for them, but I wasn't sure if trust would come from the new generation, especially considering how Shanelle always behaved when I was near. Thinking about it just annoyed the hell out of me.

I got it. She didn't like me. But, I wasn't after her man.

My aspirations were higher. I was after a permanent seat at the Syndicate table so that I could continue doing Mama's will for her children and the man she loved, Uncle Snap. Which was why I was frantic. Everything needed to happen now.

I received an e-mail alert from Navy going into the accounts and kick-starting the payments again. I was too happy about that. But then, I received another one, this time from Melissa. It was something that I wasn't expecting. What she shared scared me. Elias was on some next level crap and the family needed to be warned. So, as I rushed to the door, I flung it open. Shifting my sling bag, my gun came out with the swiftness before I realized that I had run into a familiar face who held a cell phone in my face.

"What are you doing here? You can't be here," I said, backing up.

"Since I can't deliver this personally, you can. They need it," was said to me from the short woman in front of me.

I reached for it, and thanked her. "We have another problem."

"What is it?" she asked.

"Elias plans to wipe out your neighborhood if he does make it alive from the battle," I quickly said.

"Shit! How?" she asked, following me down the hall.

We both rushed outside and I glanced down at the girl. "He plans to blow it up by a big truck of bombs. I already called Agent Monroe, and our connections are back on our side thanks to Von realizing the code. We need to get to everyone and alert them before that happens. It's time you showed up again."

"I can't. Not until it's time," she said with worry in her eyes.

"Trust me, it'll be time. Besides, he's not here with you, so I assume he's with Von?"

I watched her nod as she went to her bike. "I'll meet you there then."

Hand to my heart, I quickly hopped in my car, sent out another SOS, and sped off, glancing at a phone that I realized was Melissa's. This girl was too much. But, whatever happened, this family needed protection and Mama's contingency plan had to keep active for any of this to work in favor of Von.

Chapter 32

Javon

Everything happened for a reason. I didn't need Mama to die, or for me to take over the Syndicate to know that. Me, Uncle, my extra backup, which was comprised of a good number of the Forty Thieves, and some of Nighthawk's people from an area he controlled here in the Atlanta area all sat in their rides, waiting on my signal. Elias was in Stone Mountain. I sat twisting the muzzle of my silencer with my gloved hands thinking about everything that had occurred. It was interesting that my role as Syndicate leader wasn't going down how I originally thought it would after Mama's death.

I spent this whole time setting up the plan to get Ink distributed. That didn't go my way. Having Nighthawk and his crew be my eyes in finding Elias's location since he was already trailing him, that didn't happen. Using Melissa's information really didn't achieve a damn thing.

Mrs. Lily ended up being some low-key informant, no, protector schooled by Mama. Then she drugged me, taking control out of my hands. That shit pissed me off.

Checking that everything was good with my silencer, I laid a hand on top of my head to adjust the black wave cap I wore. Small things were successful from several of my plans during this chaotic time, though. The São-A's with Jai's help—because Jai and Shanelle just weren't going to handle it like I asked—were now taking care of Ink in getting the distribution back in our hands. Shanelle was staying back at the house to protect our child and the family.

She was probably making sure the neighborhood was protected, helping Jojo or helping Navy with the accounts because she could never sit still for shit. That was good, as long as she stayed away from fire and fighting. All I could think about with regard to Shanelle was that, luckily, she was handling business. Now, speaking of Lucky, whoever these allies were who went to him, and the fact he was acting in a manner I once only had reserved for Cory, my second, I wasn't sure how I felt about that. My trust with him was what it was. But, I had to say the efficiency in how he handled himself in this was welcomed.

My hand traced over the surface of my pistol-grip shotgun I had hidden against the side of my door as an afterthought. All of this power that was supposedly thrust on me was now being pulled from me in a surprising manner yet again. Meaning, people were falling from the skies again telling me what I needed to do and how to do it, or just doing it their damn selves. I was for lessons and all but I wasn't sure about all of this. Mama's notes weren't guiding me anymore.

I was being told that I was acting on my own, as if that was just something I wanted to really do. In my defense, I had nothing clear-cut to go by when everything went down. I felt like a chicken with its head cut off with every attack from Elias. A brotha couldn't get real time to sit and look at the bigger pictures; it all happened in pieces. Erratic pieces.

So, I behaved erratically, thanks to all of this. Damn sure thanks to Melissa. This all had me feeling like I wasn't a leader. However, I planned to work that part of my emotion out. What Ms. Lily shared had me thinking about all of Mama's hidden connects. Little by little they were coming out the cracks. Jai was the first one. Then Trey, and now Ms. Lily. We had more to find and I was learning that Mama was complicated.

But so was I. I guessed that meant I still had a lot to learn in being the head of the table, as they say. All of these agendas, though, were pissing me off.

"You're in your head again, nephew," I heard Uncle say.

I gave a slight chuckle and shrugged. "Just making sure we are all ready and covered, old man. I don't need you dying on me next, okay?"

My gaze drifted to my rearview mirror as I made a quick count of everyone behind us. We all sat strategically positioned outside of a wooded and hilly fenced neighborhood, nestled near a row of empty lots and abandoned buildings. The area appeared to be normal, yet slightly suspect. Several old-school Caddies set with spinners were parked in the driveways of large white matching houses. There were other spot-on clues that let me know this was a black neighborhood that was probably once middle class, but falling on hard times. It was no biggie for me. It just let me know that Elias gave no fucks about the lives of everyone in that neighborhood then.

Chilling in front of a mini shopping strip, half of my people were driving through the neighborhood. Some parked way ahead of us, while the other half and I were spread out in the parking lot where it kept us hidden amid everyday black folk who rode around the area. There was a corner daycare enclosed in a fence. Behind us was a soul food restaurant; next to it, a hair and barber salon. Down some ways was a school. If you took the winding road over a set of railroad tracks, it would lead you downhill past a neighborhood to an old medical district. That was where Elias was stationed. There were several large white colonial houses across from it. Each one had black SUVs parked in front.

Uncle was leaned back in his seat, black gloves on, an African-designed crocheted beanie cap on his head, and a matching black leather hoodie coat as I had on, watching from military-grade periscope goggles at the neighborhood, more specifically the old medical building ahead. Under his coat was a bulletproof vest and a long-sleeved shirt. From his snow white clean-cut chin beard that started at his gray sideburns, and mustache, I checked out his smooth brown flesh under it. The man wouldn't look his age if he shaved.

"Naw, when my time comes, I'll know it. Mama will be in front me and you'll see the biggest smile on this old man's face ever. Don't fret about it, either, because I'll damn sure be ready to exit this flesh, nephew, understand?" Uncle casually said as if there was nothing to it.

A part of me wasn't cool with his quick self-eulogy, but it was what it was in this type of environment. So, I just shifted in my seat, popped a mint toothpick between my teeth, and started up the engine of the black Charger.

"What do you see?" I asked.

Uncle rolled down his window, stuck his arm out, and made a signal for everyone. "Nothing. Which means they are ready."

"Naw, no, they aren't," I countered. "Signal for the first wave to go through the neighborhood up the front. Since it's downhill, make some noise, because I want him to hear us. We take out anyone who will harm us and keep the hood out of this."

Uncle gave a nod. "Sounds good."

I watched a hunched-over old man pushing a wire rack with what appeared to be books, tubs of shea butter and African black shop, and African memorabilia walk past our car. He gave us a look, Uncle and I gave a nod, and he smiled, pointed at his basket, asking if we wanted to buy anything. Brotha wore a huge trench coat and it had me watching him curiously. That shit looked too clean and new to be on the old man like that.

"Hey, where'd you get that coat?" I quickly asked from the side of my window, getting hit with the smell of fried chicken and other comforting scents.

"Von, we don't have time for nothing like that, nephew. You're drawing attention," Uncle quipped behind me, laying a hand on my shoulder.

"I know, trust me," I muttered low. "Hey, where'd you get that coat?"

"Up the hill. Scared brotha. Sold him some copies of *Hidden Colors* and shea butta. You sure you don't want any?" the old man asked.

"Naw, I'm good. Thank you." I slid back in my seat but kept an eye on the old man.

"Gotta be ya brotha's keeper out here in these streets, mm hmm," I heard the old man say as he walked away.

I gave a quick sigh, revved up my engine, and backed up, while Uncle gave me an incredulous look.

"Don't say nothing. Brotha's keeper, huh?" I muttered the last part more so to myself.

We moved through the neighborhood quickly once we got the clear. Rushing the colonials, my crew broke in and went to war. I could hear gunshots going off for days, which indicated that the people in there clearly weren't your typical working middle-class family. Uncle pointed ahead at the medical building, as several people ran out with shotguns and semiautomatics. I quickly revved up my engine, hitting the gas twice, as a signal to hit hard, and I smirked. The weapons we had, thanks to Nighthawk and Sato Ayume, were all souped-up military grades. I mean, we had scopes, hand grenades, Uzis, and then some. I quickly swerved my car through the men, and parked.

Uncle reached in the back of the ride, pushing off a blanket that hid a back seat–length case that he flipped open. Pulling out a barrel Uzi, he gave me a nod, then pushed open his door, stood behind it, settled that baby on his shoulders, then aimed for the small security building in front of the main medical building. Letting off a round, we watched that shit blow up like a barbecue grill with too much lighter fluid thrown on the wood.

I used that time to climb out of my car, tie a black scarf around my face while still chewing my toothpick, then remove my shotgun from my door, and move around the back of my ride, popping the trunk. I kept focused on the people around me. More of Elias's men and women flooded out, shouting. From how they rushed us, I could tell they were surprised by the ambush. They might have wanted to get to us first, but it just didn't work out that way. I had shit to make up for, with his last surprise attacks.

Walking with a bored gait, I pointed my shotgun and began pumping off rounds at the people who came at me. I crossed my arms, and used my silencer to send bullets between the eyes of those people who didn't have helmets on. The force of flying rounds occasionally hit me as I moved around my car, but they only hit my armor.

Tossing my shotgun in the seat of my car, I kept behind the open door, and shifted the brake off with my hands. I drove my Charger forward in a slow ride, while Uncle was on the other side following. My whip was our additional armor, and we used it like a tank.

I drove it forward, used my other free hand to look to my left and shoot at a big, burly asshole. I missed and had to back away from my car, whistling to Uncle to slide in and take the steering wheel, which he did. I rolled my shoulders, fisted my gloved hands, took several quick strides, then rushed the dude. My goal was to tackle him, but he was too big. He blocked it, which had me stumble back and reassess my moves.

I sent my fist forward, hitting a ribcage, using the force to fuck with his lungs on both sides. I jabbed hard like typing on computers. Each blow had me grunting and baring my teeth behind my scarf. We were like two rams butting heads. We had a purpose, and that was to kill or be killed. That became even more apparent when the man ripped off his own mask. Before me was one of the Irish. Instantly, like a bird of prey, my focus only became sharper with anger. That motherfucker had to go down. I felt his meat fist slam into my back. I gasped, spitting out my toothpick. I then used that force to shift to the side as if doing Capoeira. All I knew from that fighting style was how to move sideways from an opponent. Because of that, it gave me a better angle and time to get my breath back.

My hand went to snatch the knives on fat bastard's vest, then I plunged each one into his flesh, breaking them off. Several more quick jabs, I then leaped up to slam my fist in a downward motion into his face. Teeth, spit, and blood spewed everywhere. I hopped back, keeping my fist up, then thrust forward again.

"You fat traitor fuck!" I spat out, sending my fist up into his ugly mug.

Luck was on my side. He fell back; however, he snatched for my booted foot, which sent me to the ground hard. Reaching for my gun attached to my thigh, I pulled it from its holster and emptied the clip. Blood pooled around my enemy. I rolled to the side, looking up to see Lucky running by. He gave me a nod, tossed me another gun, and then went at it with his hands on another one of Elias's people.

My lungs were on fire, but I didn't have time to think about that. I was close to the entryway, and I was pretty sure Elias was inside.

"Give me an ETA. I need a rundown now!" I shouted in my radio attached to my coat.

Static sparked; then I heard Nighthawk: "The south side of the building is clear and empty. No sign of Elias."

"Roger that. The east entrance is packed, but no Elias," one of Lucky's men confirmed.

"Nephew, spotted him in the main building. There's a bunch of these roaches all over the place. Send more teams to the back and come get ya pound of flesh," Uncle shouted while rounds went off.

At the front of the building was my Charger. It was parked haphazardly in a gangsta lean on the sidewalk. The door to the entrance was open, which let me know it was clear. So I sprinted forward, then glanced to see Lucky.

"I got you. Keep your front. I got your back," was all he said.

Thanking him with a nod, I peeked around the door and saw several of my people inside. Goggles on, I pulled out flash and smoke grenades. Before tossing them in, I made a signal sound for my people, then rolled them grenades in, waiting. My wait didn't last long. The loud pop and bang had me rushing into the smoke. I clocked several of Elias's men trying to run from the mustard gas cocktail. I smoothly yoked them up then slammed them to the ground, pumping out another round.

"Gotdamn, that's some nasty stuff," I heard Lucky say somewhere near me. "But it got the job done."

We laughed, and I rushed around looking through the clear spots in the smoke. I could see why Elias picked this spot. It was large with balcony walkways, a huge fountain, and a small elevator. The place was open, yet compact, which gave him many advantage spots to see us come in. It also messed him up, because it left his men open. I could hear my men and women going at it. They entered from the back. Took down sharpshooters, took down whatever melee popped off in front of them, and helped to clear the place out.

Impressed, I rolled my shoulders, ready for the main event, then shouted, "Elias! What was this shit about? Now it's your move. Where ya at, my friend?"

"Near your left," I heard in my ear.

Thrown off, I turned and felt a punch at my right. Then a large boot kicked me square in my chest. I stumbled and hit something that I knew was a fountain, because water splashed over me. The hulking shadow of Elias trailed me, but I wasn't worried about it. I gave a smirk, then took the shotgun I still had strapped on me and aimed it at him. I got the satisfaction of seeing him fly back away from me. I hopped up, and followed, only to have him get up later. Bastard was covered from head to toe in a vest and protective gear, like I was. His long hair fell over his face.

He snapped it back from his face as if he were a wrestler, and motioned to me. "Do you know that you just handed me the keys to everything I wanted?" he asked in a taunting tone.

Narrowing my eyes, I shifted in a low pose ready to fuck him up. "I haven't handed you a damn thing yet."

"Oh, but you will, and the Syndicate will be all mine as is my birthright." Elias grinned, then came at me full force.

I stood there then glanced to see Uncle Snap taking down several young dudes with his fist. That old man put so much force in it that it knocked his targets back on their asses. The old man still had it. It put me back to being in front of Mama's house, learning to fight better with Uncle's lessons of Fifty-two Blocks. Every summer, we kids would stand in the heat, as he taught us to sharpen our jabs. Watch our personal space with a 360-degree perspective, and using that as a means to attack our foe. Those memories had me reading my fist in front of me and readying for an opponent I knew would use any dirty method he could to take me down. For all intents and purposes, I would allow it only to get close enough to kill the motherfucker.

Leaning back, I ducked from Elias's punch, which revealed a blade in his hand that he attempted to reverse and swipe back along my face. I extended my fist, and hit him with two blows. Rotating at the waist to reverse my own upper body hits by reaching behind me, I sent my fist into his pretty face with my back to him. This allowed me the advantage of snatching his hand, twisting his wrist, and breaking it while grabbing his knife. All of that happened in a span of a blink. I rock-stepped out of his range once he let out a sharp scream; then I was met with his knee in my jaw.

Nigga was on some Capoeira shit.

Because the air was clear of the gas, I pulled off my scarf and face mask to assess any damage.

There was a cut on my jaw, but that came from the force of his kick, breaking my mask. I shook my head, dismayed, while he held his wrist, glaring at me. An amused chuckle came from me, and I rolled my shoulders.

"Okay then. You're on some extra shit. Got it," I said, spiting blood to the floor.

"As are you, my nigga," Elias countered, then came at me. "Guess I have to end you quickly."

Quick like lightning, he reached behind him and pointed his gun, squeezing off rounds. When I ran back to Dodge, I found myself surrounded by several of Elias's people. They formed a wall and I turned to assess the situation. In our fight, I realized that Elias has purposely sequestered us in another room. A smaller one. One where he could control what went on instead of me. Basically, he set me up to figure me out, while trapping me. Smart dude.

I had none of my people near me. Everyone was in the front. I could hear Lucky shouting my name, to which I returned the favor and shouted out my location. "Far left, back way, my man!" I hoped he'd hear me.

My reward for that was the butt of a rifle against my temple. The room spun from the force and I held my hands out to balance. "Damn, you stay sneaky. Can't fight me one on one, so you resort to this," I said, breathing slowly to clear my head.

"But of course. That's what leaders do, Javon. You're so young and new at this. Weak at this. Never schooled or trained in this, that through all your tenacity and street smarts, you could not foresee your own stupidity. That's why you're going to die by the hands of my people, with me watching. I'm a true leader. You aren't." Elias snapped his fingers.

I felt myself being snatched and slammed to the floor on my stomach. I struggled but that only resulted in pain. Face smooshed in the floor, I grunted, "Don't think this will stop me. I'll find a way. Just like my Mama did when she shot you in the shoulder. That's why your punches were so weak, huh?" I laughed, and Elias scowled.

"Your mother was nothing but monkey shit to me. Her little gunplay was child's play. My moves were chess!" Patting my face, Elias glared down at me as he squatted over my head. "You should have seen how betrayed she looked when your sister revealed herself at my side. I'm pretty sure her heart was ready to go out. Hell, when she saw our guns, the joy and rush I felt at that sweet betrayal was priceless. But you don't know nothing about that, as you all say, or do you?"

Fury had me rustling to move. I kicked my leg up and was satisfied at the scream I heard. See, the force I used helped me release my legs so that I could push a few off of me. The scream? I really wasn't sure about.

"I will when I kill you!" I spat and struggled. "Melissa was foul for fucking with you!"

"Oh, but she enjoyed it. Too bad she's not here. Foul whore ran out on me, but I'll find her." Elias's gaze was no longer on me. There seemed to be a spark of confusion going on over his features. He tapped me with his fingers, then slowly stood. "Shoot him in the head like he did my mother. For which, I do thank you."

"Huh?" I asked, trying to see what had Elias's attention as another scream sounded.

It was then that I remembered, "Oh! Shit, Delanna? She's your mother, that's right. Your brother gave his thanks, too, when he took the chair you have no right to."

"Fuck my weak brother!" Elias spat out, rage sparking. "He is next and his pretty wife will be my bitch! Kill him, I said."

More screams filled the room until somehow I was free.

"Kill him? How? I already have their heads," a voice spoke from somewhere in the room. "Clean, easy shots with a lovely gun with a silencer I found in the hallway."

Shock overtook me. My hands started to shake, and I felt my heart beat a million paces. That voice was one I'd never forget. Considering the fact that the owner of that voice should have been dead, a ball of anxiety was in my stomach, but also one of immense joy.

As I slowly stood up still facing Elias, I quietly said in Filipino Tagalog, *"Bunso?* Little brother?"

"Oo, kuya. Ngunit isa akong ghost. Yes, big brother. But I am a ghost," I heard him say to me.

For whatever reason, Elias was frozen in place and I wasn't mad about it. It gave me time to figure this out. "I'm sorry," I quietly said, still speaking without turning toward the voice.

"No, you're not. You just miss me and I'm good with that, *kuya.* I love you for that."

"You should hate me, *bunso,"* I added once the voice stopped.

"Yeah, but I deserved what I got. Besides, I'm my *kuya's* keeper. Always."

When he said that, my mind went back to the old man, then I turned, wide-eyed. "You were the cloak!" Facing my baby brother again, the reality of how he survived hit me. "How'd you do it?"

Cory stood pointing two guns at Elias and he shrugged. "Better people than me can explain it. It happened too quickly."

His once handsome face was marred on the left side of his jaw by burns. His left eye was slightly shut from a gash, though the eye was functional. He stood in protective gear, no cloak in sight. The dead bodies of Elias's men was around us, and he gave me his old cocky, lopsided smile.

"Still, you were the cloak? The damn ghost, bro?" I said, incredulous and partially mad at him for hiding. I was about to ask about Inez but he interrupted me.

"Yeah. I couldn't leave you assed out just because we fought. We always fight, man. This time my death had to drag me back to reality, along with the truths I found out along the way. You really shoulda checked out the basement, fam." Cory gave a chuckle then turned his gun and began shooting off rounds.

"Your left!"

Reacting, I moved to rush Elias. Elias ran like he was gunning for the Olympics. Taking my gun, I shot at him, hitting his leg then shoulder. A sense of balance came over me with my brother at my side. While I rushed Elias, he swung back and cut me across the neck. Luckily, it wasn't exposed, so he hit nothing. Unfortunately, he took that moment to stab me on my side with his other hand.

I stumbled back, holding my side. Elias rushed me and we went to blows, fist for fist. I slammed my head into his face, knocking him back. I then grabbed him, palming his face to slam it against the floor. All anger came over me. This shit was for my family, but mainly this was for my mother.

"You took my mama. You came for my family, and you think that you deserve my seat and the Syndicate? Fuck outta here with that bullshit. I'm the king of this land and you're nothing but my shit being flushed down the drain."

"And you still won't save them," he shouted out in a strained grunt with clenching teeth.

Guns ricochet around us. I felt a bullet graze my neck, but by then it was already too late. I pulled off my belt while Elias struggled; then I wrapped it around his neck. Cory appeared in front of me. I handed him the end of it, and he pulled on it as I stood up. I watched as Elias kicked and tried to pry the belt off from around his neck, but it was of no use. Cory had a hold on him and he was going nowhere.

"You thought you could come and take what belonged to my family by killing our matriarch. Our queen. Only you made us stronger," I spat out, following as Cory dragged Elias through the building and back to the front. "I'd like to thank you for aiding in guiding me to be on course, because you forgot about one thing when it comes to family."

I glanced at Cory and he gave me a nod as he said, "McPhearsons can't be killed."

Standing over Elias, I ripped off his vest, then pressed my Glock over his heart. I could feel Uncle standing over my shoulder as I squeezed the trigger then shifted to press it against his skull. "For Mama Claudette."

Blood splattered everywhere as Elias's clawing hands dropped. I sent several more rounds into his skull as Uncle walked away, hopped in the car, and hit the gas. Elias's head ripped from his body thanks to the belt that was tied to the back of my car. I stood by Cory, and we all stared at the man who helped kill our mother. The moment felt like poetic justice until I thought of Melissa.

"We need to find Melissa," I quietly said once Uncle came back, glancing at his cell phone then frowning. I noticed he didn't look surprised about Cory being alive, and I took note.

"Naw, she's right here," Cory said, stepping away.

He came back later with a bag that he dropped carelessly near Elias's body. When he unzipped it, my mouth dropped as I stared at the face of a dead Melissa.

"Loved that gal, but I hate what she became," Uncle said with anger and sadness in his voice, clutching his phone. "At least she did us one solid when she died. We gotta get to our family, sons."

I glanced at Uncle Snap, wondering what was up but not questioning it; then I looked at my brother. "He's right. We all need to clear out now and work on ending the lives of all the people who helped these two. We need to go home." I paused as I turned to look at Melissa again. "I need her and Elias's heads. And I could have ended her."

"It was you or her," he said and looked at me from his hooded coat he put on. "I knew you couldn't make this type of call for us. She was fam. But I could. Whatever you can't do, I will. Again, *kuya,* I'm not perfect and shit, but I'm your keeper."

Chapter 33

Shanelle

Waiting for word from Javon was like nails on a chalkboard. I was worried. I couldn't front. I needed him to come back home. We had this child to raise, take care of. We had little brothers to see after. Everyone else was behaving like it was a normal day. Rize was outside the house. Navy had been in the bunker for hours. I'd taken him food and water, but he hadn't been up yet. Dani and Jojo had been arguing on and off all day.

Dani didn't understand why Jojo didn't want to say what had happened to him. Jojo didn't get why she didn't get he didn't want to talk about it. He explained to her that there were some things she just couldn't do to him. Snatching the covers off of him was one of those things. Dani had a big busted lip and a scowl on her face. Jojo had been moody the whole time, but he had been in the bunker most of the day as well. He and Navy were working on whatever Javon wanted.

Monty and Trin kept an eye on me like Javon asked, which was comical. I didn't think Monty nor Trin could stop me if I really wanted to get out of the house. But I stayed put. Javon had called me on a promise that I'd made to him awhile ago. It was a year after I'd lost one of our children in a street brawl and two weeks after I'd had an abortion we both agreed on. It was my idea for the abortion, but Javon agreed. We couldn't take care of a kid then. The money wasn't right and, try as we might, we weren't either. But I made him a promise that day that if I got pregnant again, I would keep the baby. I'd give him the chance to be the father he never had.

Jojo came from the bunker from a different part of the house. Neither Dani nor Trin knew the way in from the fireplace. They just knew Jojo, Navy, Monty, and I kept magically appearing from different parts of the house. I hadn't really had a decent conversation with my little brother. All I'd been focusing on was the overgrown whore who had been sleeping with him every night. Felt like I was alone in that fight. Neither Uncle nor Javon hadn't really said much about it. I had no backup to get Dani up out of here without losing Jojo.

"You okay?" I asked him.

He bunched his nose then slid his glass up before scratching his head once. He always did that when he was annoyed. "I'm cool," he said.

He was looking through the drawer next to the closet. It was where he and Navy kept spare wires for different things. Chargers, adapters, aux cords, et cetera, were kept there. I stared at his back in the black T-shirt that read I CAN'T BREATHE on the back. As always, he was in baggy jeans and white Nike Air Force Ones.

"Look, Jojo, I'm sorry about . . . about the way I've acted."

He stood then turned to look at me. There was no expression on his caramel-colored face.

"I care about you, Jojo. I love you, okay? And to see you with her, it . . . it bothers me."

He asked, "Why?"

"She's too old."

"To you. Nobody else said nothing but you," he said, a frown now etching across his face.

"Why do you seek out older women, Jojo? You ever asked yourself that?"

He shrugged nonchalantly, holding adapters in his hands. "Because I like them."

"Yeah, but why?"

"I know what you're trying to do. You do that same shit Mama's crazy doctor used to do."

"Crazy doctor?"

"Yeah, the fucking shrink Mama used to make us go to. Don't do that. Don't try to get in my head. I know how old Dani is, okay? But even if I thought about walking away from her, now I can't. She's carrying my kid," he said. The frown left and his face turned to stone. "And there ain't no way in hell I'm leaving my kid behind."

"Jojo, you're seventeen! You're not even supposed to have a kid," I said, talking with my hands, too.

"Yeah, but I do now, Shanelle. Look, I get it. I understand you love me or whatever," he said like he wasn't sure he believed it. "But, this is me. This is my life. Let me live it. If I fuck up, I just fuck up."

I wanted to say so much to him in that moment, but I didn't. Words escaped me. Truth be told, there wasn't shit I could say to him that would make him see the error of his ways. Not when Dani had walked down the stairs. She had on yoga shorts that sometimes rode up her ass. She had to keep adjusting them. The fishtailed thin T-shirt she had on made Trin frown anytime Monty was around. Dani didn't have on a bra. I'd never seen her wear a bra. She reminded me of Melissa when she did shit like that. I frowned.

Any time I thought of Melissa, grief, pain, anger, disappointment, all of those emotions fought for dominance in me. I was about to say something about the way she dressed around my other brothers, but Jojo beat me to it.

He was already annoyed. I could tell by the way his upper lip twitched and his eyes darted around the room before settling on her. "You gon' put some clothes on, Danielle?" he asked her, his voice low and even.

Dani stopped at the foot of the stairs, and glanced at me then back at Jojo. "What's wrong with what I got on?" she asked.

Attitude hid just behind her words. She tried to catch herself, but couldn't. Sometimes she didn't come off like a college student. At times she sounded like she belonged on the avenue formally known as Stewart, asking if men wanted a blow job or anal. Dani sometimes sounded as if she still belonged in high school. It was not what she said, but how she said it.

"My brothers are in here, Dani. Put some clothes on," he said.

"I have clothes on," she shot back.

Jojo took a deep breath, and glanced around the room for a bit. He gave a slow blink then said, "Will you at least put a bra on?"

She folded her arms across her chest. "No. My titties are sore and a bra makes it worse." Her bottom lip was big because of the punch Jojo had inadvertently given her. She was still upset about that. I knew that because she told Jojo it would be awhile before she got over it, especially since he wouldn't tell her why he did it.

Jojo put the adapters down then pulled his jeans up. The boy always wore a belt but seemed to have to always pull his jeans up. Navy and Monty always did the same. "Fine. Since you want to be asinine then don't be mad about them giving you the cold shoulder no more. Don't come crying to me when people ignore you and won't talk to you," he told her as he picked the adapters back up.

He headed toward the fireplace. I stood. He remembered not to go that way then turned to head toward the back of the house.

Dani sucked her teeth, rolled her neck, then put her hands on her rounded hips. "Whatever, li'l boy," she said.

My lips turned down like something stunk. "You knew he was a little boy when you spread eagle for him."

Dani scowled at me. Monty came from the kitchen. Saw Dani, took in the way she was dressed, and then turned back around.

"For your information, he doesn't fuck me. I fuck him," Dani spat at me.

Before I could think straight, I flew across the room. Monty grabbed me, but not before I snatched that bitch by her hair, dragging her down the rest of the stairs. All I saw was red. If Monty hadn't been there, I would have beaten Dani to death. I'd forgotten she was pregnant just that quick.

"Shanelle, let go, sis. Let go," Monty growled. He had placed himself in the middle of me and Dani.

"I'm going to kill this bitch," I said through clenched teeth.

Trin rushed from the kitchen. She tried to help Monty pry my fingers from Dani's roots. I was incensed. Rage that I hadn't felt since I'd killed my way out of my mother's house took over. Dani's squeals and flailing arms didn't bother me. But for as hard as I tried to get around Monty, his big, swole Native ass wouldn't let me. So I tried to yank Dani's ass bald in the process. I bit down on my bottom lip while snatching her hair until I tasted blood.

Monty and Trin finally got my hand out of Dani's hair. Monty walked me backward while Trin stood in front of Dani. My eyes had watered. I was so pissed, I had a good mind to toss Mama's favorite vase across the room at that bitch.

"You'd better not," I heard.

It was like Mama was standing right next to me. I heard her voice as clear as day. I jumped and looked around. That sobered me a bit.

"Leave her be. Life will handle it," I heard. *"Someone's at the door."*

I moved to the left of Monty. I didn't hear anyone at the door, but I for damn sure knew I heard Mama's voice. It scared the shit out of me.

"You okay, sis?" Monty asked me.

I closed my eyes for a few seconds then opened them again just to be sure I was awake and not dreaming. "Did you hear that?" I asked.

He looked around. "Hear what?"

I shook my head. "Never mi—"

Before I could finish my word, there was a tap, tap, tap at the door. "I got it," I said.

Monty moved a bit, but not far. I guess he wanted to keep himself between me and Dani.

"That's the last time anyone in this house puts their hands on me," she spat before charging up the stairs.

Trin shook her head, but she had an amused smirk on her face. I yanked the door open to find members of Rize and members of the Forty Thieves surrounding a cloaked figure standing in the yard. I signaled behind the door for Monty and Trin that something was going down.

"Who is that?" I asked.

"She says she has some information you need. Won't show her face, though."

I stepped onto the front steps. She was wearing a cloak, but it didn't look like the one on the person I'd chased before. She was wearing wine-colored boots. The person I'd been chasing had on black military-grade combat boots. The other person didn't have tits and hips, either.

"What do you want?" I yelled at her. "Whatever you have, say it or show it. You got five seconds or you're dead."

The woman walked closer. Guns cocked. She stopped. Slowly, she pushed the hood back on her cloak. The side of her face was heavily bandaged. Her left eye had a patch. The left side of her head was shaved and I could see the stitches there.

My hands started to shake. "Who are you?" My heart knew who it was or who I thought it was, but my mind wouldn't catch up, didn't want to believe it.

"A sister is both your mirror and your opposite," she said.

Her voice made Monty snatch the door farther open and step out. Navy came bolting from somewhere in the house. He was outside with Jojo. They had guns, but they didn't move. The looks on all their faces mirrored mine. Tears burned, welled up in my eyes, and fell down my face. I stepped, clumsily so, down the stairs.

"Ms. McPhearson, you sure you want to—" one of the guys started, but I held a hand up to silence him.

"You're not dead," Navy said.

He moved quicker than I did. Jojo was right behind him. I was still staring. Didn't have time to process it all when Javon and Uncle Snap pulled up to the front of the house. Javon hopped out before the truck stopped moving, it seemed. He rushed to me first then turned his attention to where our eyes were trained. Uncle Snap stepped from the truck, leaned against it, and lit a cigar. Blood, scrapes, bruises, and the like decorated both him and Javon.

Too much was going on at once. I didn't know whether I should be happy Javon and Uncle Snap made it back home or if I should run and grab the ghost in front of me. It was only then I realized that Javon, although he looked puzzled, wasn't reacting the same as the rest of us. Neither was Uncle Snap.

"What's going on?" I asked.

"Second chances, baby," he said then pointed toward the truck.

A pair of black combat boots could be seen hitting the ground. Then the cloak I'd been chasing. Two and two snapped together for me quickly. If Inez was here then the person who got out of the truck had to be Cory.

When he pushed back the hood of his cloak, my breath caught in my throat.

"Oh, shit," I whispered, then rushed to Inez.

When she opened her arms for me, I broke down right there. Right in the front yard with neighbors watching, right there with Ms. Lily watching with a knowing smile on her face, I cried. No, I sobbed. Shoulders shook, body shook and, when Cory came over, I did the same with him. We all did. Right there in the front yard.

It took me days to realize that Ms. Lily wasn't who or what she seemed. But that night, when Cory and Inez came back home, we all sat down as a family. There were no outsiders. Just us kids and Uncle Snap.

"Not all the people in this neighborhood are what they seem," Uncle Snap said. "Mama had a system, a well-oiled machine. Just like the notes she left can only take Javon so far, the notes King left her only took her so far. She had to make up some shit as she went along. And as the years passed, she built a kingdom. I said all that to say that the day Cory and Inez left here and the Irish attacked them, Ms. Lily and few neighbors were out there. They saw the car Cory and Inez were in flip over. Helped them out of that wreck. Took down those Irish who had attacked them. Put them in Ms. Lily's basement. Since Mama was dead, though, the other neighbors were afraid to expose themselves any more than helping her get Cory and Inez into her basement."

Monty snapped his fingers. "That's why she always wanted Javon to come to the basement."

Uncle nodded.

"It makes sense now," Navy said.

Javon was about to say something until Cory pulled two small glasses that looked like shot glasses from his pouch. Inside was what appeared to be black water or some kind of dark liquid. He passed one to Inez and they both took the liquid down like a shot of liquor.

Once they saw we were all watching, Cory said. "Helps with the late-night chills of withdrawal." No one said anything at first. It didn't slip our minds that they'd had a drug problem. But we refused to bring it up until now.

"You two good?" Javon asked.

Inez, who I noticed avoided sitting anywhere in front of anything that would show her reflection, smiled. "Getting there," she said.

I was so nervous. Scared, actually. I didn't know how I should act. I wanted to hug Inez more. Squeeze her hand, let her know I was there. I wanted her to know I'd be a better sister and friend to her from now on. I wanted to apologize to Cory for taking his big brother away from him so much. I wanted to right the wrong they felt I'd done to them, but I didn't know how.

"The late-night chills are the worst," Cory said. "But what we took, it helps."

"Yeah, besides, Ms. Lily is a hell cat. The woman is crazy, like a warden. She helped us a lot. Had doctors coming in and out to patch us up, but Uncle Snap told her we had a drug problem," Inez said.

"From there, she was on us like stank on shit," Cory added.

"They been doing pretty good. No pills or none of that other crap they were taking," Uncle said.

"So you knew they were alive this whole time?" I asked him.

"Not the whole time. The old battle-ax cornered me one morning and demanded I come to her basement. Didn't even know she and Mama had a relationship beyond Mama feeding her and checking in on her from time to time. But, yeah, since that day I've known."

"Anybody seen Melissa?" Monty asked.

We all turned to Javon, waiting.

"She's dead," he said.

"Did she really do it?" Jojo asked. "She really got Mama killed? Had something to do with it?"

Javon nodded. We all sat statue still. I was hoping I'd have gotten the chance to kill her, but it was all just the same. She was dead. Gone, just like Mama.

I took a sip of the sweet tea in my glass then looked forward. "She see you do it?" I asked.

"He didn't do it. I did. Caught her in the club trying to kill Elias herself," Cory said.

I frowned. "She had some fucking nerves," I snapped.

"Guilt was more than likely riding her, niece," Uncle Snap said.

"Fuck her guilt," I said back. "I don't give a fuck about her guilt. I wished she would have told us why she did such a cowardly fucking thing."

"We'll never know now. I put bullets in her," Cory said then shrugged. "I love her, loved who we thought she was, but fuck her."

Javon took my hand and squeezed it a bit. He changed the subject. Told us that Elias was dead and that he would be busy for a long while now. Asked us all to handle things on the home front while he did this behind the scenes with the Syndicate. He had to get his product to the table and out on the street.

This was our life now. We had our family back, minus two. That would hurt and haunt us for a long time, but we would make it work. For now, though, we had lost two and gained two back. We'd miss Melissa, but we would get over it. We would never get over losing Mama. That video of her death would always replay for me. As I looked at my brothers and the only sister I had left, I let my tears fall.

Chapter 34

Uncle Snap

The woman on the video sniffed and wiped snot from her nose. The red she had dyed her hair made her look more like Amber Rose than ever.

"I'm sorry," she croaked out. "It wasn't supposed to go like this," she said. "I fucked up. I fucked up and it got Mama killed. I could . . . I could tell y'all why I did it, but it's so stupid in hindsight. So fucking stupid. Elias, I thought . . . he said he wouldn't kill her. He used me. I had an idea and then he took over. It was supposed to be just like a robbery, to hurt her, put her in the hospital so I could get put over her accounts. I needed money."

Melissa cried hard for a few minutes. Sounded like somebody was killing her. Anger riled up inside of me. Out of the many years Mama had taken in kids, adopted them, cared for them, I'd never wanted to harm them the way I wished I could have done to Melissa. The moment it was confirmed she'd had a hand in my woman's demise, all those feelings of protector and caregiver flew out the window.

"I'm so sorry," she wailed. "He tricked me. I fell for it. He used me. I had no idea who he was—"

Melissa's face froze in a distorted figure and she tumbled off the table. Shanelle screamed as she stomped the portable DVD player that was showing Melissa's taped confession. I didn't think any of us got how much Mama's death had hurt Shanelle. An hour after our talk at the dinner table, Jai had shown up with this video and paperwork from Melissa.

"Stupid cunt. Stupid, stupid, *stupid,* Melissa. So gotdamn stupid!" she screamed.

I didn't know if it was the damn hormones from her being pregnant or what, but niece had been emotional a hell of a lot.

"Baby," Javon called out.

"No. No. Mama was wrong. Mama assumed it would be the Syndicate or someone in the streets to take her out, y'all. And it was one of us. One. Of. Us. One of the kids she took in. One of the kids who she loved and cared for. That shit hurts."

She looked around the room with red, wild eyes like she was about to panic.

"She took her. She took my mama. She did it and for what? I hate her so much. It wasn't her time. I still had . . . was supposed to have time to love Mama some more. She called me that day. I rushed her off the phone because I was busy at work. She told me she loved me but I didn't get a chance to say it back. My phone, it hung up and I didn't get a chance to call back."

Shanelle kept shaking her head and talking with her hands. She kept looking around the room like she was expecting Mama to pop up from thin air. Like she wanted one last chance, a chance wasn't none of us about to get. She was sobbing, sobbing worse than Melissa was on that video.

I'd never seen her broken like the way she was in that moment. There wasn't a dry eye in the room, but to see Shanelle break down like that was something else altogether. Jojo dropped his head. Navy looked everywhere but at Shanelle. Monty had turned to face the wall. Cory had his eyes closed and Inez sat unmoving, but not looking at Shanelle. Not even Jai could look at her. Jai sat at the table, head down, one hand covering her face. After a while, I couldn't look either.

Javon stood and went to his fiancée. She was barely standing. Bent over holding her stomach, Shanelle let out a wail that shook all of us to the core. Guessed it was time. Guessed it was fucking time for her to mourn. None of us really had time. Everything came all at once.

"Why? Why?" she cried while Javon lifted her into his arms and took her from the room. We could still hear her crying long after Javon had closed them in their room.

God had always been cruel to me. Any woman who ever loved me, He took away. My grandmother, my aunt, and now Mama. I didn't know what I'd done to the old Man Upstairs to make Him be so cruel to me. He had even made it so I brought my woman's killer to her. I was cursed. Had felt that way since I was that fifteen-year-old who King had taken off the streets and gave work to. The only light that came into my world was that night, long ago, when I was twenty-five and Mama had been waiting on me in my tiny apartment. Five years after King died, my world came alive.

Later that night, where no one could see me, I sat alone in the room I'd been occupying. Couldn't bring myself to sleep in Mama's room again. Naked on the floor with the moonlight shining down on me through a crack in the curtain at the window, grief crept into my room. He took a seat beside me.

"Claudette, for so long you were the reason I fought to live. My saving grace. I fought to stay alive each day 'cause of you. Today, I thought about dying. Thought about letting a hail of bullets bring me to you. But the kids . . . I know you don't want me to leave the kids. I'm tired, baby. All my life, this is all I've been and I ain't got no problems with that. But gotdamn I swear this shit too hard for me right now. To know I, me, I brought your killer in this house . . ."

A gust of wind breezed through the window. It was cold outside, but the wind settled around me like a warm embrace. Felt like the way Mama used to hold me. She liked to hold me from behind, lay her head on my back, and we would sway to some unheard music. I got ready to say more, but couldn't.

Moonshine in hand, in the mason jar I'd never let go, I let my tears flow freely. I let go. I mourned. Finally, I mourned.

Chapter 35

Javon

Sometimes, time can be healing or harmful. Throughout everything that had happened to my family, we all learned that lesson well and experienced it like an iron fist. I stood in the family room where Mama's picture sat staring out of the huge bay window. My mind ticked away with the rise of the morning sun while looking out at the neighborhood in its small enclave of support while holding a cup of coffee to my lips. In my thoughts, I mentally went on rewind over all the lessons, the stumbles, the problems, the fights, the near-death experiences.

This family had lost so damn much, but we were back together, still broken, but together. There was a lot that we had to work on, shit that I was pretty sure would take many years to heal and grow through, but in honor of our mother, I planned to do my part in keeping us glued together. Besides, we had Uncle Snap to watch over now, and the two youngest in our family, Jojo and Navy. We had to get our family together in order to keep everything else in our lives in check, and I wasn't just speaking about the Syndicate.

Relishing the taste of my coffee, I heard light footsteps. "You stay trying to sneak up on me, *bunso,* but it's only worked one time and you had to die for that to work."

Light, deep laughter came by my right side as Cory slide into my peripheral vision. "True enough, *kuya,*" Cory said, reaching and taking my coffee from me to drink it. "Hmm, good today. Not crappy and bland like usual. You've changed. And you look like shit." We spoke in our typical language when it was just us: Spanish-Filipino Tagalog.

I took in my reflection, noting the bandages on my bare upper half while crossing my arms over my chest. "At least I'm not looking like the Elephant Man wiped his ass on the right side of my face."

"Kiss my ass! My Afro-Filipino sexy still shines through," Cory said in light laughter.

There was an undertone of sadness in his words and I knew why. Though neither Inez nor Cory had said it, the accident took a lot out of them. The act of their choices would forever be etched on their flesh even after the surgeries they were going to get to correct it some. It would always be there as a reminder. It hurt to see it and I knew it hurt for them to live with it. Which was why Cory and I hit each other with our dry humor. It was the only thing we knew to do when dealing with personal pains.

"Yeah, it does, and I hate it. Now you got that mystic and shit," I said, chuckling. I grew silent after that, going back to my thoughts of the family, of Mama, of everything.

"What are you planning?" Cory asked, knowing me better than I knew myself.

"First thing, I want you back at my side; but, for now, until you can get clean and work to stay clean, Lucky will be in your seat holding it for you." I slightly turned to see Cory quietly drink my coffee while looking out the window.

"So, I'm on punishment? Timeout?" he said, not in a sour, jealous tone like he'd usually do, but in a quiet, understanding, jolted tone.

"For now. I missed you and I need you at the table. But I can't have you falling back where you were and I can't have what we do lead you back there."

Cory turned to look at me, then gave me slight nod and a shrug. "It's what I'd do if I were you. Even though it pisses me off. I'm very mad at how you did me and Inez, know that. I get it, but it hurt. So, breaking from y'all, I'll do that. Just to show you my ass to kiss when I come back full throttle."

My brother gave a silent pause as if thinking then locked eyes with me with intense seriousness. "I mean, if Uncle's method of detoxing can help us, then I'll do what I can. I do this for Mama's memory because I can never be like Melissa."

I knew what he was saying. That he'd never betray me in that way, though we may hurt each other through our own bullshit in life. That was enough for me. He had to get my trust back, but on some real? It really wasn't gone. My brother was a real deal addict and with that life came challenges. It was just up to him and Inez to see how they can manage it.

"Don't be like Ike Turner, either, a'ight? Mama would—"

"Mama would shoot me in my pinky toe for that type of betrayal, I know." Cory laughed, sighed, and then ran a hand through his silky hair. "I know. It's all part of the rehab Uncle and Jai are planning for me."

"Ah, yeah? Didn't know she was in on that. She stopped the van from coming in and blowing shit up. I appreciate her for that. Crazy that she was in on you and Inez as well."

Cory blew out steam and glanced back at the window. "All of that was the old lady Ms. Lily. Called her to get whatever information and money we needed to stay on the low. If she hadn't I would have blown our cover long ago. Both women are resourceful."

Nodding my head in agreement, it brought me back to Cory's question. "So, what am I planning then? Like I said, you and Inez heal up. I need to talk to Shanelle about this next part but, if she's down, I want you to move in our apartment while we move in here."

"Yeah? Why move?" Cory asked.

"With Mama gone, only one staying is what? Uncle Snap, Jojo, and Navy? Monty every now and then? They are the youngest. Especially Jojo. Uncle Snap can't carry this all on his shoulders and he shouldn't. The house belongs to him in name and I'm next on it; then it goes down from there. This is our home. So we need to keep it like that. Besides"—rubbing my neck, I sighed—"we need to change the bunker around and split the entrance just in case we get raided again, and we all need to keep an eye on that Dani chick."

My brother quirked an eyebrow and frowned. "Yeah. Speaking of, what are you going to do about that?"

"Kick her ass out this crib, and set her up next door," I said nonchalantly. "Not setting her up or nothing, just setting Jojo up and keeping an eye on her. He'll pay for it out of his paycheck that I give him for his work through the Syndicate."

Cory let out a boisterous laugh. "A'ight. Next?"

"Next. We handle Melissa's body."

I watched him make a face and as he made the face, I smelled moonshine, and I knew Uncle was coming in the room. He stood by my left and stayed silent.

"How much you hear, old man?" I asked without looking.

"All of it and some of it. Fuck Melissa," he said with ease.

Part of me wanted to wipe her from my heart, but that just wasn't going to happen. "True, but I'm dealing with her body. We'll cremate her, put her in replacement of Inez and Cory, then—"

"Then what, nephew? Give her a eulogy? Pump her up yonder?" he sarcastically spat out in anger. "She killed my Claudette."

"And she loved her in the end," Cory added. "Mama's name was the last she said." Backing up with his hand up, Cory gave Uncle a passionate look. "Just hear Von out. Remember I killed the ho, but I remember the little sister who held us down no matter what."

Uncle growled low and wearily looked my way. I reached out and laid a hand against the crook of his neck. Gently squeezing the nape of his neck, I spoke up. "We'll cremate her. I'll go, and no one else has to. After, I'm going to Brazil to deliver her and Elias's heads."

"How soon is this?" Uncle asked.

"In a couple of days."

"Not alone," he added.

Shaking my head, I gave a smile. "Not alone. I'm planning this for us all. Just for a week, then we'll come back. With our security around us, and keeping the neighborhood safe. Besides, I have to make sure the pipeline is still good now that everything is distributing correctly."

Uncle understood what I was speaking about with regard to Ink. "A'ight, nephew. Handle things then. Don't do nothing special for Melissa. Burn her and that's it. Punt the fucking head over a fence and handle business."

I watched him take a swig from his mason glass. Then Cory held up the coffee mug in a cheers. I shook my head with sadness in my heart over Melissa's traitorous ass.

"Before you go, nephew, I will say this." Uncle reached out to clap a hand on Cory's shoulder and he looked my way. "This old man is very glad the family is back. We now can heal up and take care of business. Family business."

"Indeed," I said as Cory nodded his head.

Moving on, I took my time and walked barefoot with my drawstring pants sitting low upstairs to Shanelle. They were down for the plan, I just needed to check on my fiancée. Once in what was once Mama's room, and now our room, I quietly listened at the door. Light sniffles could be heard. I knew then that Shanelle wasn't sleeping at all. Her grief was in charge here and it was my duty to hold her down. After all the risks she took for me in our new life, that was the least that I could do for her.

Quietly, I strolled into the room, and closed and locked the door behind me. Shanelle lay with half the blanket and sheets off her body. I stood there taking in the beauty that was my woman.

Shanelle usually, no, always became easily hot at night. So thanks to that, while standing there, I was blessed with a glimpse of her thick, naked thighs, and sepia brown skin. My gaze traveled to her bunched-up tank, and hip-cut white briefs with the Pink emblem upon them. Her hair was wrapped in an intricately folded silk scarf. It sat tucked on top of her head as if it were a crown. Eager to feel her in my arms, I immediately walked up to the bed to slide in behind her and pull her against me, folding her in my embrace.

Damn, she smelled like peace. As I held her, I knew that she wasn't asleep anymore, just from the way her breathing changed. "We should talk about what we're doing next. What I also have to do next," I gently said against her earlobe.

"I'm listening," was all she managed to say while I shared with her my ideas on us moving in.

"What do you think about us moving in?" I asked, holding off on the Melissa and Brazil stuff.

"The family needs us. I don't want to lose this house, and we need to take care of it. As long as we can keep our own place for privacy, coming home wouldn't be a bad thing." Shanelle turned in my arms and glanced up at me. "Besides, it has more room here for our baby as well."

She made my heart feel good. Shanelle understood me the best. That's why she would forever be at my side. I smiled then kissed her forehead. It was wild to me; through all of this madness we had made life. I intended to protect our child and Shanelle with my life, though I knew they would be my weakness in this criminal world.

I accepted everything that came with that. My hand slid down against the curve of Shanelle's belly and, for the first time since everything, I was able to let the gravity of the reality that we were going to have our own child sink in. A brotha felt misty-eyed about it. Mama wasn't going to be here to see this, but at least her presence would be around us.

"That's where my mind was going with all of this as well. Outside of keeping an eye on Jojo and Navy, and Uncle Snap, we'll have to start sorting out our baby."

"We'll move in then. . . ." Shanelle said, trailing off. She rested her head against my chest and I closed my eyes.

"So, I'll keep working. Keep up appearances because we need some normalcy. My job is my normal, but I may flip some things and become my own boss with that. It'll be easier, considering . . ."

"Considering being head of the Syndicate?" Shanelle finished for me.

"Yeah, exactly. Which leads to what I need to do next. Melissa—"

Shanelle shot up so fast that I thought she might hit me in the face with her head. "Fuck her!" she spat out with tears lining her eyes.

"Damn, baby, chill! Just listen!" My hand shot up and I tried to stop Shanelle from getting out of bed. Quickly, I ran down everything I planned to do. When I mentioned Brazil, that's when Shanelle stopped her stubbornness and looked my way.

"You want to take us to Brazil?" she asked, raising her eyebrow.

I knew I had to sweeten the pot so I slid to the edge of the bed, licked my lips, and rubbed the side of my aching waist. "Yes. I mean, not only does a brother have to handle boss business and finish this shit off, but I also need to take care of family business and move us forward."

Reaching up, I ran my hand over my waves then looked into Shanelle's eyes. "That would mean taking you to the Escadaria Selarón steps and making you my wife. You game?"

Suffice it to say, she was game. My girl rushed me and we fell back into the bed. She kissed me and gave me the best head ever, not that she could ever give me wack head. I then returned the favor, pleasuring her and making her sing several of octaves with my gift of the tongue. After, we made love, reminisced about Mama and other things, and the night turned into day. Then the days turn into several. I privately took care of Melissa's body. Shipping a head overseas could be difficult, let alone two heads and a mangled body, but the Syndicate helped me with that.

We all headed to Brazil minus Uncle Snap, Jojo, Navy, Inez, and, of course, Dani. It was their duty to watch the house, along with Rize and a handful of the Forty Thieves. Inez couldn't bring herself to go because of the damage the wreck had done, which was why I had her set up to go to a plastic surgeon while we were gone. I needed to take care of her and we would. Uncle Snap stayed specifically behind for Inez and our younger siblings, as well as to keep an eye on the Syndicate.

I owed that old man a trip one day and I planned on bringing him here after everything chilled. Once we landed, of course the views were the typical ones we saw in movies, but it was so much more than that. Black, brown, and white were all around us, including other immigrant races. My mind reflected on family as we rode in a private car through the streets of Rio.

Cory was on the fence about Inez being back home. He had wanted to stay by her side, but with Uncle Snap staying, we agreed that I'd be his anchor, while Uncle was Inez's anchor, in keeping him grounded away from the drugs;

and he with Monty would be my protection at my meeting. We all were dressed in our finest. Shanelle wore a light blue sheer, flowing dress with a large diamond on her left hand. Her hair was in twisted braids that rested over her shoulder, while I wore a light gray suit with a touch of blue that matched Shanelle.

We all had just left the stairs of Escadaria Selarón. The memory of it made me feel mad good. Shanelle stood poised on the colorful mosaic stairway as if she were a straight-up model or queen. She flowed down those stairs coming toward me. By my side, watching with me were Cory and Monty. We looked like royal warriors in wait. Shanelle's simple yet elegant dress flowed behind her, lightly lifting in the gentle breeze, as she was led down to me by Trey. Light washed over her, framing her as if she were an angel, and I felt Mama's presence in that moment. Once she took my hand, we turned to stand in front of an older brotha with a white beard as we were married in front of half of our family. We decided after everything to hold a second ceremony back home once we returned.

Shanelle's peaceful smile and the way she looked in her dress basking in the sunlight danced across my mind in memory. It made me warmly smile. I briefly looked toward her, only to look away and return to my plans for the meeting. The location was set up by Jai, who rode in the front with Trey. We made sure to set the meeting up in several different locations around Rio, with only one true meeting place. Amen and Cintia Gallo would be brought to me, instead of me meeting them. Which was the case as we finally all sat in a glass modern-style house that overlooked the beautiful hills and mountains of Brazil.

Amen and Cintia were lead in by Monty and Trey, along with two of our Forty Thieves. I glanced at Shanelle, who sat center with me, then at Cory, who lounged back with a glass of black liquid. I knew he was focused on protecting me, so I was good to fall into my role. Standing from my seat on a long white couch I then held out a hand, motioning for the couple to sit.

"We welcome you to Brazil," Amen said while walking up to me, grinning wide. Brotha strolled in like a king. His huge, fluffy ponytail fro bounced behind him. He wore a fly suit with an African motif in the colors of Brazil while his wife seemed to step from the pages of the Nigerian *Vogue*. Her beauty had me watching her hard, especially how she walked in like a queen herself.

She smiled my way, as her husband took my hand then shook it. I watched him turn it to kiss my ring; then Cintia followed suit.

Both greeted everyone who watched them. To the far left of me sat Jai, along with Lucky as a second representative of the Syndicate. To the far right sat Nighthawk. Both had covered my ass out there in the battle and this was my way of giving thanks, and proof that I could handle leading the Syndicate. Amen and Cintia then elegantly took their seats, and I stepped back to take mine. Once I sat, I nodded. Monty and Trey disappeared then came back with large sheet-covered steel drums. They set them down in front of the couple with their gloved hands, removed the sheet, reached in, and pulled out two Plexiglas jars. They then stepped back.

Cintia gasped and looked away. "I can't."

"Forgive my wife. She has a soft constitution with this nature of the business," Amen said while glancing at the floating heads in the jars. "So here he is and his accomplice."

"Fair exchange has been held. At this point, I now want something from you," I calmly stated, then sat forward.

"But of course. I'm listening," Amen said, looking my way.

Hand sliding in my pocket, I pulled out my cell, flipping it against my palm while holding it. "It's come to my attention that, in this battle, both of our families made our business affairs difficult. Betrayals ran on both sides of the fence; however, yours ran just a little deeper."

As soon as those words left my mouth, both Amen and Cintia were snatched by their hair, necks exposed, with blades pressing to them.

Leisurely, brushing my pants off as I rose up to stand, I played with my cell, flipping it with one hand then hitting play. Anticipation was everything. Voices immediately started and my conversation with Elias played back for Amen and Cintia to hear. In it was his reveal of his mother aiming to take over the Syndicate and him following in on the plan.

"Wait! We have no part in that. On my life, and on my bloods' blood." Amen held his hands up.

"My husband came in to stop the corruption that was flowing through the family business. Like you, Javon, he was tired of the blind egos that were destroying the positive in the old ways. He is fresh blood. We are the new age. Please. We aren't here to take from you, but we are here to build with you," Cintia spoke up, pleading.

Amen held his hands up and locked his gaze on me. Brotha showed slight fear but he also showed the steely look of someone not to fuck with but who was also honorable. I respected that. So I listened as he spoke.

"She is right. We are here to keep the São Africana intact and at the table that honored us in giving us our mother's seat. Our city is at war because of her machinations. This has made us lose too much equity, and too many allies. Let us prove our worth," he continued. "We are not Elias. We pride ourselves in being honorable and dependable. We don't roll around in bull-shit."

I rubbed my jaw, then sat back down. I leaned to listen to my brother whisper in my ear; then I flashed a smile. He really didn't say shit. It was just an intimidation move on his part that I played along with. Resting my arm against the back of the couch, I laid my finger against my temple then glanced at them.

"This is what you owe then. Fifty percent of your shares with the Japanese Yakuzas in distributing Ink in Japan is now cut in half, to fifteen percent profit of anything they do in Brazil. They now do business with me."

Amen's hands fisted then he gave a nod.

"This is for an intermediary period and I'll be up front with you. This is just a slap on the hand. I'll revert it once your people can all be trusted."

Keeping a steady gaze on the couple, I continued, "As a result, your distribution shares to France, Spain, Portugal, and the Islands, all of those stocks will be divvied up to each of the members in the Syndicate. Once this penalty expires, you'll have your shares and your voting rights back."

Cintia looked my way in shock. "This will break us!"

Amen laid a hand on his wife's lap, took her hand, and kissed the back of it. He shook his head and spoke softly to her. "No. This is how it goes. If we are good, then we will buffer this and not break."

"Exactly," was all I said.

"How long will this be?" Amen asked, returning his attention to me. Brotha was angry, but I could see that he understood it. Even if he didn't, I'd kill him if he fought against this.

"Don't worry about the length. This is about what you all can do as my pipeline. If this helps you all shape up, then focus on that. You'll know with the ban is lifted and when you have the right to offer any suggestions to the table."

The couple sat in silence as I stood. "We can give you time to think. I'm not fond of ultimatums and the fact that you told me to bring you the head of my sister disgusts me. However, I tolerated it. Respect at the table is earned and this is me showing that; however, I'm not a motherfucker to be played with. So, I chose to be diplomatic and show you that in the nicest of ways. I mean, I could just wipe you all out and end it here, but I picked you both for a reason to take over."

Stepping in front of them, I offered my hand. "We believe in reviving the Syndicate. If you can do that, and keep it one hundred percent with me at all times, then we all will gain and grow. Understand?"

Amen took my hand in a business grasp and nodded. "Fair exchange."

"And strong unity," Cintia added as she stood and smoothed a hand down her dress.

"Exactly," I said while shaking Amen's hand.

"Then, my friend," Amen added, "we'll accept this punishment as is and take the heads of our enemies as trophies. Now we'll show you all our city and move on from this unfortunate issue."

Our time in Brazil was good. We learned who killed our mother and we watched as Amen and

Cintia burned our adversaries' heads like coal. The spirit of loss, love, and family was tested greatly, but in the end, we became what Mama wanted us to be: our own Syndicate. Our own unit. Even though we were still healing up from the fractures, we learned to never ever stay broken. Or, life would shoot us in the pinky toe, as Mama would always say.